TWISTED ECHOES

Visit us at www.boldstrokesbooks.com

By the Author

Crimson Vengeance

Burgundy Betrayal

Scarlet Revenge

Vermilion Justice

Twisted Echoes

TWISTED ECHOES

by

Sheri Lewis Wohl

2014

ISBN 13: 978-1-62639-215-1

This Trade Paperback Original Is Published By
Bold Strokes Books, Inc.
P.O. Box 249
Valley Falls, NY 12185

First Edition: November 2014

CREDITS
EDITOR: CINDY CRESAP
PRODUCTION DESIGN: SUSAN RAMUNDO
COVER DESIGN BY SHERI (GRAPHICARTIST2020@HOTMAIL.COM)

Being deeply loved by someone
gives you strength,
While loving someone deeply
gives you courage.

—LAO TZU

CHAPTER ONE

Not for the first time, Lorna Dutton wondered whose fucking idea it was to move to this place. Oh yeah, it was hers. With the sleeve of her shirt, she wiped away the icy rain that sliced across her face. She gave serious consideration to staying outside to let the rain beat her up. Somehow it was soothing to feel something, anything. Instead, she turned around and went back into the living room. The storm continued its unabated rage outside. From all appearances, she'd have plenty of time to let a storm kick her ass. Seemed like all it had done outside since she'd gotten here was rain and blow.

Inside the hundred-and-twenty-year-old Victorian, a fire blazed in the massive fireplace. The warmth almost thawed the ice around her heart. Almost didn't really count. It would help if it was a little less isolated and strange. Except it wasn't the house—lovely, old, and full of history. No, it was...well, everything. Where she was, why she was here, and worst of all, why she was here all alone. A pretty house and killer views couldn't take the edge off of any of those things, especially the latter.

In the massive bedroom that was now hers, she shrugged out of wet clothes and dropped them in a heap on the floor. With the towel she grabbed off the bar in her private bathroom, she dried her hair as best she could, then slipped into nice dry sweats. Might as well get comfortable for another night watching movies. Wasn't like she needed to dress up for anything or anyone. Old, ratty sweats were just the thing for hanging out all by her lonesome.

The only sound as she made her way back to the living room was the slap of her bare feet on the hardwood floor. She stopped and stared out the big window amazed that the rain still came down as hard as when she'd come in earlier. Did it ever let up around here? Her gaze drifted from the storm to the low table in front of the sofa. On it rested a small bottle of wine, one stemmed glass, crystal she was pretty sure, and a plate of cheese and fruit. The small kindness of the housekeeper, Jolene Austin, pushed back a bit of the loneliness. The only thing about it that rubbed Lorna wrong was the sight of the single glass. Not Jolene's fault. Just another unfortunate reminder of how messed up her life had gotten.

She poured a little of the wine into the solitary glass and sipped it. A touch of depression was no reason to let good wine go to waste. The flavors tickled her senses as she swirled it in her mouth. Not too shabby. It would appear Jolene knew her wines.

She trailed her fingers along the back of the sofa as she walked around it while studying the room. The house was so much a reflection of Great-aunt Bea. From the burgundy accent wall to the cream leather furniture to the paintings with a touch of surrealism, it all screamed Bea. Eccentric and more than a little out-spoken, she was one of the most interesting people Lorna had ever known. How she wished she'd told her that, and regretted it was now too late.

Bea left her this place, and no one had been more shocked than Lorna. She could count on one hand the number of times she'd stayed here. That made the bequest of the handsome home overlooking a gorgeous stretch of the Pacific Ocean all the more odd.

When she gave it a little thought, perhaps it wasn't such a peculiar bequest. Even if they'd spent time together only sporadically over the years, Lorna and Bea got each other in ways none of the others in the family did. They were kindred spirits. Or rather they had been.

When the news arrived about the house she could have easily refused Bea's generous gift. Lord knows there were plenty of cousins ready and willing to step up and take her place. Her initial reaction was to do just that. Beautiful as the house was, it was four hundred miles away from Spokane where she'd been born and raised. Top it off with its rather isolated location, and it wasn't the kind of gift she jumped and ran with.

In the end, she didn't turn her back on Bea's final wish. Instead, she quit her job, sold her condo, and headed to the coast. In the big picture the bequest was not only generous, it was incredibly well timed. A dramatic change was just what she needed, and it was handed to her in the form of a deed.

Spokane had been her home for all of her thirty-five years, and honestly, three and a half decades was enough. Beautiful and unspoiled, the city in northeastern Washington State had many positives. The cost of living was fantastic, and the area boasted every kind of outdoor activity possible. As an outdoor enthusiast, it was a great place for someone like her. The negative, in her opinion, was the staunch conservative base that called Spokane home. All in all, way too conservative for her taste. She felt like she'd done her part to help open eyes to the beauty of diversity, but frankly, it got tiring always having to be a crusader. After everything that happened, it was time for adventure, and Bea handed her the perfect excuse to escape.

Except it really wasn't the city she was trying to escape. Deep down the truth was she could deal with its conservative roots. She could live with small town mentality in a metro environment. She could be proud and loud. What she couldn't handle was seeing Anna day after day, and knowing that what they'd shared was over. She couldn't handle running into her having dinner with someone else. The lilt of her voice carrying across a restaurant as she laughed and smiled with another woman, or bumping into them at Huckleberry's, the grocery store they used to shop at together. No, she couldn't deal with any of that, and she took the chance to run without as much as a glance back over her shoulder.

Now, in the quiet of this place, she was beginning to think it wasn't just the coward's way out; it was the stupid coward's way out. What the hell was she going to do here? She was more than twenty miles from the nearest town and much farther than that if she wanted a real city like Seattle. She'd been born and raised in a city. This was definitely not urban living.

And then there was the rain. It was raining when she drove up, and it didn't seem to be in a particular hurry to quit. If it wasn't so damned wet, it might actually be comfortable outside.

She tapped gently on the glass. "Rain, rain, go away," she whispered, her breath fogging up the window. Her reflection was wet and wavy like a spirit dancing in the storm.

Despite the constant precipitation, the place did have an upside. Like the fact the view from just about every room was spectacular. It was like staring out at a fabulous painting every day, only this was real. Even when it was raining outside, from inside the house, the majesty of the ocean view took her breath away. This night when the weather was hideous, there was something magical beneath the icy rain and howling wind. As much as she was tempted to say fuck it and move back to Spokane, she didn't. Beneath her heartache, loneliness, and confusion was something else. The way she figured it, she owed it to herself to stay long enough to find out what it was.

"Lorna?"

At the sound of Jolene's voice, she jumped like a scared cat. Even after nearly a month living here she still wasn't accustomed to co-habitating with her. At least once a day, Jolene startled her. It had to do with her way of moving around like a ghost. Quiet didn't even begin to describe the way she floated through the house. Lorna rarely heard her coming. Housekeeper slash ninja. Good thing she was relatively young or she'd have succumbed to the big one a couple of days after moving in.

Lorna turned and tried for a smile. "Yeah?"

It must have worked because Jolene smiled back. She was one of those people who gave off warm and comforting vibes. It was hard not to like that about her. Lord knows her mother had never exactly been the warm and fuzzy type. Of course, in her defense, she was a single mother trying to raise two kids all by herself. With no one around to help, Mom was exhausted more than her share. Still, it would have been nice to have come home to a smile like Jolene's once in a while. Mom wasn't the smiling type.

"Are you hungry? I can put on something hearty if you are."

The light snack arranged so prettily on the table was still untouched, and she shook her head. "I appreciate it, but I think this will do."

Jolene's smile morphed into a frown. "That's not a proper meal. If you get any skinnier, you'll fade away right before my eyes. How are you going to do that run thing you're training for if you don't eat? Let me fix you something more substantial."

Lorna held up her hands as she laughed. That run thing was actually the endurance event Ironman. A bit more than just a run, but Jolene was trying. "Really, this is great. I'm tired tonight anyway, and I think I'll turn in early. This lovely wine and cheese will be perfect, and I promise you can fatten me up tomorrow."

"I don't know…"

"I'll be fine. I'll see you in the morning."

Jolene was muttering softly as she turned and walked away. Her words grew softer until silence once more fell. More than likely Jolene had reached the back of the house where she occupied a suite of rooms that comprised her private quarters.

"Well," Lorna said to the empty room. "Might as well drink up." She poured more wine into her glass and sipped. Dear old Aunt Bea had a damn good way with wine, and Jolene had a way of picking out exactly the right one. Speaking for herself, she didn't have the knowledge to be anywhere even close to a buff. All she really knew was what tasted good, and this was yummy. Paired with the selection of cheeses arranged in a pretty fan on the plate, it was a snack made in heaven. The nicely stocked wine cellar was going to be fun to play with.

Lorna set her nearly empty glass on the table and put her feet up on the soft cushions of the sofa. The wine, combined with the warmth of the fire, made her eyes heavy. Maybe she could lie here for a little bit and enjoy the warmth and comfort of her favorite room in the house. She might actually sleep for a little while without dreaming of Anna. The possibility of that was worth downing the whole bottle of wine. The last time she'd been able to go to sleep without heartbreak weighing her down and invading her dreams was hard to remember. Maybe tonight would be such a night. Her head felt suddenly very heavy so she slid down the sofa until she was stretched all the way out, her head resting on her arm. Yeah, nice and comfy.

Her eyes fluttered open, and for a second, she wasn't sure where she was. Her house in Spokane? No, that wasn't right. She didn't live there anymore. Then the room came into focus and she remembered. Aunt Bea's house by the ocean. Except, something was off. The living room where she'd fallen asleep looked and felt different. It wasn't like she'd been asleep that long, and yet it wasn't as it had been before she slipped into slumber. Then it hit her. The furniture, the paint, the rugs, they were all changed as if the room had been completely redone while she slept. Oddly, it seemed newer although everything about it had the flavor of expensive antiques.

She was about to push up when she lowered her head back to her arm, her body going very still. On the rug in front of the fire, two women sat close together. Neither one of them wore a stitch of clothing. Afraid to say anything, she held her breath, afraid one of them would turn around and see her. Too much like being a voyeur, and yet she couldn't look away.

Firelight glowed on their naked flesh. One woman was pale with flowing brown hair that fell to her waist. Her breasts were full and firm, her face a beautiful oval with generous, red lips. Her slim fingers stroked the flawless brown skin of the other woman whose black hair was long and braided. Slim and small-breasted, she murmured in a voice too low to hear. Whatever she said made the other woman smile. They embraced their kiss passionate. Together they reclined on the thick rug, hands stroking, lips kissing, bodies moving together. Their moans grew louder as their lovemaking intensified. Suddenly, they stopped, fear etched on their beautiful faces as they reached for clothing strewn across the rug. The brown-haired woman jumped up, her dress pressed against her nakedness. A scream rose from her lips. "No—"

Lorna came awake with a start, her heart pounding. She jumped up from the sofa and did a three sixty. Nothing. The fire was still going, although it was beginning to die down. The walls were once again pale green, the furniture comfortable modern leather. The rug beneath her feet was a thick oatmeal weave. No expensive antique furniture, no Victorian patterned wallpaper, no naked women in front of the fire. She was alone. All alone.

She sank back down on the sofa and took a big swig from her glass. The zing of the wine helped. Wow, she'd wanted a little sleep that didn't include dreams of Anna, but where the hell did that come from? It wasn't just odd; it was odd, erotic, and more than a little crazy. Maybe she was losing it after all. Difficult breakups had a way of sending a person over the edge though she always thought she was made of sterner stuff than that. Apparently, she was mistaken.

❖

Renee Austin stood next to the fire truck and willed herself not to cry. The fire raged despite the best efforts of the men and women who fought it. Flames lit up the night sky in a show of red and gold that would be intriguing were it not for the fact her home and business provided the tinder.

Her heart hurt as she stood powerless to do anything but watch her life disappear. She tried to be a good person, to do the right thing, to keep her life in balance, and to give back to her community. Obviously, somewhere along the line she'd messed up, and karma was now giving her a big fat bitch slap. Why else would her home and her business be crumbling to ash before her eyes and the eyes of all her neighbors? Ten years of hard work and persistence gone, and all that was left was a smoking pile of debris, the stench of which made her want to gag. The one and only good thing to come out of it: Clancy hadn't been inside when the building went up in flames.

"Ma'am." A firefighter reeking of smoke touched her on the arm.

She didn't flinch from his touch. Didn't respond by word. What was there to say anyway? And why in the hell was he calling her "ma'am?" Made her sound like a little old lady. She was only thirty-seven for heaven's sake. Ma'am was for older women.

"Do you have anywhere to go, or would you like us to call the Red Cross?" The tone of his voice never changed as if he was accustomed to people who stood like statues, stony and silent.

Finally, she looked up and met his gaze. He was a nice-looking man, maybe five or so years younger than she was. What bugged her right now was the idea he should be hitting on her instead talking to her like she was a delicate little flower. She opened her mouth to tell him that and then snapped it shut. Hitting on her? What kind of fire professional worth his salt would do something like that?

Maybe she was being a little bitchy about the ma'am thing. Possibly the reality she'd just lost everything she owned could be making her a shrew? All she could see in his face was concern. His kindness was appreciated even if she realized it was all part of his job. He wasn't the one out of line; she was.

She patted the hand he still had on her arm and shook her head. Her car was okay, she had her backpack with her wallet and credit cards, and most importantly, she had her dog. As for clothes and all the rest of her belongings, including her livelihood, well, those were gone.

Her eyes strayed to Clancy who was leaning heavily against her legs. She patted his head and looked back up at the fireman. "Thanks, we're going to be fine. I have family." It sucked that she was forced to run home to Mommy, but some days were like that. At least she had a mom who was there for her. How many others did not?

The concern in his eyes didn't diminish. She wasn't sure if he didn't believe her or she looked so lost he didn't think she'd be able to find her way out of a cardboard box. "Do you want us to take you there?"

Apparently, it was the latter, and she must look pretty rattled despite what she considered a noble effort at looking and sounding calm. Must not be working because he seemed more than a little hesitant to leave her alone.

She thought of her mom at the house on the cliff and the calming sound of the ocean waves outside the window. Simply visualizing it filled her with calming vibes. The drive was long, but since she'd lost her home and her business in one fell swoop, what did it matter? She might as well get out of town. There was time enough for all the paperwork and drudgery that would come with a total-loss fire on another day. That it was now nearing midnight didn't deter her either. It would be a long time before she'd be able to sleep.

"No, thank you. I appreciate your kind offer, but we can stay with my mother on the coast. If you need me—" She dug in her backpack and came up with a piece of paper and a pen. After she wrote the pertinent information, she handed it to the firefighter. "You can contact me here."

Clancy in tow, she left behind the smoldering remains of her life and headed toward her car. He jumped in the second she opened the back hatch and proceeded to whine as he pressed his nose to the window. She ran a hand down his sleek coat and leaned in to hug him. He was young, a mere five months, but he was as sharp a dog as Renee had ever shared her home with. Like her, Clancy seemed to know their life in this place was over, at least for now. It was too hard to think about rebuilding and so she didn't. Later, she'd think about it later. As long as they were together and unharmed, it was enough. He licked her cheek, did two full circles, and lay down.

The drive out of the city and toward the coast was odd. She'd made the same trip a hundred times before. A light heart and anticipation were her usual traveling companions. She looked forward to seeing her mother and had loved Aunt Bea, who wasn't her aunt at all. It didn't matter; she called her Auntie and loved her as much as if they shared the same blood. Family wasn't always defined by birth, and her relationship with Bea proved that.

Today, the journey was awash with great sadness. Who knew that a fire could make her feel so lost and alone? After all, she'd only lost *things* and things could be replaced. Thanks to a buddy who also happened to be an insurance agent, she'd been responsible and had plenty of insurance on both the business and the property. All her possessions could be replaced. The building could be repaired or replaced. Best of all, she had family who could take her and Clancy in. Unlike so many who suffered catastrophic events, they had support. None of that mattered at the moment. The blackened windows, smoking roof, and charred brick left her feeling adrift and that made her sad.

Halfway to her mother's, she pulled into a convenience store and ordered a tall latte. In her world, there was little that couldn't be fixed by a good latte. Even tonight with problems of epic proportions, it helped. The sadness retreated...a little...and as she neared the coast, the band around her heart began to loosen. In times of crisis who better to see than Mom?

At the house all but one of the windows was dark, and a strange car was pulled up in the driveway. Company? Mom did have a few friends, and since Bea's death there had been a number of folks helping out with the estate, of which the house was part. She'd never really heard much about the will, only that Mom had a home for as long as she wished. That was great because Mom loved it here. She'd been with Bea since Renee was just a toddler. In many ways, it was as much her mother's home as Bea's.

She parked behind the unfamiliar car and got out, wrinkling her nose when she realized she reeked of smoke. No wonder Clancy had retreated to the back of the SUV and stayed there the whole trip. Usually, he was panting over Renee's shoulder as if he really wanted to take the wheel and drive it himself. After the one good lick alongside her cheek, he'd settled down in the back. The only time he moved was when she stopped for a latte. She'd let him out and he'd done his business. That was it; he'd slept the rest of the way.

How long had she stood outside the burning building while billows of gray smoke wrapped around everything in sight? It had been almost like standing in the middle of a flue. Her eyes had stung, and her lungs hurt with each inhalation. The firefighters tried without success to get her to step back. She hadn't been able to do that despite understanding the wisdom of their repeated requests. It would have felt too much like she was abandoning what she'd carefully built and nurtured. Only when there was no longer a single spark of a flame had she been able to walk away. By then, she smelled just about as bad as the firefighters on the front line.

Until now, she hadn't noticed the stench. If Mom even let her in the back door smelling like this, she'd be lucky. Clancy didn't smell much better. A shower was the first thing up...for both of them.

Hopefully, Mom had something she could change into until she had a chance to buy some new clothes.

A security light kicked on as it caught her motion walking from the driver's door to the back of the SUV. She opened the hatch. Clancy jumped out and went running over to a patch of grass to relieve himself. Energy radiated from every step. Renee smiled. She loved that dog and the boundless energy that made him such a perfect companion. How people lived without dogs in their lives she couldn't understand. Without him in her life this day would have been unbearable.

A light breeze blew, carrying the scent of smoke and fire across the massive bluff. In the distance, the sound of the ocean waves crashing against the rocks was a welcome reminder of home. Not the home she'd made for herself in the city, but the home where she'd been taught to love. The home where the door was always open.

Her mother must have been watching for their arrival because suddenly there she was, her arms pulling Renee close. Unlike Renee, she smelled of soap and vanilla shampoo. "Oh, sweetheart, are you all right?"

Renee hugged her back. The feel of her mother's arms around her was exactly what she needed. It didn't matter one little bit she was pushing the big four oh. She was never too old for a mother's comfort. "Yeah, we'll be fine. Just sucks to be me right now."

Her arms dropping away, Mom stepped back and studied her. In the buttery glow of the outside light, her dark eyes were serious. "Renee Kathleen Austin, I hate when you use terms like that. Makes you sound like an unruly teenager."

Oh no, her full name. Mom only did that when she was upset with her. She almost smiled. "Sorry," she said even though she wasn't really. Mom could be so old-fashioned. It was reassuring in a way. Some things just never changed, and that was okay.

"You smell too." Her nose crinkled and her lips turned down into a frown.

She laughed a little this time. "I think Clancy was a little offended. He stayed in the back the whole way. What he probably didn't realize is that he smells as bad as I do!"

Her mother's face lit up at Clancy's name, all traces of displeasure wiped away in a second. "Clancy! Where's my boy?" At the sound of his name, he came racing around the SUV, almost losing his footing as he did, and jumped joyfully, his paws coming to rest on her chest. Laughing, Mom began to rub his ears.

It amazed Renee how much the two of them seemed to love each other. Though she'd never had a dog growing up, Renee had lived with one ever since she'd left home. Mom had always seemed to like her dogs, but for some reason she didn't understand, Clancy was special to her. Something about the black-faced German shepherd touched her mother's heart. She didn't know what it was and didn't care. It warmed her through and through that the two of them shared a tight bond, so she stood aside to let the two of them have their moment of joyous reunion.

Her mother finally straightened up, her face thoroughly licked, and held out a hand to Renee. "Come on. Let's get you cleaned up and then you can tell me all about the details of the fire. Come on, Clancy, that means you too."

After standing there smelling herself for a few minutes, the cleaning up part sounded fantastic.

The fire part not so much.

st morning she hadn't awakened thinking of Anna.
that? Things must be looking up.

hirt and a faded pair of sweats might be ugly, but
t for a sweaty workout in a little bit. First things first
nd a bagel. She skipped down the stairs following
hly brewed coffee. God, it smelled like heaven. No
Aunt Bea was so fond of Jolene. She hadn't been
d she was already in love with waking up every
e's kitchen magic.

ber was a strange reality for her. Her family never
money that would allow for such a luxury. Her
vell for Lorna and her brother. Solidly middle class,
vhat they needed, and much of the time what they
lad she been the kind of girl who blended into the
lemories of growing up would have been all good.
eded didn't include a housekeeper. With no one to
h, she was taught very early to be self-sufficient.
re, she cleaned her own house, cooked her own
d her own clothes. She never thought too much
and never minded doing for herself. Still, she had
to coffee and a clean house was pretty sweet.
e around for company wasn't too bad either. At
would be uncomfortable having another woman
g in her home. That lasted about ten minutes.
bout her that made everything comfortable, and
atural. Now Lorna couldn't imagine not having

hrough the kitchen doorway with a cheery
Before she uttered a single word, she stopped
but together all the pieces of the picture she was
eated at the kitchen table. No big surprise there.
ter what time Lorna got up, Jolene was already
he coffee made. That isn't what made her stop

her enough to derail her mission for coffee was
itting across from Jolene whose features made

CHAPTER TWO

From the shadows, he watched the two women and the dog. Wrapped in the darkness, he was but a whisper. Something seen from the corner of the eye yet never fully formed. It had been that way for him since the time of his fall.

His wait had been long, but deep in his heart he had known she would come. Had understood they both would come. They had to. For it had been written in the stars so many years ago. The familiar crash of waves against the rocks filled the night with a lullaby of sorts. The sound had been his constant companion year after year, its steady beat a comfort in the endless procession of nights as he watched and waited.

His eyes drifted back to the massive house that had stood on this spot for more than a century. Old in the human realm. But a blink of time in his existence. Inside, one slept, her slumber no longer troubled. No more on this night would he send her dreams. His work for now was complete. He had given her what he could, and it would have to be enough. She would wake and begin to wonder. It was the wonder that would bring her understanding and knowledge.

Not open to him yet, the other one he would not trouble for he could not. Her time would come, and her soul would open to him. Until then, he would wait and watch just as he'd been doing for so long. His patience was endless. His time to make this right was not.

Once before, he had failed, and two had been lost. His fault. Their damnation. Ever since, he had been waiting to bring them home. Only then could he hope to find his own salvation. Alone, he could do so little. Together with the two women now beneath the roof of the old house, they could do so much. In his heart, he dared to hope.

But still he was afraid.

The wind picked up and blew around him in a swirl of dead grass, golden leaves, and fine beach sand. It did not touch him. Neither did the rain, the cold, or the heat. Nothing touched him except the ache of the lost. As their souls suffered in a limbo they did not deserve, so too did his. Guilt was a heavy burden, his rightfully to bear.

He wished a thousand times it could have been different. That he could have stopped the evil that saturated this place and hurt two who committed no greater sin than to love each other. He wanted to bring them home, and more than anything, *he* wanted to go home. His failure kept his feet on the earth, his soul waiting. Until he could bring them with him, the gates would never be open to him.

Tonight, two came, and for the first time, a flicker of hope pushed away a little bit of the darkness in his heart. Outwardly, little changed for though he neared seven feet tall with a body rail thin, no one saw him. Ever. A blessing. A curse. His fate.

No more could be done this night. With his eyes still on the windows of the old house, the Watcher took several steps back into the deepest shadows and faded as if he had never been there at all.

❖

Lorna rolled over and groggily thought she heard a dog barking. Must have been a dream. Somebody's pet would have to have gotten really, really lost to end up clear out here. It wasn't like they had close neighbors. The isolation was one of the things that appealed to her when she decided to make the move. One of the things that scared her too.

The sleepy fog cleared and the barking continued. The sound should have annoyed her because it meant someone's dog was far from home and she'd probably have to find its owner. Strangely

it obvious the two were related. The kind of whoa baby moment that usually happened in clubs, not her kitchen. Funny, until this moment, she'd not considered how beautiful Jolene was. Seeing the younger version made her breath catch.

Jolene jumped up beaming, and seemingly unaware that she'd been struck speechless. "Lorna, good morning. I hope you slept well. This is my daughter, Renee. I don't know if you remember her. You two played together a couple of times when you were children."

Daughter? A vague recollection of a skinny girl a year or two older with crazy red hair who talked a lot flitted through her mind. Yeah, maybe there had been a daughter but certainly not this vision of hotness sitting at her kitchen table. "Good morning," Lorna said. She sure didn't remind her of that wild little girl who annoyed the hell out of her back in the good old days. If she was, then that little girl was long gone, replaced by a graceful beauty.

Renee stood also and extended her hand. "It's been a long time. I think I was about eight last time we saw each other. I remember you being tall with braids I liked to pull. I bet that annoyed the hell out of you." Her laugh was soft and musical.

Lorna shook the outstretched hand, liking the way her fingers touched her palm. She didn't look even remotely like that Raggedy Ann little girl of her memories. Not even close. This woman was, to put it bluntly, gorgeous. The crazy red hair was gone, replaced by long, wavy tresses a shiny shade of auburn somewhere between red and brown. Her green eyes were large and bright, her pale skin sprinkled with just a few freckles.

"Hi," was all she could think of to say, and she hoped her mouth wasn't hanging open or that she'd have to wipe drool from her chin. Lorna wasn't a big talker on the best of days, but today she appeared to be particularly verbally challenged. Really, she should be able to come up with something besides a one-syllable greeting.

Renee didn't seem to notice that she wasn't just staring but staring stupidly and displaying the vocabulary of a one-year-old. Instead, she sat back down in the chair she vacated to offer her hand in greeting, took a sip from the hefty coffee mug sitting on the table in front of her, and then sighed. "I hope you don't mind me crashing here. My place burned down last night."

That statement, said so calmly, shocked her. If her house burned down, she'd be a damn wreck, and yet here Renee sat at her table looking cool and collected like it was just another morning with family and friends. A twinge of guilt hit her as she thought about how depressed she'd been over her breakup. Seemed kind of dramatic when compared to a house fire.

Jolene handed Lorna a cup of coffee in a mug just as big as Renee's. "I was going to ask you today if you'd be all right with Renee staying just a bit until this fire mess gets straightened around. Since we're all here, might as well ask you now. I realize I'm putting you on the spot and in front of my daughter, but would you mind terribly if Renee stays with us?"

"Well, me and Clancy." Renee added with a wry smile. "And it won't be for very long. I'm sure my insurance covers temporary lodging. We'll be out before you know it."

Lorna held the big mug between both hands, not yet taking a drink, and asked, "Clancy?" Her boyfriend maybe? A shame. Despite her recent breakup, Lorna found Renee's face entrancing. Wouldn't it be sweet if she was, well, like her? Fantasy.

Renee smiled, and the way her face lit up made Lorna's heart skip a beat. Having her stay was a no-brainer, but if she smiled at her very often, she wasn't sure she could take it. Right now, she better sit down before her knees buckled.

"My dog. A pup really, not quite six months old. He's a dream, and I promise he's very well behaved. You won't even know he's around." As if on cue, a sound came from the kitchen door, and Renee got up to open it. A young black and tan German shepherd raced in, came right up to Lorna, and jumped up, his two front legs draped over her knees. His tail wagged, smacking the table leg with a thump, thump, thump. Thank goodness she'd set the big mug on the table or she and the dog would be wearing the coffee.

If he was only six months old, he was one big boy. Handsome too with his shiny black and tan coat. She laughed and petted him between the ears, her fingers touching damp fur in his undercoat.

Seeing him certainly explained the barking earlier. "He's beautiful." Her smile was only half for Clancy. So far, no boyfriend. She liked that.

Renee pushed the thick hair off her shoulders. "Thank you. I'm pretty fond of him. He might be a little wet. We both had to shower or we'd still smell like a campfire."

Her hand still stroked Clancy as she asked, "Your house burned down?"

"Yeah, my house, my business, my everything pretty much. I own a building in Seattle. Downstairs is my natural foods store and upstairs is where Clancy and I live. Well, I guess it's more like where Clancy and I lived. Everything was lost last night."

"What caused the fire?"

She shook her head. "I don't know and the fire department folks weren't saying much last night. They probably think I started it."

"You? Why?"

Renee shrugged. "No reason I just figure that's what they always assume in a situation like this. The owner did it."

"That's fucked up. Oops, I'm sorry. I mean, ah, um, tell me about the fire." God, what an asshole she could be. Who talked that way in front of strangers? Beautiful, sexy strangers?

Renee didn't seem to miss a beat. "I'd closed up for the night like I always did, then Clancy I went to the dog park..."

As she talked, Lorna couldn't help but think how different they were. Renee was taking the loss in stride, something she didn't think she'd be able to do. She told the story calmly as though she were an observer rather than a victim. Everything the woman owned was gone, and yet she sat here drinking coffee and smiling as if she were on a happy holiday break. She even seemed to take in stride the idea that she might be considered an arson suspect. Her first impression was this was one amazing woman.

Made her embarrassed at how mopey she'd been since getting here. She'd been dumped, and that hurt more than she'd believed possible. Even so, she still had a home, her belongings, and a job. Everything that Renee had lost in a matter of hours last night. If she could still smile and see hope in the world, then Lorna didn't have much of an excuse for not pulling her head out. She'd been dumped by her girlfriend, BFD.

By the time they polished off a second pot of coffee, Lorna was trying to remember the last time she'd enjoyed a morning so much or felt so relaxed. Both of these women made her feel comfortable and alive. She didn't want it to end even at the expense of her training.

Across the table, the fatigue clearly showing in Renee's face made her feel guilty. Even taking her tragedy with incredible grace, Renee needed rest, and here she'd been blabbing for at least an hour. She was a horrible hostess and not a very good caretaker.

"Why don't you bring in whatever you were able to save and get settled?"

Jolene squeezed Renee's shoulder as she walked behind her. "I'll get clean linens on your bed, sweetheart. You need to lie down and sleep for a bit. It's not that I'm not thoroughly enjoying being here with both of you, but, honey, you look dead on your feet."

Renee smiled at her mother and then looked back at Lorna. Her eyes were sparkling despite the weariness etched into her features. "You're sure it's okay if Clancy and I stay for a little bit? It's a terrible imposition. I promise though, we'll stay out of your way as much as we can."

After Anna's devastating rejection, Lorna was leery of being around someone she found attractive. What would be the point? Even if something did miraculously come of it, odds were it would end on a bad note. She was good at a lot of things, but gracefully ending a relationship wasn't one of them.

Still, as she gazed into Renee's mysterious eyes, she couldn't bring herself to refuse her shelter. She was lovely and energetic, the kind of distraction that was good for the soul. Especially a soul battered by the crushing loss of a loved one. In short, a breath of fresh air. God, how she needed fresh air and a bright light.

It didn't make sense. Here was a woman that tragedy chose to dump on, and yet she almost glowed with light. Lorna was drawn to it like a moth to a fire. To hell with first reactions, she hoped it was a long time before Renee was able to go home. Besides, thinking there was a chance in hell they'd have a relationship was just plain stupid. The probability that she liked men was far greater. It was the way the world worked. Well, it was the way her world worked anyway.

"Yeah," she said softly. "I'm sure."

❖

The last thing Jeremy felt like doing was driving I-90 across the state. Tired and grumpy, what he really wanted to do was to drop into bed to sleep for a week or two. The marathon meetings had been a real bitch, and exhaustion weighed him down like a bag of bricks slung over his back. When he had this brilliant idea to go into business with his best friend, Lorna should have slapped some sense into him. Never in his wildest imagination did he see how it would all turn out. It wasn't that they failed. On the contrary, their contracting business had taken off like a rocket.

So had the time he'd put into the business. Anywhere from sixty to seventy hours a week had helped to make the business flourish and make him an old man at thirty-five. He had money, he had status, and he had lots of friends. No time to do much with any of it though. His world was more work than much of anything else.

Even that wasn't so bad. In the beginning, it was also exciting enough that he found a way to make it all work. The turning point came the night he caught Nate and their office manager, Melinda, in the storeroom. Both were married to other people, and they'd been going at it like a couple of kids. It wasn't that Jeremy was the morality police. Not in a million years because he wasn't the kind of guy who threw stones at glass houses.

No, it was everything. The crazy hours. The stress. The way his best friend changed from a nice guy into a money-obsessed player. Their success had changed his friend into a guy he didn't know and one he didn't like. These days Nate wasn't the kid who'd sat at the kitchen table with him drinking cheap beer and dreaming of what they could accomplish together. He missed that guy a bunch.

Combine that with the mess he'd managed to make of his personal life, and everything seemed to be blowing up in his face.

Living like this wasn't something he wanted to do anymore. He'd been coasting along too long now, and if he was honest with himself, pretending he was making everything work. Changes had to happen, and he couldn't wait around to see what they were going to be. The only choice he felt he could reconcile with was to make his own changes. So he did.

He owed it to the memory of his mother to do the right thing for himself and those around him. It was, after all, the proceeds of her life insurance policy that gave him the freedom to quit his first real job and go back to school. Armed with his graduate degree, he and Nate had launched their business. That Mom was gone too soon hurt his soul because she didn't live to see what he'd built. Even so, he knew that what he'd done with the legacy she provided him would make her very proud.

Things were different now. Living a life that was a lie would not make her proud regardless of the monetary success. That had to come from the heart, and his had called for a change. Mom would take one look at him and would know in a flash he was not a happy guy. He was beyond pleased at what two regular guys had been able to create and nurture, and if he'd been able to find a balance that worked would have been able to look his mother in the eye. Instead, he failed in that department and now had to make it right.

Now, however, before he could work on his own life, he had to get Lorna her gear or she was bound to have a heart attack. Ironman wasn't that far away, and she needed her stuff to keep her training on track. Granted, it would be easy enough for her to find a wetsuit to practice in, but the bike was a whole different story. The one loaded in the back of his SUV cost more than his first car. It still made him shake his head every time he thought about it. Lorna swore it made a world of difference in her biking speed. He wasn't so sure. After all, a bike was a bike was a bike…right?

Whether or not he was a believer didn't matter. This was her gig, and he respected her for taking on the huge challenge of the endurance race. If she said the bike made a difference and was worth the cost, then who was he to argue? Besides, bringing this bike to her was a small price to pay to give her a little pleasure. Though she tried to hide it from him, he could tell she was suffering. That bitch Anna had dropped her like she was nobody special, and he hated her for that. Lorna was awesome, and Anna should have been thanking her lucky stars a woman that wonderful loved her. Not Anna. Instead, she runs off with some pretty little artist, breaking his sister's heart in the process. His patience with people who cheated was slim at best. When the person cheated on happened to be his sister, well, his patience was non-existent.

All he could do to help was be there for her. If she asked him to pick up her uber fast bike from what she characterized as the only guy in the Pacific Northwest who could tune it up right, and bring it to her, then he would. It might seem like a big favor to ask, but he didn't feel that way. It's the kind of thing a person did for someone they loved. He loved Lorna even if he didn't say it often. He'd try to work on that.

In the middle of the Vantage Bridge, a gust of wind hit him like a hammer to the side. Every time that happened, he wondered why he didn't end up in the Columbia River. Hadn't happened yet and probably never would, but that didn't mean the wind was going to give up either. He hated that bridge.

The long and winding hill up past Vantage with its sagebrush and basalt rock always made his imagination soar. He could envision the wild horses that used to roam the hills and the Native Americans who camped on the shores of the Columbia River. These days, all that rose from the earth were hundreds of giant white windmills that looked like aliens standing sentry.

Finally, he made it past the hills and windmills and to the wide-open flatlands that announced Ellensburg. Farmland and cattle ranches replaced the desolation he'd just left behind. At the second exit, he put on his blinker and pulled off. He had to get out of the car and stretch.

He pulled up to the gas pump at the Exxon right off the exit and got out. Waiting for the tank to fill, he raised his arms over his head and stretched. Man, that felt good. Out of the corner of his eye he noticed a little boy maybe three, four tops, racing across the parking lot. He also caught sight of a car turning in and it wasn't slowing down. The little boy was smiling and running as though he didn't have a care in the world and as if he was in a park instead of a terribly busy service station. Without giving it a second thought, Jeremy took off in a full-out sprint and managed to grab the boy around the waist. He spun away from the incoming car just in time. It missed them by inches.

"Oh my God, Michael," a young woman screamed, dropped her purse, and ran from the other side of the lot.

"He's all right," Jeremy said as he handed the squirming boy—Michael—to his frantic mother. Her lips were quivering and her hands shaking as she took the still cheerful toddler out of his arms. Happy to return the little one to his mother, only then did Jeremy realize his heart was beating like a drum. It hit him how close they'd come to being struck down by the car.

"Thank you, oh thank you," she said on a sob. Her blond hair flew around her face as wind gusted through. If not for the fear still etched in her face, she'd have been a beautiful young woman.

"Tank you," the smiling boy echoed. His blue eyes crinkled with the joy of innocence, and he reached out with a pudgy hand to pat Jeremy on the cheek.

He laid his hand over Michael's. "You're welcome."

The woman started to turn away and then turned back. With one arm still around Michael, she used the other to give him a hug. "Thank you," she said again softly before hurrying back to her car holding her son close.

He watched them go, an ache in his heart that he didn't understand. These people were strangers, and their paths crossed only because they'd happened to stop at the same service station. Saving the little boy didn't make their connection any deeper. All he'd done was what any decent person would. So why did seeing a mother hold her child give him such an empty feeling?

He ignored the emptiness that settled in his stomach and instead focused on the drive ahead. Snoqualmie Pass was just ahead, and he always looked forward to driving the ascent that would take him to the top of the mountains. Each time he hit the summit, he smiled because it brought him that much closer to the beautiful and vibrant city of Seattle. Didn't matter that he was born and raised in Eastern Washington, the west side of the state had its own special charms, and he wasn't immune. He loved crossing the mountains.

Even given how much he liked coming across state, Lorna's move to the coast was weird because she was an Eastsider too. Not that he was saying her move was a bad idea. On the contrary, getting her away from the possibility of running into Anna and her new little *gal pal* would help her heal. Time and distance were great for that. Not a bad idea for him either.

So, if taking his first weekend off after the epic showdown with Nate to drive over to the coast with Lorna's stuff was an inconvenience, he'd live with it. Besides being a great excuse to get out of town, he really wanted to help make certain she had everything she needed to kick ass in Ironman.

CHAPTER THREE

"Mom," Renee said while watching Lorna through the kitchen window as she stretched and readied for a run. "She's special."

"She's a lovely young woman," she agreed. "Sad though. She hasn't said too much to me, but I see it in her eyes. She's hurting over something or someone. She's bright enough when she knows I'm looking. It's when she thinks no one will notice that sadness drops over her like a blanket. Breaks my heart."

Renee was shaking her head as she turned around and watched her mom clean up the coffee cups from their morning around the table. "That's not what I mean. I'm with you. I see the sadness in her, but it's something else. She has an aura I haven't seen in anybody for a long time. Maybe never when I really think about it."

"You think she has some kind of power?" It was said absently, her attention more on cleaning up the kitchen so it sparkled.

Mom never really did buy into what Renee could read in people. She passed it off as her daughter's eccentric nature. In some respects, it was true. Renee couldn't deny that she wasn't exactly the *normal* daughter. That was true even before she stopped pretending. For as long as she could remember, she stepped to the beat of her own special drummer. Life worked for her that way. It still did.

It didn't, however, explain away what it was she could see. From the time she was very little, she was able to see light around people. As a young child, she thought everyone could see the lights.

It was quite an eye-opener to learn very few could actually see them, and it made her feel like more of an outsider than she already did. It didn't take very long before she discovered that it was best not to talk about what she saw. Easier to keep friends if they didn't think she was the local crazy kid. Eccentric, people could tolerate. Crazy, not so much.

When she learned it was auras she could see, it actually made her feel a little less nutty. After a while, she even learned to love her unique ability. Strangely, it made her feel special. She was teased plenty about being the odd kid, but that little bit of special was all she needed to help reconcile with herself. By the time she was an adult, she found the talent pretty handy. Good, bad, and everything in between had a tendency to show up for her. Made it easier to know who to trust and who not to trust.

What she was seeing in Lorna this morning made her very curious. The tall, muscular woman with the short blond hair was interesting for a whole lot of reasons, but it was the fusion of color surrounding her like a rainbow fog that was filling Renee with a desire to know so much more. Even if she weren't homeless, she'd want to stay here and find out Lorna's secrets.

"I don't know, Mom. Could be power, could be something else. It's unique, I'll give her that. Haven't seen that kind of color on anyone else." She'd seen auras of power before, and Lorna's wasn't like that. In fact, it wasn't like any she'd seen before. It made her all the more curious to find out what made Lorna tick. Professional curiosity only, of course.

"Maybe you're just seeing something because of what happened to you. Stress of losing your home and business. That kind of stress would be difficult for even the strongest of people. You're also tired and that's affecting you more than you know." She continued to put dishes away without looking at Renee.

She closed her eyes for a second and counted to ten. As much as she loved her mother, her subtle innuendos got on her nerves at times. The truth was she'd never reconciled with Renee's decision to live in Seattle after the incident on the rocks. Only once did she try to explain it all to her mother. She'd been full of empathy and concern, but she hadn't understood. Nor had she been able to grasp what had driven her to that awful night. She stopped trying to make her understand. Instead, she'd packed her things and moved to Seattle, leaving everything in her rearview mirror.

At first, it had been difficult. A hundred times, she'd thought about throwing in the towel and going back home. A hundred times, she stopped and found the strength to keep trudging forward. In the end, she'd embraced the freedom to be the person who'd lived hidden inside her soul.

It started that night on the rocks with the ocean pounding the stones with a fury that matched the way she'd been feeling. She'd come within a breath of embracing the violence and giving her body to sea. To this day, she couldn't say what it was that pulled her away from that irreversible decision. Whatever it was, she was grateful. She'd climbed down from the stones and changed her life. She no longer hid her sexuality or her desire to give her heart to a woman, and that drummer's beat became a lot funkier. The quiet discontent always rippling through her disappeared. Scary as it was, she embraced the courage she needed to be free. She was happy.

That long ago night was not something they talked about. Mom was great in so many ways, but when it came to Renee's idiosyncrasies, she chose to pretend they didn't exist. Like her ability to see auras. She might mention them, might give superficial attention to Renee's visions of them, that's it. Belief was another thing altogether and something she really didn't possess.

Renee wasn't going to go into it with her now. It was easier just to roll with the superficial acknowledgement. "Yeah, you've got a point, Mom. Losing everything sucks, and it's more than a little stressful though it doesn't affect someone else's aura. Lorna has something very cool going on, and I'm really curious to find out what it is."

"Well," she remarked as she picked up a bucket filled with cleaning supplies. "Remember, this is her house now, and despite her warm welcome, remember you're a guest. She may not appreciate your voodoo ideas, so probably better to keep those to yourself."

Renee smiled and kissed the top of her head. "I promise I will not bother our hostess with any voodoo."

❖

The second she stepped outside and the fresh air filled her lungs, Lorna smiled. For some reason, running always made her feel alive and real. It wasn't that she liked to run all that much. On the contrary, getting herself out the door and on the road was more often than not an exercise in sheer determination.

The funny part was once she got going, all the resistance melted away, and she took off with a feeling of energy and light. When she first began running, she'd felt like a heifer trying to run with a cougar. Her friend Sophia had pestered her until she gave in. The first few months were pure torture, and if not for Sophia, she'd have quit the first week. As good friends often do, Sophia gave her the encouragement she needed to keep going. Who could have guessed all the wonderful side effects?

Still, even after months of logging mile after mile, she could recall thinking she was nuts to even consider finishing a 5K. The idea of a triathlon was nowhere on her horizon until Sophia got a wild hair that they should do Valley Girl, an all-women spring triathlon. A third of a mile swim, a twelve-mile bike ride, and a 5K run.

Turned out to be so much fun, she was hooked before she realized what had happened. Three years later, after watching Ironman in Coeur d'Alene, she caught the fever. Next thing she knew, she was a regular volunteer working with the awesome athletes as they made their life-changing journeys. The logical step following her years as a volunteer was to sign up to be one of those athletes. Caught up in the high of last year's event, that's exactly what she did. Expensive commitment made, the only choice she had, in her opinion, was to give it the best shot she could.

A couple months after making the decision to go all in, she'd gotten bold and decided to go big guns. With only a twinge of guilt about spending so much on a bicycle, she plunked down a bundle for the red and white Cervélo. One hundred and twelve miles was a long way to ride, and if she could give herself an edge, she was all over it. Any remaining guilt slid away the first time she went out.

The miles glided by, and it was the first time she began to believe her Ironman dream might become a reality.

Of course, at the time she had a great job, a beautiful home, and was deeply in love. In her mind, the stars had, to her utter amazement, aligned for her. Boy, had she been wrong. Everything blew apart as if she'd been hit by a freak tornado. By the time the dust settled, she'd quit her job, sold her home, and tried to figure out how to keep going forward with a heart broken into a thousand pieces.

Could be she had a little guardian angel lurking above her because after all the turmoil, things started to fall into place. She inherited this house and even a fair chunk of change to keep it going. Her skills and experience as a technical writer came together to create a new career that allowed her to work anywhere. She worked from home these days making nearly as much as she had working for corporate America. Both the home and the work-at-home career gave her the time and place to train. If not for the heart that still hurt like hell, her life might be pretty sweet.

With her pre-run stretches complete, Lorna stopped thinking about the state of her life and began to run, her pace easy and relaxed. The sun had decided to peek through the clouds, and the scent of the ocean wafted in the air. This was so different from the hot, dry air in Spokane. Not that it was unpleasant. On the contrary, it was exactly what she needed. No reminders of what she'd lost and what she'd left behind. This was a one hundred and eighty degree new beginning.

Once she made her way down the long driveway to the road, she stopped and inhaled deeply. It was breathtaking here in a completely different way from Spokane. How the family ended up on this gorgeous spot of land between Neah Bay and Clallam Bay was a mystery. It was so out of the way on one hand and so incredibly stunning on the other. What she didn't get was the isolation. They were a rich, interesting family, and it seemed to her they would have wanted to be part of the vibrant Seattle society. Instead, they settled here far away from the city and pretty much anyone else for that matter. Given her current state of mind, that part was welcome to her and maybe that's what they were looking for too when they stopped here and decided to build.

She took a sip from the water bottle on her fuel belt and then took off again. No more easy. In the race, she'd have to complete 26.2 miles, so wimping out at a couple miles wasn't going to cut it. She pushed even as her legs ached with each strike of her foot on the unforgiving asphalt. It was her fault for ignoring most of her training during the last month. The body had a way of expressing its displeasure at her abandonment of the plan she'd been faithfully following until recently.

With her race coming up in a few months, she didn't dare allow her training to slide any longer. If she didn't focus, she'd be lucky to finish the endurance test within the allowed time limits. And with strict cutoff times on each leg, it wasn't like she could make up time for a weaker segment in one where she was stronger. No, it was out for the count if she missed her time by a single second in any of the three. Not an option.

So shut up and run was what she was thinking right now. And it's what she did. After a few minutes, she found her rhythm, and the pain in her legs began to ease away. Despite her whining about the stiffness in her body when she started, it usually ended up this way. Ten minutes or so into the run and her attitude shifted from reluctant runner to willing participant.

After about five miles, the road veered closer to the ocean though still decidedly inland. A side road lead away from the main highway and to the cliffs overlooking the waters. This was a much nicer road to run on without the worry of high-speed traffic. Along the side road, she ran on until she veered off the road and onto the wild grass of the bluff. Her breath coming in labored puffs, sweat beading on her forehead and trickling down her chest between her breasts, she stopped. Hands on her quads, she leaned forward and caught her breath as she looked out on the breathtaking view.

A glorious cool breeze blew off the water cooling the sweat on her skin. Despite the unaccustomed dampness to the air, it was delightful. All the way over here from Spokane she'd wondered if this was the right move and whether she'd be able to acclimate to a coastal climate. With each passing day, she became more and more convinced that she could. It was different but in a good way.

Besides, wasn't that exactly what she'd been looking for? Her life on the east side had become painful, and everything she thought she believed, altered. Coming here gave her a chance to start over without distractions, and more importantly, without having to worry about running into Anna. She didn't think her heart could take that despite her conviction that she was a tough bitch. Just didn't think she was quite that tough.

As she watched the ocean ebb and flow, the spray of the waves touching her face like fine mist, she considered why it had been so important to run away. That wasn't like her really. And it wasn't like this was the first time her heart had been broken. Anna had dumped her for another woman and that had its own kind of sting. But it was something more than simply being dumped.

She'd believed what they'd shared was forever, and discovering how terribly wrong she'd been hurt more deeply than she imagined. The courage to love that completely might never come to her again, and that was one of the reasons she ran. Not so much from Anna but from herself. Hidden away on the ocean shores, who could touch her here? No one, and that made her feel safe. Eliminate the temptation and the problem was solved.

With a sigh, she decided that rather than stand here psychoanalyzing herself, she should probably keep running. She was, after all, due for a twelve-mile loop today, and according to her Garmin, there were almost seven more miles to go.

It was hard to work up the energy to leave this place. The grass was green, a big overhanging tree provided lovely shade, and the ocean waters were clear and beautiful. Perhaps for just a little while, she'd sit and rest. Enjoy the moment, the journey, and then finish her run.

She lowered herself to the ground, slipped out of her running shoes, and took off her fuel belt. She leaned her head against the tree trunk and closed her eyes. So peaceful. A girl could get used to this.

The wind howled, the sea raged, waves crashing against the rocks with the roar of a wild beast. She stood on the rocks, the spray soaking her dress and chilling her skin. Tendrils of her long hair whipped around her face, but she didn't move. The crash of the water against the rocks was deafening. She gave little notice to any of it as she stared across the ocean waters, waiting and watching.

Even the rage of the lightning and the crack of thunder in the far off sky, could not dull her senses enough to block out the sound of her beloved. When she sensed her spirit, her heart soared. The night had called her, and she'd come. She always did. Love had a way of speaking to the heart, no matter what else happened. Soon they would be together again.

The wind tore the pins holding the thick mass of her hair, and it fell free, whipping around her face as the wind carried it. The ocean spray soaked her gown, and it clung to her every swell and curve. She shivered as she stared into the dark sky, the beginnings of a storm rolling across the sky until all the blue was pushed away. None of it mattered, for she could feel her spirit on the wind. Out here where nature roared and raged, she felt closest to the one she'd lost. That if she reached out, once more their fingers would entwine.

Another sound cut through the night, and she whirled, her gaze turning toward the bluff where earlier she had walked. A figure, large and menacing in the growing darkness, moved with speed and determination. Her scream cut through the growing wind, the raw pain of it clear even to her own ears. Knees buckling, she crumpled to the ground as she pressed the necklace she held in her fingers against her face. Great, wracking sobs shook her body.

He came across the bluff, his strides never slowing. She did not need to raise her gaze to his to know that his dark eyes never wavered from her. The grim set to his face would not be one of compassion or caring. Anger would darken his features just as the storm darkened the day. She had seen it a hundred times before. When he reached her side, he did not put a comforting hand on her shoulder. Instead, he gripped her arm and dragged her to her feet heedless of her cries of pain.

"Enough," he bellowed through the howling winds. "Someone will hear you, or even worse, see you with this thing!" He ripped from her hand the necklace she'd been holding to her face.

"It's mine," she screamed. "You have no right to take it from me." She lunged, trying to take it back. He held it outside her reach.

"No more!" He flung it far away, and when she tried to run after it, he wrenched her hard in the opposite direction. "Do not cross me, child. I will have no more of it."

She twisted back and forth in her attempt to break free of his cruel grip. "It's mine. It's all I have left of her." In the darkness she could barely make out the flicker of white beads as they bobbed and floated in the ocean surf. If she didn't get to it quickly, it would be gone.

He dragged her in the opposite direction, the fabric on the sleeve of her gown tearing away to leave bare skin to take the brunt of the rain that now came down in a torrent. "No more," he yelled through the wind. "No more."

She stumbled, a sharp pain knifing through her ankle. He dragged her without regard to her footing or her tears. One shoe slipped from her foot, and still he did not pause. Hot blood mingled with cold rain when a stone tore the tender skin on the bottom of her foot. "I hate you," she screamed back at him, heedless of the pain and the blood. "I will always hate you."

Her eyes stayed on the ocean as he hauled her away. His hatred could not destroy what was in her heart. She could not fight him and win, for he was bigger and stronger, but neither would she bend to his will. Her heart belonged to one and one only. It mattered not what he did; that would never change. He could never destroy their love. She would make certain.

The waters stirred up by the storm roiled with a fury that matched that of the man whose fingers dug into the skin of her arm and drew blood. The last thing she saw as he hauled her away was the beautiful whalebone necklace discarded amongst the craggy, surf-battered stones at the edge of the beach.

CHAPTER FOUR

In the shade, the Watcher stood tall enough to brush the branches rising seven feet from the grass-covered ground. A leaf snagged in his hair and he brushed it away. His focus was on the woman whose gaze was locked on the bluff overlooking the ocean shore and the waves beyond. The expression on her face was hard to read. Shock? Disbelief? Fear?

He'd waited so long for both women, and he'd nearly given up hope that they'd come. His fall had taken him many places and across many oceans. In a multitude of faces, he'd searched for the power and grace. Time and time again, he prayed for redemption. Time and time again, he failed.

This time he prayed it would be different. Each had their part to play, and if they did, his work would at last be complete. First, she must open her mind and see the past. Only in understanding what came before could she make the future right. That was her destiny if she went deep for the strength to embrace it.

If she opened her heart and helped, then perhaps he would at last be given the chance to go home. His sins would at last be forgiven. Alone, he was powerless. He needed her. They needed her.

Across the palm of his hand, a necklace dangled. Since the night he'd found it in the sand, cold and wet from the slap of the ocean's waters, he'd kept it close. At the time, he'd not understood why he felt compelled to keep it with him. Only later did he come to know. He had failed to help her that night, and in every night since, and it was a constant reminder of why he was here. Not that he'd forgotten for an instant. He thought of her every day and every night. He wanted to bring her home and grant her peace. She deserved at least that much.

To make it happen, this woman had to see. Her power to pull aside the veil separating the worlds was critical to bringing the lost ones home and to helping him find his way to forgiveness. The trinity needed to make it all happen was within his reach at long last. If they each fulfilled their destiny, he and the two women, all would be as it should.

For now, she'd seen what he needed to show her. He could show her but not make her understand. That she had to do herself. He hoped she hurried. He worried their time was short and that the other one might once more grow strong.

A cloud passed before the sun blotting out the bright sunshine. The sudden change seemed to draw the woman back to the here and now. She shook her head as if to clear it of cobwebs. She slipped her shoes back on her feet, tied the laces, and stood. With her back to the ocean, she once more began to run down the lonely quiet road.

For several minutes, he stood watching until he could no longer see her as her long legs moved with a strong, steady stride. The urge to do something more was strong, yet there was nothing more he could do. For now, he'd done all he could. It was in her hands. As the cloud began to move past the sun, he stepped further back into the shadows of the shady tree until he became one with them.

❖

Renee ended the call and slowly put her phone on the table. Tears pricked hot at her eyes. Yesterday, when she'd witnessed her life going up in flames, she'd felt a whole heck of a lot more philosophical about the unfortunate tragedy. After all, what she'd lost were just things. She had her dog and she was alive and well. That was all fine and dandy until now. Suddenly, she didn't feel quite so Zen. The vastness of what had been destroyed was beginning to dawn on her.

Her insurance agent was kind and helpful…to a point. It didn't matter that she'd been a responsible client and paid her premiums on time each and every year. It didn't matter that she'd never been in trouble; not even a speeding ticket. Nope, none of it made a darned bit of difference when it came time to put the policy into action. It seemed a business burning down was suspect regardless of how squeaky clean the proprietor might be. Until the Seattle Fire Investigator cleared her from intentionally setting the fire that destroyed her home and business, she was screwed. No place to live, no business to run, no income to live on.

"What is it, Twinkle?"

Despite the overwhelming urge to burst into tears, she actually managed to put on a smile. The childhood nickname helped ease the tightening in her throat. It spoke of unconditional love, and she needed that right now. "Red tape, Mom. From the sounds of things this whole fire mess is going to take longer than I thought."

Quickly closing the distance between them, her mother wrapped an arm around her shoulders. "You know you can stay with me as long as you need to, Twinkle. I know Lorna will tell you the same thing."

She kissed her mother's cheek. "I do know and I appreciate it. It's just that all of a sudden I feel incredibly powerless. Who knew that losing everything would set me adrift like this? I never realized how attached I really am to my stuff. Makes me sad on a bunch of levels."

"Stuff we can replace. You and Clancy are irreplaceable, and I, for one, am glad you're here with us for a while. Even so, honey, it makes sense. It isn't just stuff that you lost; it was your home and your business. If you didn't feel like you'd been punched in the stomach, I'd be worried about you."

"Well, in that case you sure don't have to worry about me. I do feel like I've been on the losing end of a prize fight."

"It'll all work out. You just wait and see. In the meantime, you just stay here with us."

"I can't help the feeling that I'm imposing on Lorna's hospitality." She liked being here, and she liked being around Lorna.

At the same time, it was an incredible imposition and that she didn't like. It was one thing to come visit for a couple of days. It was something entirely different to show up with no expiration date and with a dog in tow.

"It's a nice kind of imposition, and honestly, I think it will be good for her to have someone a touch closer to her own age around. She's a little lost herself. Maybe you two can help each other. I know she can definitely use someone to talk to, and you've always been a wonderful listener."

"She doesn't seem very lost, and at least she has a home." Her aura had a touch of disharmony but not enough to make Renee think she was in any kind of crisis. She'd have been able to see that.

"Trust me, Twinkle, she's a lost soul at the moment."

Mom might be right except she wasn't the one who could ride to the rescue. How could she help anyone when she couldn't help herself? She had dumped every dime of the divorce settlement into the building and the shop. At the time, it had seemed so perfect—a rite of passage from her old life into the new. As usual, Bryan declared she'd lost her mind. Not that she blamed him. If the shoe had been on the other foot, she might not have taken the divorce, and the reason behind, nearly as well as he did.

Well, the lack of reasons was a better way to put it. She'd given him nothing definitive to hold on to because at the time she'd not been able to voice it herself. All she'd known was that it was time to walk away. She loved him and probably always would, except it wasn't the kind of love he needed and deserved. Any passion she worked up was hollow and insincere. For years, she'd tried to want the same things he did, wanted to crave his touch and long for his kisses.

It never happened. Somehow, when they were together it was more like being with a close friend than the love of her life. After a while, the lie was too heavy. She couldn't carry it anymore, and she had to come clean with him. He'd been shocked and hurt—at first. When he'd had a little time, he seemed to be brighter, lighter somehow. It was as if her lie had been a burden unconsciously weighing him down as much to him as to her. They'd divided up their assets, signed the papers, and started fresh. He with a lovely uptown attorney and her with a brand new vocation.

Of course, he still had his attorney and she had nothing. Even though she'd let go of denial and embraced what her heart had known all along, love eluded her. Karma appeared to be giving her one well-deserved big bitch slap. For every action there is a reaction, and perhaps for her it just took a little while.

Her mother interrupted her whirling thoughts by taking her face between her hands. "Stop thinking and just accept. You will stay here until things settle down and it will be fine. I promise." She kissed Renee on the tip of the nose, making her smile. "Let's make the best of a bad situation and enjoy the gift of time together."

"Okay," she agreed and kissed her back, on the top of her nose. Moms always knew best, right?

❖

All right, Lorna was either going crazy or something was totally messed up with this place. At the house, she'd been exhausted and could write off what she'd seen as her too-tired mind working in strange ways. Not exactly the case at the moment. She was up, alert, and feeling damned good. All around her were clear skies, bright sunshine, and fresh air. What was she going to blame it on this time?

She was pretty sure she wasn't crazy…although wasn't that what all crazy people say? Still, stress aside, she was as stable now as ever. Her broken heart hadn't sent her so far over the edge that she was seeing and hearing things. Anna's cruelty didn't have that kind of power over her.

So, if it wasn't her, it had to be the house. At least that's where it all started, and now it appeared it was stalking her.

Or at least that's how it felt. First at the house. Now out here on the bluff. It was a little like a miniseries that was broadcast exclusively for her. Lucky Lorna.

Not.

The really scary thing was something about what she was seeing and feeling gave her the creeps deep down into her soul.

It was more than just thinking she was losing her mind. First of all, it was too real. It had a depth and substance to it that made it feel alive. Secondly, the woman made her heart ache each time she gazed on her face. Especially today. The rage mixed with agony was something Lorna could relate to. She'd felt the same way when Anna left her. Powerless and alone, she'd wanted to scream and sob at the same time. Nothing made her feel better. No one could help her. If she'd had a bluff overlooking the ocean, she'd have been there too letting the power of the sea carry her sorrow out with the tide. Until the man showed up to drag her away, the young, sad woman had longed for release of the sea. Lorna had felt it as deeply as if it had been her own desire.

And what was with that guy? She'd instantly hated him with an intensity that made no sense in the logical world. It was as though he'd been a real living and breathing man harshly gripping her arm and spewing his hateful words in her face. It didn't make sense to hate an apparition, and yet that's how she felt.

Shake it off. Dwelling on this was stupid. She was probably just imagining things anyway. Her imagination had always been vivid, and these visions or dreams or whatever in the hell they were most likely were nothing more than her creative imagination working overtime. Besides, it was going to take a while to settle in and blow off the stress of her former life. This was time for new beginnings, and the sooner she made peace with that, the sooner her life would settle into what was ultimately going to be her new normal. She was looking forward to the new normal.

With her shoes back on, Lorna stood, did a quick stretch and then hit the road again. It was past time to release a few endorphins—a sure way to banish any lingering feelings of desolation. One of the greatest things about all the workouts was it never failed to elevate her mood. It was a way better alternative to the chemical solution to depression, and that solution was an absolute last resort.

Two hours later, she'd returned to the house. According to the Garmin on her wrist, she'd just finished up a thirteen-mile loop. Just shy of half a marathon. Her legs were burning in a good way, and sweat drenched her jersey and shorts. Even after the bumpy start, once she got into the run for the first time in months she'd one hundred percent been in the moment.

Maybe it was the odd experience on the bluff or maybe it was just time to get back into the groove of her training. Whatever it was, a thread of optimism threaded through. She'd found a rhythm that carried her for miles, and it was fantastic. If she could capture this same enthusiasm come Ironman day, there was no way she'd fail.

Strange vision aside, the outing was a roaring success. Now all she needed was her bike and she'd be back on the Ironman trail. She'd sculpt her body and focus her mind; she'd meet the challenge, all one hundred and forty point six miles. Optimism buoyed her spirits. This was all going to work out.

CHAPTER FIVE

"A bout damn time." Jeremy stopped in front of the big house and shook his head. A mere four wrong turns, twelve miles out of his way, and at least an hour spent trying to find the place, and he was finally sitting in front of the little cottage Lorna now called home. Ha, little cottage indeed. The house was large enough for a couple of families to live in without getting in each other's way.

Seriously, it should have been easier to find. Not to mention he'd been here before. Both he and Lorna had spent a little time with their great-aunt, but then again he'd been just a kid. The last thing he'd paid attention to was how they got there. He'd been far more intrigued with the ocean shores and the endless hours of exploring the massive grounds had afforded him. His memories were of a little boy's heaven. Driftwood, seashells, rocks worn smooth by the ocean. It made him smile even today. Of course, that had been more years ago than he'd like to admit. He might remember the house, but he sure didn't have a clue how to drive here. It was a lot more complicated than when Mom drove and he rode in the backseat drinking soda, eating chips, and playing games.

Despite being geographically challenged by the drive, he finally made it and even still had gas in the tank. There was a lot to be said for small favors and all that. Now to find his sister and his mission would be complete.

Her moving so far away and to such an isolated location was the kind of extreme that might just work. To say she hadn't taken the breakup with Anna well was sugarcoating it. His always strong, tough-as-nails sister had been crushed. It made his heart hurt as much as hers because he couldn't do a damn thing to ease her pain.

On one hand, he was angry with Anna for what she did to Lorna. Among other things, it wasn't nice. Then again, he'd never thought Anna was the one for his only sibling. It was nothing he could point to and say, "ah ha," more like a feeling that always nagged at him. He couldn't help thinking Lorna could do better even if he never would have said as much to her.

That his feeling turned out to be true didn't make him feel any better. Lorna was hurting, and if he could make that pain go away, he would. He couldn't and knew the only two things that could make it better were time and a chance to meet other women. Time was easy enough. Getting her out to meet other women wasn't going to be so simple, particularly considering where she lived now. Couple that with her clear reluctance to even meet anyone new, and his work was cut out for him.

The one thing he could do for her was deliver her coveted Cervélo to the front door. She was so looking forward to the challenge of Ironman, and he'd do anything he could to help her succeed. He was the first to encourage her in every aspect of her training, and he'd be the first at the finish line in June when she ran across to the announcement, "Lorna Dutton, you are an Ironman." He wasn't crazy enough to ever do the endurance event himself, but he had no problem sharing the moment with Lorna.

The bike in the back of his car was more than just an expensive piece of gear; it was her pride and joy. She'd worked long and hard to be able to afford it. From both a technical and mental standpoint, it gave her an edge. With it, she'd be able to fly along the coast as she trained for the big day.

Once he got out of the car, he stretched his arms high over his head. Everything sort of went snap, crackle, and pop. Made him sound like an old man. After all the hours in the car, it felt good to work out the kinks and it made him feel a little less like the old guy.

Man, this place was something. His childhood recollections were of a huge house, and even with the passage of time that brought him to adulthood, it hadn't really gotten much smaller. It was a friggin' big house for one single woman. Sweet too. Now that he was here, it made him a little jealous.

He wouldn't have had to think twice if Aunty had left it to him. Spokane was a nice place to live, and he loved the boundless outdoor activities the area offered. With four distinct seasons, he was able to play all year round, from swimming in the summer to snowshoeing in the winter He had all the toys a guy could ask for. Golf clubs, a kayak, snowboards, and for his style of cycling, a mountain bike.

Still, it was spectacular here, and it just plain felt good. The air was filled with the distinct scent of the ocean; the sky was crystal clear and beautiful blue, and the grass with thick and green. Lorna's decision to move here was a good one. He could think of far worse places to mend a broken heart.

"Junior!"

Despite himself, he smiled. He *hated* being called Junior, and Lorna knew it, which is precisely why she did it. Didn't matter how old they got, she still liked to poke the bear anytime she got the chance. He'd growl at her for the poke except he couldn't. The sound of her voice, clear and happy, did something good to his heart. Right now she could call him asshole, and if she did it with that note of joy in her voice, he'd still be smiling.

He stared into the blue sky and tried to look serious. "I hear something but can't quite make it out."

She threw her arms around him and hugged tight. She was sweaty and smelly. Anybody with half a brain would back away. He hugged her back. "You smell like an old sock," he said into her ear.

"Yeah, I do. Now you do too."

"Good to see you too, sister."

She stood back and smiled. He decided she looked better than the last time he'd seen her. Even though her voice was light and happy, her eyes held a haunted look he didn't recall seeing before. His hopes for a quick period of healing fell. He'd anticipated that moving here would restore the energetic, beautiful woman she'd been before the Anna debacle. Maybe his hopes had been unrealistic.

It was more than the look in her eyes. She was skinnier too. Not her best look. Neither one of them was ever going to be runway ready. The stock they came from was tall and sturdy. Skinny just wasn't in their bones, and it didn't flatter her now. He wanted his sister back, healthy and strong. Good thing he had some time on his hands because he had some work to do here. He wasn't leaving until she was back to being healthy and happy.

"Got your rocket," he told her.

The way her eyes lit up lightened his heart. She kissed his cheek and then ran to the back of his vehicle, grabbing the handle to the hatch and yanking on it. "Have I told you lately that I love you?"

He laughed and helped her get the bike out of the back. "Yeah, yeah, yeah, you say that to all your handsome brothers."

❖

Renee didn't have to ask her mother who the attractive man in the driveway was; he looked just like Lorna. A little younger and, well, a guy, but he still resembled her enough to make the possibility of a mistake remote. Jeremy. She hadn't seen him for a very long time. The last time she recalled him being here, he'd been a grade schooler playing pirate on the beach. No pirate now, he was tall and handsome.

She also didn't have to ask if Lorna was thrilled to see him. She'd been watching her run up the driveway, and while she appeared happy enough, the sight of Jeremy getting out of the loaded SUV had put a glow on her face.

The joy of reunion was so strong it made Renee smile just watching them. It was infectious even from a distance. No warring siblings in this family. It made her both happy and sad. Happy for them. Sad for her. An only child, she'd always longed for a brother or sister. Both, if she were really lucky. She'd kept that wish locked away in her heart knowing instinctively that her world was different from most of her friends. One great love had been enough for her mother, and though he'd died far too young, he'd left her one child to love. There simply wasn't going to be a little brother or sister. As a single mother, Mom had given her the best she could, and in the big picture, it had been plenty,

It was true she'd grown up in another woman's home, this home, as a matter of fact, but that was okay too. Despite the fact her mother was employed here, it always felt like a real home. Looking back, she could see how much care Aunt Bea took to make it right for her as she grew up. Her little bedroom at the back of the house had been hers and hers alone. The choices of paint colors, furniture, drapes were given to her making the room all the more special. She'd grown up happy and well-adjusted thanks to both Mom and Aunt Bea. That was enough.

Except in moments like this when she stood like a peeping tom watching others in the exchanges that only siblings understood. She'd wanted that, still did, and no matter how many years passed or how mature she became, that little girl in her who longed for a younger brother or sister, reared her head now and again. It probably had a lot to do with why she'd married Bryan. He came from a large, close-knit family, and she'd enjoyed his brothers and sisters to no end. With the divorce and his subsequent marriage, her contact with his family became infrequent. It wasn't that they disliked her, and she certainly held no ill-will toward any of them. No, it was just the inevitable consequence of a broken marriage. The loss was always more than just the bonds of husband and wife; it was the loss of friends and family as well. It couldn't be helped and wasn't something she wanted to linger on. He'd moved on and so had she. Sort of.

Again, the feeling of being adrift wafted over her as she studied Lorna and Jeremy. She hadn't been completely honest with her mother earlier when she'd said it was all because of the fire. This feeling of being lost in the world had been coming over her for a long, long time. It was partly why she'd had to leave Bryan. Things weren't right between them, and it hadn't been fair to him or her. He at least had picked up the pieces and moved on. He'd found what he'd been looking for all along, and she wished him many years of love and happiness. She wasn't so convinced it was going to be in the cards for her.

That night on the rocks so long ago still haunted her. In a perfect world, she'd like to believe she'd been able to reconcile with everything that had driven her to that moment. Unfortunately, her world was far from perfect and she was far from convinced. Especially at moments like this. Doubts lingered, and she shook her head to dispel them. She wasn't going back to that dark place ever again.

Frankly, she didn't know what she wanted. Most of the time she felt a little lost and very much alone. Her saving grace was Clancy. He kept the loneliness from becoming unbearable. And he was a funny guy—that helped more than she could explain. His gentle and comedic disposition was a godsend. It was hard to understand people who didn't share their lives with pets. If Clancy wasn't with her, she was pretty certain there'd have been some serious drugs in her cabinet to keep her from returning to the rocks. Not a road she cared to go down.

Her attention was drawn back outside where Lorna had grabbed her brother's hand and was dragging him in the direction of the front door. Renee spun away from the window. The last thing she wanted was for either of them to see her puppy dog expression. As she whirled away from the window, she smacked right into her mother who went "umph" before landing on her behind on the floor.

"Oh God, Mom." She leaned down and grabbed her arms, helping her back to her feet. "I'm so sorry. That was so stupid of me. You okay?"

Brushing off the non-existent dust from her backside, her mother smiled. "You know you used to have that same look on your face when you were a little one. You'd stand at the window and watch other children playing down on the beach. I'd tell you to go play with them, but you always said no. I never understood why you wouldn't go out with the other children."

Vague recollections filtered into her mind as her mother spoke, and visions of Makah kids running along the beach began to jell. "I remember," she said slowly.

"So why was it you'd never play with them?"

It was on her lips to say she didn't know, and then she paused, recollecting the days when she'd stand at the window watching the kids play, wanting to run along the beach with them, and knowing she wouldn't. She remembered it as if it were yesterday instead of a lifetime ago. "I was afraid."

Her mother's brow wrinkled as she studied her face. "Afraid of the kids? They were all a great bunch. Many of them still live nearby. I never would have suggested you go play if I thought a single one of them would hurt you."

"No, Mom, it wasn't that. Getting hurt was never something I worried about." Old fears wafted across her heart like a cold wind. "I was afraid they wouldn't like me."

Her mother took her face between her hands and placed a kiss on the tip of her nose. "You were always such a sensitive child. Who wouldn't like you? Then or now? You are one of the most wonderful women I've ever known, and I'm not saying that just because I'm your mama. You underestimate yourself, Renee. You always have."

Warmth threaded through her, pushing out the icy memories, and she wrapped her mother in a hug. "And you always know what to say to make me feel better."

"I love you, Twinkle. Always have, always will. Come on, now. Let's go say hello to Jeremy. I haven't seen that boy in eons. I plan to give him the what for."

"I haven't seen him since he was just a little kid."

"I'm not surprised. He wasn't here as often as a child and even less as a teenager. The last few years, both he and Lorna phoned in now and again to check on their aunt. It was a sweet thing to do, and I doubt either of them have a clue how much it meant to Bea."

Lorna and Jeremy came toward the house, their arms linked together. Their auras blended together in colors warm and filled with love. Sometimes her gift made her heart light.

Sometimes it didn't. Threaded through the vibrant red, yellow, blue, and green aura was a streak of black.

Chapter Six

God, Lorna was glad to see Jeremy. When she made the decision to come over here, it didn't occur to her how much she'd miss her brother. At the time, all she could think of was how much distance she could put between herself and Anna. That living here would essentially separate them by the entire state seemed perfect. That it would also put that same amount of distance between her and Jeremy didn't occur to her as she was packing up the moving van.

Even in the time she'd been here, it had been okay. She was lonely, sure, but at least she hadn't had to worry about running into Anna and her new girlfriend if she stopped in at the grocery store. There was a great deal of peace to be found in that. Now, seeing her brother's smiling face brought tears to her eyes. Missing him hit her hard.

Something wasn't quite right though. It was in his eyes. Ever since he was a little kid he always thought he could fool her. If he put a goofy smile on his face, he figured she'd be none the wiser. He'd been wrong then, and he was wrong now. He wasn't fooling her, and before he headed back to Spokane, whatever it was, she'd get it out of him.

For now, though, it was party time. She was so excited to see him and her tri bike…she could bust out dancing, and that wasn't something she did every day. Rather than scare everyone with her sad attempt at dancing, she figured a shower and a beer on the patio would be a whole lot better. She'd drag Renee and Jolene out too. It would be a regular party and maybe, just maybe, she'd feel a little like the woman she'd been before she ran away from Spokane.

Or not.

In her heart, she believed that woman was gone forever. She'd been trusting and gullible then, something she vowed never to be again. All the shit Anna had dished out about love and forever, she'd bought into hook, line, and sinker. She'd been a fool, and that wasn't going to happen again. The woman she'd been when she was with Anna wasn't the kind of person she wanted to be anymore.

What she wanted more than anything was for the pain to go away. To feel free and alive and happy instead of suspicious and gloomy would be incredible. But the suffocating sense of betrayal lingered like a cold that wouldn't respond to antibiotics. No matter what she did or where she went, there it was. The elephant in the room. She'd never thought of herself as a sensitive woman. Practical and even-tempered was what she liked to think even if lately it hadn't been her M.O. so much. She wanted that woman back, and today, for the first time, it felt like a glimmer of hope dangled out there just waiting for her to grab it.

Yeah, a shower and a beer. It was going to be great. With a kiss on the cheek for Jeremy, she walked with him into the house, and then left him in the massive living room while she took the stairs two at a time. In her room, she threw her sweaty clothes on the floor and stepped into the huge, dual-headed shower that made her feel like a queen every time she used it.

❖

The pounding of Lorna's feet on the front stairs made Renee smile. She liked the way she moved. It was more than her obvious conditioning. She was an athlete through and through, yet it was something beyond athletic training that made Renee take notice. There was a grace in the way she walked and ran that was unique to her. It captured the eye, and Renee found herself entranced each time Lorna was around.

It was definitely not out of the realm of possibility it was her first real girl crush. Lord knows she'd tried to be the woman everyone expected, and any time there was a twinge of attraction toward another woman, she'd stifled it the second it raised its head. She'd told herself it was no big deal to feel attracted to a woman. Every once in a while every woman felt that kind of pull, right? When her marriage ended, so did the lie. She'd felt free for the first time in her life. Funny thing, though, with freedom came a sort of solitude she hadn't expected.

In her head, she'd expected the world to open up to her. To make peace with who she really was and come out to friends and family was sure to topple the barriers to happiness or so she'd believed. Deep in her heart, the seed of hope that she'd find the kind of love she'd always desired began to take root. Her life would take bloom and grow because she was brave and fully alive for the first time ever. It didn't happen. In fact, it was pretty much the opposite. The world seemed to have gotten smaller, and love, well, that didn't even show up as a blip on the radar. Nothing. Nada. Nyet.

She was more alone than she'd ever been. The truth had set her free and had become her isolation. That might be a bit of dramatization about her world these days, but it wasn't too far off the truth either. Most of her friends still stood by her, and her mother had taken the news with the grace of a saint. It didn't change the fact that her reality was skewed. At times, old friends seemed awkward around her as if they didn't know what to say or do. Some of her girlfriends appeared downright nervous as if they expected her to jump their bones. Not likely to happen because though she loved her friends deeply, she didn't love them like *that*.

Damned if she did. Damned if she didn't.

Maybe that was why the shop burning down didn't send her into automatic crisis mode. It was an unexpected excuse to get away from her day-to-day life for just a little while. A break was, if not needed, greatly appreciated, and this was a perfect place to take it.

Except for Lorna. No matter how she looked at it, Lorna was trouble on a pair of shapely legs. Renee could make all the excuses she wanted and it wouldn't change anything. She thought Lorna was the most intriguing woman she'd met in a very long time, and was attracted to her in a way that made her hot in all the right places. Yeah, it was most definitely her first serious girl crush and that realization made her smile.

Lorna, on the other hand, was polite and friendly. Just like any other casual acquaintance who felt absolutely nothing beyond friendliness. Figured she'd be here in this big house with the first woman to light her fire and the feeling was one-sided. Her timing seemed to suck no matter which team she was on. With that thought, she didn't feel like smiling anymore.

Oh well, she was a big girl, and like all first crushes, this too would pass. Give it a few weeks and she'd be back in Seattle rebuilding her shop, and Lorna would be here training for her big race. She would pick up her life in the big city and let fate roll the dice. Lorna wasn't the only game in the Evergreen State. Surely there was at least one woman in Seattle who could share Renee's feelings. Or at the very least be up for a hot love affair. She didn't need the forever kind of love, but she certainly wouldn't turn away heartfelt companionship.

She stopped in the doorway to the living room. Jeremy was staring out the big windows at the ocean as the waves rolled toward the sandy beach. The sky was growing dark from yet more incoming storm clouds. They were in for another rainy night. She didn't mind. The rain was comforting, and that's probably why she never moved farther east than Seattle. If she got too far away from the ocean or the volatile weather that made this area so special, her heart felt empty. Some people found rain dreary. She didn't. It was soothing to her.

"Hi," she finally said after watching him for what had to be a full minute. The aura of color that surrounded him captured her completely because now it was an aura barely troubled by the wave of black she'd seen just minutes before. Vague as it was, the streak was still present in his otherwise joyful aura. That it had backed off in intensity was a good thing. That it was there at all wasn't. She didn't like it, and before she headed back to Seattle, she would find out what it meant. A man like this shouldn't ever be troubled by something like that.

At the sound of her voice, he jumped a little before spinning in her direction. His face at first was sad, serious, and then a smile banished the dreary expression and his eyes sparkled. "I remember you," he said as he strode in her direction, his hand extended.

"You do?" She was shocked. He'd been so young last time and she wasn't usually the person people remembered. Her ability to blend into the background was legendary.

"Oh yeah, you're Renee, and when I was six I thought you were coolest girl ever. I told Mom I was going to marry you some day."

She laughed and all her somber thoughts of a moment before banished. "Well, I am single."

A shadow briefly crossed his face, quickly replaced by the high-wattage smile. "Sweet, maybe I should propose." His eyebrows rose in an expression of teasing suggestion.

His hand was warm in hers as his long fingers wrapped her hand. She loved the warmth and friendship the simple gesture conveyed. "Jeremy, you are just the prescription I needed."

He frowned slightly, his eyes searching her face. "You've been sick?"

She shook her head, letting go of his hand. "No, just displaced. My place burned down, and your sister has kindly opened her home to me while I wait on repairs."

"Oh, man, that sucks. How did it happen?" He stuck his hands in his pockets and rocked back on his heels.

As much as she hated thinking about what happened to her beautiful building, she recounted the gritty details of how she and Clancy ended up as grateful recipients of Lorna's hospitality. When she finished, he was shaking his head.

"Wow, you're handling it better than I would have. I'd be a mess if I'd lost everything like that. Sounds pretty shallow, but I'm kind of attached to all my things."

She shrugged, and her earlier distress over the insurance and fire investigation began to fade. "It was just stuff."

"Cool stuff."

She nodded. Her shop had been awesome and her inventory unique. It was going to take years to build it back to the level it had been just yesterday. "Definitely cool stuff."

In a way, it wasn't all bad. Yes, it had taken years to build the inventory. They had been incredible years filled with impromptu trips, excursions to estate sales, and accidental finds. Every find, every treasure, had been a joyous discovery. The shop had been more than simply a shop. It had been her own world of bliss. The fire had indeed taken her things. It had not destroyed her bliss.

Her eyes were drawn to his hands that were fiddling with his phone as if he wanted to call someone but didn't want to offend her. She knew the move, had been guilty of it herself more than once. The curse of the electronic world was its instant access to everything. It was a lure hard to resist. He was doing an admirable job though she decided it was time to leave him be to make his call or send his text or do whatever it was he wanted to do with his phone. She was glad she'd come in to say hello and even more glad that he was such a bright light, but there was wisdom in letting their pleasant reunion be at short and sweet.

A storm was surely on the way, and before it came, she and Clancy needed a bit of fresh air. With a wave and a smile, she headed outside, leaving Jeremy to make his call while she pondered the disturbing slash of black that darkened an otherwise beautiful aura.

❖

As soon as he was alone, Jeremy stared at his phone and resisted the urge to hit speed dial one. His heart said call. His pride said walk away. Merry was the one who was hiding something. Not him. She was the one who wouldn't look him in the eye. Not him.

So why should he be the one to break the silence that had now stretched on for three long days? If she cared, Merry should be the one to call him.

And therein was the rub.

He wanted to come off as the big, strong guy with a chest full of pride. He didn't need a woman to make him whole or happy, and while that sounded good, it was essentially a crock of shit. Any way he came at it, he loved her with his whole heart. He'd never met a woman like Merry, and no one had ever made him feel such extremes, both good and bad. He didn't want to lose what they had.

Whatever she was hiding, he wasn't going to like it, and that belief cut him deeply. Lorna always told him he'd know when the right one came along and she'd been dead-on. It only took him a couple of months with Merry before the light bulb hit a hundred watts. With long, curly brown hair, a build that leaned toward an extra ten pounds and green eyes that sparkled, she wasn't a classic beauty. To his eyes, she was the perfect beauty. He loved the way she looked, the way she moved, and the way she laughed. He loved everything about her.

Oh, he was hooked all right, and what scared him the most was the growing fear that she wasn't. So what was wrong with him? Why did she scurry to another room when he walked in on her talking on her phone? Why wouldn't she meet his eyes when he asked what was going on?

Worst of all? Why had she let the silence drag on? He could only think of one reason, and it broke his heart.

And that pissed him off.

Seriously, he was a big tough guy who played football in high school and college. He ran marathons and climbed mountains. Women were always interested in him. They called him and stopped by his house unannounced. He did not get teary eyed and sad because one woman ignored him. Another one would be by in five minutes. It had always worked that way for him. The cheerleaders, the beauty queens, and the pampered all loved him. They were drawn to him and he to them. Until now.

Now all he wanted was Merry, and she was nowhere to be found. He had finally caught the golden ring and it was slipping through his fingers. He desperately needed to know why. It was impossible to fix whatever had gone wrong when he had no clue what it was.

"What's with the long face, bro?"

At the sound of Lorna's voice, he jumped and almost dropped the brand new smartphone, which really would have sucked considering it cost him way more than any reasonable person should have paid. He was pretty sure it hadn't been worth the price since it wasn't doing anything good for him at the moment. It was entirely possible it wouldn't even work way out here in the sticks. Still, he was glad he'd caught it before it crashed to the floor.

Lorna was standing in the doorway, her face shining and her hair damp. In jeans, a sweatshirt, and a pair of red Converse sneakers, even he had to admit she looked great. A little thin maybe, but more like the sister he'd been missing ever since Anna had left her.

"I don't have a long face. That's just stupid." Guys did not go around wearing their hearts on their sleeves. Or at least this guy didn't. He hoped.

"I beg to differ with you, pal. You look like somebody just sacked you."

Of the all the people who might understand and the only one who wouldn't pass judgment, Lorna was the person he could lean on. She would get why he was feeling like crap. Still, he hesitated. He didn't want to sound like he was sixteen and in the throes of his first relationship. Or, rather the way it felt right now, the shock of being dumped for the first time. Besides, Lorna already had enough emotional baggage after the ugly breakup with Anna. He didn't need to add his troubles to the mix.

Her eyes were steady on his face, and he knew that look. She wasn't going to give it up. "Come on, Jeremy. Spit it out. I don't need you moping around here like a sad puppy. I can do enough of that all by myself. Don't need or want company in that department. Tell me what's wrong and I'll help you just like you've always done for me. We're family, man. It's what families do for each other."

Her point was well taken. They'd been each other's support for years, even before Mom and Dad were gone. Empathy wasn't a bad thing when he felt like he was in the dumps. He shoved the phone in his pocket and stepped over to the window. Outside, the ocean was dark and moody, the waves coming in hard and strong, spraying mist high into the air. The sight was incredible and almost hypnotic. Slowly, he began. "I think Merry is getting ready to dump me." He silently congratulated himself on not choking up after the words left his lips.

Lorna's response was machine gun fast. "Bullshit. I've seen the way she looks at you."

He shook his head. There was so much she didn't know. "You haven't seen the way she looks at me lately."

"Meaning?"

He closed his eyes, seeing her face and her beautiful gray eyes as they turned away from him. Until recently, her gaze was always steady on his, and in it he'd seen a reflection of his own heart. "Meaning she won't look at me at all."

"So talk to her."

"I've tried." Any harder and he'd be a begging mess. Not exactly the image he really wanted to portray.

"Try harder." Lorna abruptly left the room. He didn't have to wonder why very long because she returned a couple minutes later with two bottles of beer she'd obviously snagged from the fridge. After twisting the top off one, she handed it to him. She opened the second bottle and took a long pull.

The icy cold beer in one hand, he rubbed his eyes with the other, and sighed. "I don't know what else to do. She's not picking up my calls, I haven't seen her in almost a week, and I haven't talked to her in three days. We haven't been apart this long since we met, and even then we talked every day. I've left messages, called about a bazillion of times, and driven by her office enough times I'm surprised they haven't called the cops on me." Still looking out the window at the ocean as the incoming storm made it rumble and roll, he took a drink of the beer.

When Lorna didn't immediately come back with another snappy response, he turned around. Her silence was unnerving. She stood watching him with one hand on a hip, the bottle of beer pointed at his chest. Her expression was bland, almost bored looking. "What?" he asked.

"That's it? That's what you base this whole *she's dumping* me scenario on?"

"Yeah, well, that's what it feels like."

Lorna laughed, a big rolling sound that was full of merriment. "Put on your big boy panties, bro, and call the woman. Trust me on this one; don't let something little blow up into something huge. It's not worth it. Swallow your man pride and call."

"I want to…" he muttered as he rolled the bottle between his hands. God, did he ever.

"Oh, for Christ's sake." Lorna smacked her beer on the fireplace mantle before shoving her hand into his pocket and ripping out his phone. She did it so fast he didn't even have time to react before she was scrolling through numbers. The phone up to her ear, she said "Hey, Merry, it's Lorna. How you doing? I'm great. Say, you got a couple minutes? My brother wants to talk to you."

She shoved the phone in his direction and mouthed "talk to her." He took it and for a moment just stared at the display. "She answered?" It was unbelievable. He'd called her so many times he'd lost count and not once had she actually picked up.

"Merry, my brother is a dork," Lorna yelled as she spun and left the room, the beer once more in hand.

He put the phone to his ear. "Merry?" Was that really his voice? Sounded more like a twelve-year-old.

"Hey, baby," she said softly.

The sound of her familiar rich voice brought tears to his eyes. "Are you upset with me?"

"No, baby," she said firmly, though her words were still full of the sweetness that always made his heart happy. "But we have to talk…"

Chapter Seven

L orna decided that sometimes when they were around each other it was like they were ten and twelve again. Lorna in her role as the big sister and bossing Jeremy around, little brother Jeremy wanting to resist but not able to defy the older sister he loved so much. And she loved him. They'd had each other's back forever, and now as adults it was the same. No matter what, he would be there for her. She would always be there for him. Like right now because it was clear from the second he got here that he needed her. It was her turn to step up.

A person would have to be deaf and blind not to see how much he loved Merry. She was glad too. All his previous girlfriends had been...well, *fluffy* for lack of a better description. Nice enough she supposed, but no substance to them. They just liked hanging on the arm of the pretty boy who was a football star. He'd loved the attention, but even way back when, Lorna had known he needed more. Jeremy was much deeper than the stereotypical handsome jock he appeared to be at first glance. That meant he wouldn't survive the long haul on fluff.

Merry was the more that he needed. She was cute and alive, smart and engaging. She made everyone around her feel the joy of life, and was exactly the person who could fill that empty place inside of Jeremy. It was more than that though. Merry wasn't the brief fling kind of woman for Jeremy; she was the forever kind, and

Lorna wasn't going to let him fuck that up. Guys could be, well… such guys! Her brother included.

He might think he was big and tough, but that was just a well-crafted façade. Inside, he was all heart, and if he realized he wore that heart on his sleeve, he'd probably want to die. It made her love him all the more. God may have given her challenges in her life, but by giving her Jeremy, he'd put a giant plus in her column. Now it was up to her to keep him going down the right path, and that meant with Merry.

His voice held a huge note of hope as she'd quietly closed the doors to the hallway. Let him have his call in peace. Obviously, the two of them had things to work out. They would. She felt that in her bones. They were, she was quite certain, going to make it for the long haul. All they'd needed was a little nudge, and she was more than happy to oblige. Of course in Jeremy's case the nudge was more like a big fat kick in the ass.

The sun was beginning to set when she left the house to take a walk outside. The air was cold and fresh with a hint of storm that was gathering to the west. Maybe coming here was running away from life and maybe not. Sometimes she had the feeling she was meant to be here all along. Everything about the place felt so natural that it made her wonder if coming here was her destiny.

She walked to the edge of the bluff where the land dropped off sharply and stared down. Dangerous if one weren't looking. Beautiful if one were paying attention. With her legs draped over the edge, she sat and stared out across the water. The scents so particular to the ocean shore wrapped her in their now familiarity. Yes, she still missed Anna, but it occurred to her that every minute she spent here, the ache eased away a little more and a little more. She wondered if there was magic in the water, the air, the land. Whatever it was, she liked it.

"Can I join you?"

Lorna jumped, and a shaft of fear shot through her as she wobbled on the precarious lip. Strong hands steadied her shoulders. Renee.

"I've got you," Renee said softly into her ear. "Sorry I startled you. I wasn't trying to sneak up."

When her heartbeat returned to normal, Lorna looked up at Renee. "My fault. I was so wrapped up in my own thoughts I didn't hear you or Clancy." She really must have been inside her own head because she hadn't heard so much as a hint of two feet or four paws. She was normally quite aware of what was going on around her.

"You looked a little lonely sitting out here so I took a chance you might want some company. Clancy and I have been out on a walk. I wanted to get him out for a good run before the storm hit. Looks like it's going to be a zinger."

Lorna couldn't help the smile even though by all rights she should be annoyed. After all, she'd come out here to be alone, but all of a sudden, she welcomed Renee's presence. She didn't even mind the damn dog, Clancy, who was right at the moment racing along the bluff, jumping into the air, and trying to catch leaves that were being tossed around by the stirring wind. Nope, she didn't mind the dog one tiny bit.

"Company is good. The solitude has been pretty nice all things considered, but having others around isn't so bad either. Keeps me from becoming the local area hermit."

"I don't see you ever being a hermit, local or otherwise. You know, it was lovely seeing your brother again after all these years. He was just a little guy the last time I saw him. Boy has he changed. Bet the ladies knock on his door at all hours of the day and night."

"You know it, sister. It started in junior high and he loved it. Now days, he might look like a big, strong man, but he's still a little guy inside."

Renee's laughter was a beautiful sound and made her all the more pleased to have accepted her offer of company. "Aren't we all?"

"Yeah, I suppose we are." Wasn't it the action of a little girl to pack up all her toys and run away? Couldn't deny that's exactly what she'd done. Could be that sometimes it was okay to be a little girl inside.

The rays of the sun were beginning to slant down through the clouds, sending a shaft of light onto the beach. Something glinted in the increasing gloom, and Lorna squinted trying to bring it into focus. A necklace? "Do you see that?" She pointed.

Renee leaned out a little and, like Lorna, squinted. Her hair floated around her face in a silky veil. It was beautiful, and it took a great deal of self-control not to reach out and run her fingers through it.

"It looks like jewelry," Renee said.

Lorna's gaze returned to the surf and the mystery treasure bobbing in and out of view. "That's what I thought too. You up for a trek down to the beach?"

Renee jumped to her feet, a smile on her face. "Absolutely," she said and then reached out a hand to Lorna.

In the long shadows cast by the darkening clouds, the Watcher stood with his face turned up. Above him, the two women sat and talked, voices too low to make out the words. The day was growing shorter, the spring storms coming more often. Tonight, the air was turning brisk with the approach of rain and the threat of thunder. Soon darkness would fall.

He was not discouraged by the encroaching darkness or the approaching storm. The glow that surrounded the women was the light he'd been seeking for a hundred years. It was the sign he'd waited and hoped for since he'd come to this place. Hope surged through him.

The two women were the answer. One possessed the power of the spirit needed to cast aside the constrictions of the earthly world and look to the other side. There, and only there, would the truth reveal itself. When it did, what was wrong would once again be brought right.

The other woman was the strength needed to keep her true. She was the believer, and through her, the other would embrace the truth. One could not do it without the other. Of that he was certain and there was not much time. If they did not heed the call soon, the chance would once again pass by. The gates would stay closed to his eternal entreaty to walk through, and those who were lost would not find their way to the light. Another year would pass him by, and another year he would stand in the shadows hoping for a chance at redemption.

At the edge of the beach, pools of glistening water formed when the waves flowed to shore. He studied the whalebone necklace as it floated in the swirling pool where he had dropped it. The bone, so smooth and white, captured the light of the setting sun. To let it go for the first time in a century was a loss he felt to his soul. The beautiful piece had been in his hand since the awful night when two souls were denied love and worse, life. He'd always known the day would come when it would slip from his fingers and be lost to him forever, and yet he hadn't understood how desolate it would make him feel.

All he could hope for was the loss would bring him that much closer to bringing them home. If these two women failed to understand the significance of what he left for them, he'd lost it all for nothing. He prayed they would see, and more importantly, would understand. It started with a simple question, and that would be enough to drive them in the direction they needed to go.

With the question, their minds would open even more. That's all he needed to touch their spirits and their souls. Then together, they would make right the tragedy that had stained this ground for far too long.

When the women rose and started down the bluff toward the shoreline, he nodded to himself and stepped deeper into the shadows. His work on this day was complete. He could do nothing more. Now it rested in the hands of the one with the sight, for she must touch the past and push aside the veil to see. When she did, it was up to the other to make her believe.

❖

Bottom line? If this was her first girl crush, Renee liked it. Sitting side by side on the bluff with Lorna talking like they were old friends was wonderful in a way she didn't even know she was missing until it happened. If it were possible, she could have sat next to her all night just talking.

Then again, that shiny thing down in the swirling pool between the rocks was way interesting. It was the kind of treasure she'd loved to capture for her shop. If she still had a shop that is, but she didn't want to dwell on that ugly fact at the moment. It was too pleasant out here in the fresh air with Lorna, and now they were climbing down the steep bank on the search and recovery mission.

Once they hit the beach, Renee gave Lorna a sideways glance and then sprinted toward the swirling pools. Balanced on the slippery rocks, she reached down and grabbed what turned out to indeed be a necklace. An old necklace. Her victory complete, she held it up. The condition was amazing considering it had obviously been in the water for a while. How in the world did it stay in such pristine condition after being washed ashore and battered by the rocks? Spray from the crashing waves quickly soaked her, and she shivered as she tried not to slip into the whirling pool at her feet. It wasn't deep, but she didn't need to get any wetter than she was already.

Carefully, she made it back to the beach and for a moment studied the lovely workmanship. It was a whalebone piece, which meant it had to have come from the Makah. Did someone accidentally lose it? The more she studied it, the more she was convinced her initial impression was dead on. It was old. The workmanship was exquisite and detailed. This was not a necklace one would find in a tourist shop. No, this was the real deal and no way should it have been floating around in the Pacific Ocean. It made her sad to think it had been lost this way.

"It's beautiful," she said to Lorna as she turned it over, examining each bead. "And old. Someone spent a great deal of time making this necklace. It had to have been very special."

"Why do you think that?" Lorna peered over her shoulder.

She loved the feel of Lorna so close she could feel her breath on her neck. "Mainly it's the workmanship. I've seen this level of skill in the museums. That's not to say folks today can't do this too. They can. But the materials they use are a little different. This screams old and traditional. Here, take a look." She handed Lorna the necklace, laying it in the palm of her hand. It was pale against Lorna's tanned skin.

At the sound of Lorna's sharp intake of breath, her head snapped up. Lorna's face had gone paper white and she was trembling so hard, Renee reached out to take her hands. Before she could stop her, Lorna crumbled to the sand, the necklace held tight in her fist.

CHAPTER EIGHT

Jeremy sank to the sofa, his phone still clutched in his sweaty hand. Tears sprang to his eyes, and it was all he could do not to burst out in sobs. Good God, guys didn't break down and cry like big babies. Not at his age anyway. But honestly, that's what he felt like doing. What Merry had told him was still ringing in his ears as if she was screaming it from an inch away.

Was he really that clueless? Apparently, he was because he managed to miss all the signs. The only halfway decent excuse he had was he'd been too wrapped up in his own world to notice anything. Regardless of how chaotic his life had been lately, it was no excuse, considering until recently it had almost been as though they lived together. Either he was at her place or she was at his. They were rarely apart. So much so he'd planned to ask her to move in together. It didn't make sense for them to maintain two separate houses when they were with each other so much. Then everything got wonky and her behavior changed when he was around. He'd been baffled and hurt. A little pissed off if he was really being honest.

Now he understood and none of it mattered. Not his confusion or his hurt feelings. As for his irritation, that was just plain out of line.

Tears welled up in his eyes again, and this time he let them fall. Screw being a big, tough guy. Everything he'd been feeling before the call, everything he was feeling now, well, it was too much to be contained. Even the toughest guy was entitled to a good cry after a call like that. Never in a million years would he have believed he could feel this way.

"Are you all right?"

Jeremy took an unsteady breath and turned to look at Jolene who stood in the doorway with an expression of worry on her face. It had been years since he'd seen Jolene, and yet the moment he saw her it as was as if it had only been a matter of hours. It had always been that way with both Jolene and Aunt Bea. Now, her voice, her expression, were those of a caring parent. All of a sudden it hit him how much he'd been missing that since losing Mom and Dad.

He smiled at her through the tears and his heart soared. He'd never been more all right than at this moment and was delighted to share it with her.

"Yeah, Jolene, I'm great 'cause in about six months, I'm gonna be a dad."

❖

She walked along the beach, the night sky streaked black and blue, the air cold and powerful. Her braids whipped in the wind, her skirt pressed wet and heavy against her legs. She didn't worry if the water was ruining her gown and didn't care. Her heart was light; she didn't even try to stop the smile.

In the distance, she could see the other woman who came toward her with long, dark hair flying as she raced across the sand, her bulky skirts held up in her hands. From this distance, her feet seemed to barely touch the sand as she ran straight down the beach in her direction.

Her own step grew quicker until at last they came together in an embrace that was far more than friendship. Their bodies touched, pressed as closely together as possible. Their lips met in a kiss that rang of passion and love. The intensity of the kiss took her breath away and she trembled from head to foot. It was that way every time they touched.

"I cannot stay long," she said as she ran her hands down the silky black braids.

"I am happy for even a moment."

She tried not to let her fear show. *"He will find me. He always finds me."*

"Let us not waste even a second. Come, my love. I have found a place of solitude."

She knew she should return home before he missed her. A wise woman would not tempt his fury. She didn't want to be a wise woman. Hand in hand, they walked down the beach, turning at an outcropping of boulders. Moonlight cut through the darkened sky sending a shaft of light to shine on them. Around her lover's neck gleamed a whalebone necklace.

Lorna sat up straight, her hand so tight around the whalebone it cut into the flesh of her palm. "I think I'm going crazy," she said in a husky voice. "I really think I'm going crazy."

"And I think you scared the living daylights out of me. What just happened? Where did you go?" Renee asked. "One second you're standing there clear eyed and strong, the next you drop like a hot rock to the sand and I don't know where you've gone. Freaked me out."

The necklace lying in her lap, Lorna pushed the wet hair off her face. The day was quickly turning cold, and after her little drop and roll on the wet sand, she was now chilled and soaked through. The way things were going lately, it would be just her luck to end up sick after this, thereby screwing up her Ironman training.

She took a deep breath and blew it out slowly. "I don't know what happened or where I went, but the last couple of days, it keeps happening."

Renee's brows drew together as she looked at Lorna. "What keeps happening?"

She didn't want to admit to Renee exactly what had been going on. She'd think her certifiable, which might not be that far from the truth. What else could explain the things she'd been seeing? These dreams where she was her but not her along with the beautiful woman that she obviously loved were so realistic it was freaky. Nothing too crazy in that.

Nope, she didn't want to tell Renee any of it.

Then again, if she didn't tell someone, she really would go off the rails. She'd never had anything like this happen to her before. Even given the stress of her breakup with Anna, it hadn't been enough to send her over the proverbial edge. And truthfully, she didn't feel crazy…like anyone ever did. Except for the few minutes when the visions, or whatever the hell they were, happened, she felt pretty damned normal. So what was going on? Was she really losing her mind or was it possible there could be another explanation?

Renee was stroking her hands and she liked the way it felt. "Come on, Lorna. You can trust me. Tell me what happened. I can help or at the very least, I can try."

She looked into Renee's dark eyes and her reservations flowed away like the outgoing tide. Reflected in their depths wasn't judgment or fear but rather compassion and truth. Though they might now know each other well, she believed in her heart that she could tell Renee anything. She wanted to trust her. So she did.

After five minutes of babbling, she took a breath and closed her eyes. There was no denying it felt good to be able to articulate what had been happening to her. At the same time, she was afraid to see the look on Renee's face. Undoubtedly, it would show compassion— the kind reserved for the mentally unstable. That was more than she could handle, so she kept her eyes tightly closed. Better not to see.

Still holding onto her hands, Renee gently pulled up to her feet. "Come on," she said in a hushed voice. "We're getting cold and wet, or in your case, colder and wetter. Let's go dry off, make a pot of coffee, and then you're going to tell me all of this again in detail. We'll figure it out together."

She was forced to open her eyes when she got to her feet, and she was shocked to discover her fears about what she'd see in Renee's face were unfounded. Instead, what she saw was curiosity, and that gave her hope. Even so, she said to her, "You think I'm crazy."

Renee's smile was warm and genuine without any hint of condescension. She nodded and patted her on the arm. "Maybe a little, but not in the way you think. Training for an Ironman, now that's crazy. Having visions, on the other hand, is pretty awesome if you ask me, and I want to know more. So come on. Let's get dry and warm, a little coffee, and a whole lotta talking. Besides"—she held out a hand—"I have something I want to share with you and then we can decide which one of us is really crazy."

Unbelievable. She fully expected Renee to think she was suffering from some form of mental illness and instead she seemed genuinely interested rather than appalled. Oddly, it made her think of Anna and how she might deal with this turn of events. Not like this, was her first thought. Her second thought was that she was grateful she was with Renee rather than Anna.

Before they left, she reached down and picked up the necklace where it had fallen to the sand when she'd stood. For a second she hesitated worried that it would send her into another vision as soon as she touched the whalebone bead. It didn't and she slipped it into her pocket. Together she and Renee headed back up the bluff and toward the house. She could hardly wait to sit before the fire and tell Renee her secrets.

Inside, Jolene had laid a small fire in the fireplace. It gave the room a warm and cozy glow, and it chased away the dark shadows of the storm that began its assault before they were safely back inside.

"Okay," Renee said as they sat in front of the fire. "So tell me what has you thinking you're going crazy."

Lorna took a deep breath, let it out slowly, and began. "I can see two women. They're obviously in love and yet they're being torn apart…" She continued to describe the visions to Renee hoping that she didn't scare her too much. When she finished, they were both silent. Lorna was worried that Renee had concluded that her fears of mental instability had merit.

She was surprised with Renee smiled and touched her hand. "Kind of cool when you think about. I think spirits are reaching out to you for some reason. There's something they want you to know."

"No," Lorna said. The last thing she possessed was any kind of paranormal ability. She was as down to earth and grounded as they came. She didn't believe in anything like that.

"I think you're wrong and I'll tell you why. You'll more than likely think I'm the one who's crazy, but I'm not and neither are you.

Ever since I was a kid I've been able to see colors around people's bodies. When I was little I thought everyone could. Imagine my surprise when I discovered almost nobody could. I quit telling people when I figured out few thought it was a positive personality trait."

"You were just a kid."

"That was the problem. I had a habit of blurting it out, and people did not respond in a positive way."

Lorna was intrigued. There were so many layers to Renee; it was exciting to see them peeled back. "What was it you were seeing?"

A little smile turned up the corners of Renee's mouth. "Not was, Lorna. Is. What I still see are auras."

"No way, that's just some new wave voodoo." As soon as the words were out of her mouth, she regretted them. They were the words of a rude and narrow-minded person. Not very nice of her considering what she'd just unloaded.

Renee's smile didn't falter. "Now you get why I quit telling people?"

Lorna couldn't help but smile herself. "Oh yeah, I get it. You really see auras?"

"I really do."

"Can you see mine?" Renee's smile finally faltered, and a feeling of unease rippled through her. "What? What's wrong with me?"

Renee reached out and patted her on the arm. "Oh, girlfriend, you're fine."

"Except?"

"Except for the little shade of black rippling through your aura."

"Black? That can't be good."

She shrugged. "If it was all black, I'd be very concerned. It's not so it's more like a touch of something not quite pleasant is circling around you and your brother."

"Jeremy?" A shot of alarm went through her.

"Sorry, yes. It's around him too, and I'd like to know why it's touching you both. We'll figure it out and make it all right. After what you've told me, it's probably something to do with your visions."

"Doesn't sound good." Not to her anyway.

"No worries, Lorna. I'm sure it will be all right in the end."

Maybe Renee was confident. She was a little less so. The last thing she needed was one more problem. She was busy enough taking care of the ones she already had.

Chapter Nine

Renee went to her room a little after eleven. The storm picked up steam while they sat in front of the fireplace the last few hours, and now the wind and rain pounded against the windows. For some, the sounds of a storm were disconcerting. Not to her. She loved the whistle of the wind and the patter of rain. In a way, it was a lullaby that reminded her of a wonderful childhood in this house.

Tonight, she traded blue jeans and a sweatshirt for sweats and a T-shirt thinking the switch to comfort clothes would help her relax. By all rights, she should be tired. Clancy certainly was. The ability to run free of a lead was a huge treat for him, and he ran the beach and grounds until he was so tired he could barely eat. It was like that every single time they came here. Today was no exception. Now, he was stretched out in the middle of the bed, breathing deep and even. It was bound to be a struggle when it came time to try to claim her half of the bed or whatever portion of the bed she could get him to give up. Not yet though, the battle for the domination of the bed would have to wait a little while. She wasn't tired. On the contrary, her mind was whirling with thoughts about what Lorna had shared with her as they fed the small fire and listened to the building storm.

Lorna might have gone into the conversation thinking she wouldn't believe her. She would have been quite wrong. While Lorna had been a visitor in this house during her childhood, Renee had grown up in the big house with more rooms than one family could use. Always in the back of her mind lived the suspicion that they weren't exactly alone. Not that she'd actually seen any ghosts or had any visions as Lorna had. No, it was more a nagging feeling that never quite went away. Something that she would catch out of the corner of her eye and yet when she'd turn her head, it was gone. She had no trouble believing what was happening to Lorna was quite real.

After listening to Lorna and considering the black ribbon that threaded through her aura, she no longer wondered whether or not they were alone here. Something, or rather someone, had never left this place. For some reason, it picked Lorna as its conduit. What they had to find out is why. It was an adventure far more preferable to pursue than the kind of adventure that started with a fire. Gave her something more interesting to think about.

Restless, she pushed her feet into a pair of slides Mom had loaned her and left Clancy snoring away to head downstairs. It struck her as funny how every time he sank into a deep sleep, he snored like an old man. She never realized German shepherds snored until Clancy joined her little family. Made him more endearing to her than he already was, if that was even possible.

In the kitchen pantry, she rooted around until she located several bottles of wine. Her pick was a nice cabernet from one of the state's noted wineries. Even though it was a good wine, it was still nothing too fancy or expensive so she didn't feel guilty when she uncorked it. Raiding the wine cellar for one of Aunt Bea's high-end wines didn't seem right. One of the cheaper versions, well, she'd was okay with imbibing. Giving it a few minutes to breathe, she went to the cupboard where the wine glasses were kept and picked out a pretty one with a dark blue stem.

The house was still and quiet when she took her wine into the living room. She didn't turn on any lights. Instead, stood at the French doors and watched the storm batter the balcony, spikes of lightning cracking across the sky far out over the ocean. The way Lorna described the first vision, it was here in this room on a night much like this one. Seemed awfully coincidental that it would be the same on the night she decided to share her secret.

"So," she said quietly as she turned and gazed into the empty room. "What are you trying to tell her? Who are you? I know you're here, and I know you've touched her. I've seen your fingerprints."

No one answered. No visions came into her head. Only the stillness of a house at rest. In the fireplace, embers glowed red and yellow, the dying remnants of a fire her mother had built earlier in the evening and that she and Lorna had fed during their long talk. The air still held the scent of burning tamarack and the warmth only a wood fire could create. It reminded her of long ago nights when she'd sit with Bea who read her wonderful stories. *Little Women, Pride and Prejudice,* and sometimes works a little darker, *The House of Seven Gables,* and one of her personal favorites, *Frankenstein.* It was a good room with many wonderful memories.

Still, even with all the warmth of the past wrapped around her heart, the feeling that all along there was more, just wouldn't leave her. Who were the two women Lorna saw in her vision? Why were they coming to Lorna? Renee wasn't going to be happy until the mystery was solved.

"Come on," she urged. "You can trust me. I won't tell your secrets. I want to help you."

She laughed quietly thinking she sounded sort of drunk even though she'd had only a few sips of the wine. She was obviously a lightweight, which wasn't a big surprise. She didn't imbibe very often. Tonight just seemed to call for something a little harder than the iced tea she usually drank.

What she'd really been hoping when she went in search of wine was that it would relax her enough to open her spirit. Overall, she was pretty darned open and receptive to things unseen. In this case, it didn't seem to be enough so why not help things along a little? If someone—or something—was trying to get through to Lorna, why not her too? She had a willing heart and a spirit that believed. She wanted to know and understand the heartbeat of the house. For some reason, she had a strong sense that what Lorna had seen was important to this place. Somehow, she'd have to dig up the truth.

Even after the glass of wine was gone, nothing changed. There was more in the kitchen, and maybe she should fill her glass again. She didn't move. Alone in the dark, nothing even remotely paranormal happened, and she didn't think more wine was going to change that. Whatever secrets the house had to spill, apparently, it didn't want to spill them to her. Lorna appeared to be the vessel of choice.

Renee retraced her steps to the kitchen. She touched the open wine bottle and thought about another glass. Just as quickly, she rejected the idea. The tiny buzz she earned with the first glass would help her sleep even if it didn't open the door to the household spirits. Sleep was going to have to be enough for now. She found a stopper for the wine bottle, washed up her glass, and turned out the kitchen lights. Back in her room, she slid under the covers and pushed, fighting a reluctant-to-move Clancy for her six inches of the bed.

❖

From the darkness of the balcony, the Watcher studied her through the windows, the rain blurring her features. Even with the rain distorting her face, she was a pretty woman. The wine had opened her to him and he'd been able to look inside. Her heart was good and she would be useful, though not like the other. The power to part the veil dividing the worlds of the living and the dead was not within her. She would not see the women who longed for peace and could not find it. She would not step into the memories of another to discover the love or the tragedy that brought them to this place. But she would give the other strength, and that was a priceless gift. In fact, it could be the one thing that would bring this all together at last.

His hopes rose in a way that made his heart lighter. He turned his face to the sky and let the cool rain mingle with his hot tears. Above all, he longed to grant them peace, and to release their souls into heaven. They deserved it, and that it had been denied them was so dreadfully wrong.

Alone, he had been ineffectual in his quest to right the awful wrong visited upon the women in this very house. But he was no longer alone. Despite the fact they were unaware of the roles they were to play, they would unite in a common quest. All the positive signs to the contrary, he'd worried they would not see or understand their path. Tonight, all worry vanished like a fog that suddenly lifted to let in rays of sunshine.

Pure hearts. Honorable motives. For eons, he'd been a solitary figure. Then she came and there were two. Today, it changed again. God had smiled on him at last, and now there were three.

A blast of cold struck him in the face as though a hand slapped him. With a gasp he put his palm against his cheek. The skin was warm to the touch. Fear knotted in his gut. This was not possible. None could touch him. Not in the realm in which he existed. It was his alone.

He whirled, seeking the source of the assault. He scanned the world around him only to discover nothing and no one. He was alone in the darkness and the rain. A shiver slid down his spine. Time was running out.

❖

Lorna sat on the edge of her bed and stared at the necklace. In the light of the bedside lamp, it glowed beautiful. In perfect condition, it was as beautiful as if it had been crafted just yesterday. She felt deeply that wasn't true and there was a bit of research to back it up too. After she'd left Renee and holed up in her bedroom, a little Internet searching had offered up a bit of information. Odd as it seemed given how perfect the piece was, it was an antique. The archive photos placed it at least a hundred years old, probably older.

Yet something about it wasn't right. How could something this delicate be so perfect some ten decades down the road? It didn't make sense. Lorna leaned over and gingerly picked it up. Her hands shook as it lay against her palm. Red and blue beads were strung between the finely carved whalebone, pale and milky in the light of her bedside lamp. Someone had spent many long hours crafting the piece. To her, this felt like a labor of love. It might be her imagination, but then again, it might not. Deep emotion had a way of staying around even in an inanimate object...like a necklace.

Her fingers still trembling, she rolled the beads between her fingers. When she'd touched it at the beach, everything had swirled dark and crazy before dropping her to the sand. Her knees had buckled so quickly she wouldn't have been able to stay on her feet no matter how hard she tried. Then, she'd seen the women as if they'd been right in front of her close enough she could have reached out to touch them. The same women she'd seen in the living room.

By simply listening, Renee had taken a huge burden off her shoulders…sort of. Renee's claim to be able to see auras was, well, interesting. In the past, anyone who said they had preternatural abilities was written off in her book. She just didn't believe in that kind of crap.

Still didn't want to believe. Except now, her steadfast belief in the natural world was beginning to waver. What had been happening to her since she'd come to this house had only two possible explanations: declining mental capacity or preternatural inclinations. The latter actually seemed to be the better option at the moment.

And what was with a black streak in her aura? At least that's the way Renee described it. A spirit trying to connect with her. A couple of weeks ago, she'd have declared it bullshit. Tonight, she wasn't so quick to call it BS. She didn't know about swirling colors that surrounded her body; she sure didn't see anything even if Renee swore they were there. As to the spirit trying to touch her, she was starting to think there could be something to that. The part that bothered her the most was the black streak. Just as she'd researched the necklace, she'd done the same thing with auras. Renee was right; black wasn't a good thing.

"What do you want?" she whispered as she stared down at the finely carved whalebone. "What do you want from me?"

Darkness began to tinge the edges of her vision, and her stomach turned. Her fingers tingled where they tightened around the whalebone beads. It was happening…again.

The flickering glow of the fire was the only light in the room. Upon the bed, they were entwined in each other's arms. The velvet spread in a glorious shade of burgundy was in a pool at their feet.

Their voices were low as they kissed and whispered. She didn't want him to hear.

"We must leave here, Catherine." Her need to get away from here was a desperation that almost hurt.

Shaking her head, Catherine said softly, "My beautiful Tiana, I cannot, for this is my home. It has been the home of my people for more lifetimes than I can count. I would not know how to live without both you and this place."

"They will tear us apart." She knew it would be so. Even together they were not strong enough to fight him.

"Please, please do not ask me to give up my home. I cannot."

She kissed her head and held her close. "I will not do that. I love you, dear Catherine, and I will be at your side always no matter where we are. I will not let them take you away from me. You are my heart."

Tears began to streak down Catherine's face, her sobs quiet in the darkened room. "I cannot leave here. I cannot leave you, and yet I feel danger touching my shoulder. I worry harm will come to us both."

The fire crackled as one of the windows crashed open, a strong draft of cold air making them shiver and grab at the velvet spread.

Tiana pulled the spread up and around Catherine's shoulders. Tears glittered in her eyes as she gazed upon her. "I will be with you always. I promise."

Lorna dropped the necklace, and her room came back into focus. The bed beneath her was soft and warm, the hard wind battering at the closed window. The rest of the house was quiet. Everyone had turned in for the night as darkness had taken the storm even darker, heavier. It was much like the dream or the vision or whatever it was.

The same heaviness lay on her heart, and she didn't really know why. Or did she? By all appearances, she was losing her mind. Visions were coming at her like gunfire. Sane people didn't see the kinds of things she was seeing and hearing.

As disconcerting as it was, at her core, she felt anything but crazy. Instead, a sense of profound sanity enveloped her. Yeah, she was seeing things...or more precisely, seeing and hearing two women. The same two women over and over. Nothing about it appeared random, and if she were truly losing her mind, surely things would be more chaotic. Right?

The fact that nothing like this had ever happened to her before coming to this house made her wonder even more about the possibility of other realms. She wasn't a big fan of the spooky reality shows so popular these days, and yet she questioned if there was something to them that she'd blatantly discounted. Perhaps a little too quick to pass judgment on things she didn't understand.

Renee's claim that her aura showed signs of a spirit connection had her thinking. Maybe there was something to it. At least it was a partial explanation to the things happening to her and why touching things from the past seemed to bring the past into Technicolor reality. Sure sounded better than her losing it.

The bigger question was: Why her? She wasn't anyone special and had no claim to any unique abilities. A private life was a perfect life. No visions, no connections, no complications. That's the way she liked it, especially right now. Getting too connected and too close was how she ended up here in the first place. Maybe some errant spirit thought she was an easy touch, but it would be wrong. All she had to do was keep her mind closed and that should take care of things. That black streak would have no choice but to find another host to bother.

No time like the present to start being carefully closed up. With a pen, she picked up the necklace from where it had fallen to the bed top and laid it on the nightstand. If she didn't touch it, no visions. Easy peasy. She opened the bedside table drawer and dropped it off the end of the pen and into the drawer. Take that, spirits.

With the necklace safely out of the way, she pulled back the covers and slid beneath them. After turning out the lights, she laid back against the pillows. For a long time, she stared at the ceiling watching the play of shadows as they danced.

CHAPTER TEN

Jeremy came into the kitchen before the sun came up. He'd managed a few hours of sleep, though not many. It wasn't just the fact that in contrast to his apartment in Spokane it was incredibly dark and quiet here. He kept thinking about what Merry had told him, and it was all he could do not to jump up and drive back to Spokane. He wanted to see her face-to-face. No, he needed to see her.

Over the phone, she didn't sound completely convinced about how he really felt. How he gave her the impression that he'd be upset over a child was beyond him. More than anything, he wanted to pull her into his arms, kiss her deeply, and tell her how wonderful it was. Once she looked into his eyes, he hoped like hell any doubts she had would disappear.

A baby? How incredible was that? His childhood had been great, and he'd always known that someday he'd have kids of his own. He hoped they would have the same kind of rough and tumble fun that had made him and Lorna so close. All he had to do was see her and he could make it right.

When he stepped through the kitchen door, he was smiling broadly but so wrapped up in his own thoughts he didn't realize at first that the lights were on. Right after he did, he fixated on Lorna sitting cross-legged on a chair, her laptop on the table in front of her. A soda can, a coffee mug, and a box of crackers littered the table in a halo around her computer.

Geez, how long had she been up? Or had she even gone to bed at all? The obvious clues said she'd been here for hours. Like the fact the coffee carafe was half-full and it didn't smell fresh either. That pot of coffee had definitely been on the warmer for a while. The acrid scent made him wrinkle his nose.

"What's got you up so early?" he asked as he thought about pouring himself a cup of the sludge in the carafe in spite of the strong odor. He changed his mind after he picked up the pot and got a good strong whiff. It was way worse close up, and no way was he putting that sludge in his body. He dumped it down the drain and began making a fresh pot.

"Doing a little digging." She didn't look up from her computer, just reached over for her coffee mug and sipped while her eyes still scanned the computer screen.

"What kind of digging? You working on a new project?" She was a technical writer who always had more work than she could handle. It was one of the perks of being good, reasonable, and punctual. With an impressive list of clients who were always sending work her way, Lorna had carved out a niche for herself in a competitive market.

She still didn't look up. "Not exactly. This is more personal."

He pulled out a chair and sat at the table. "Care to share?"

Finally, she looked up at him. His question as to whether she'd been at this all night was answered by the dusky circles beneath her eyes.

He studied her face. "Did you go to bed at all?"

She shrugged. "Sure I did. Got an hour or two."

An hour maybe. "Seriously? That doesn't count as going to bed. That's a nap."

"Nap. Sleep. All the same. Besides, I couldn't turn my brain off and didn't see the point in tossing and turning when I could be doing something more constructive."

"Well then, you gotta tell me what's so fascinating you opted to blow off a whole night's sleep. Not like you to give up the zzz's."

She turned her gaze away from him, and for a long time didn't say a word. Finally, she said slowly, "I don't know…"

The smell of freshly brewed coffee filled the room, and sun began to stream through the window, a great sight after the stormy night. Together with his excitement over the baby, he should be feeling on top of the world. The vibes rolling off his sister, however, set him back. "Lorna, it's me. You've told me everything since before I could even talk."

That brought a ghost of a smile to her face and banished the weariness around her eyes in a heartbeat. Better. "True story, but if I tell you this, you might have me committed."

"Naw," he said with a big smile, hoping to encourage her to share whatever concerned her enough to forfeit a full night's sleep. "Not until I have you sign everything over to me first."

Her laugh sounded wonderful. "Gold digger."

He nodded and gave her a thumbs up. His uneasiness faded. This was sounding like the sister he knew and loved. "Yup, guilty as charged. Now seriously, sister, what are you up to?"

Her smile vanished and her eyes grew serious again. "You really are going to think I'm nuts, Jeremy, and I won't blame you a bit. At first, I thought I was losing it too. Things took a turn yesterday, and while I still don't understand what's happening, I'm pretty certain now that I'm not ready for the psych ward."

"Honey, don't mean to burst your bubble, but you've been ready for the psych ward since we were kids. I love you anyway 'cause we're family."

"Ha ha. Seriously, J, this is some crazy shit that's real and not real all at the same time."

His news was going to have to wait. Lorna was so obviously troubled by something, and he needed to be here for her. Dramatic wasn't her style. Neither was mysterious. He'd listen and they'd figure it out together just like they'd always done.

He put a hand on her shoulder. "I love crazy shit, so tell me."

❖

As much as she'd wanted to make the call last night, Renee opted to be a good friend and wait until a decent hour in the morning.

As far as she was concerned, this was a decent hour. She picked up her cell phone and punched in her friend Mia's number. If anyone could give her insight and clarification on everything happening around here it was Mia.

"A glorious morning to you, my little strawberry sunshine."

"Mia, you make me laugh."

"Of course I do. It's one of my gifts. Now, where are you? I drove by your place or what's left of it. That horrid fire was a tragedy of monumental proportions, but you will be fine."

"You think?"

"You know better than to ask me that. I know you'll be fine. What has you calling me before my second cup of tea?"

"I have a friend…"

"Why, yes, you do."

"Not that kind of friend."

"Not yet."

"Mia…"

Her laughter was full of joy. "All right, all right, explain so I know how to help you."

Renee told her about everything from the tainted auras to the visions Lorna shared with her last night. When she finished, she asked, "What do you think?"

"First, your friend. She's psychic, or have you figured that out already?"

"I had an inkling."

"More than an inkling. She's got it and she's tapped into what I think are trapped spirits in that house. Until she was in an environment that was rife with spirit presence, her talents hadn't manifested themselves. Has she had a recent traumatic event?"

"From what little Mom has told me, she just got out of a long-term relationship and it was quite painful."

"That would do it. You couple extreme emotion with a psychic talent and spirits who need help and there you have it. She's come into her own, and the spirits are trying to reach out to her. There's always a reason, and she has to find out what it is before she'll find peace in that house."

"Wow, that's quite a charge."

"She's up to the task. I can feel it."

"You don't even know her."

"I know you, and even from this distance away, I sense what you do. She's special, Renee, as are you."

"You're prejudiced because you like me."

"I am at that. I'm also right. My only caution to you is to be careful with your heart. Love is near and you can embrace it and let it change your life."

"Or?"

"Or you can turn away and regret it for the rest of your life."

"Sometimes you scare me, Mia."

She chuckled. "Sometimes, Renee, I scare myself. Come see me when you get back to town."

Renee set her cell on the nightstand and smiled. "I knew it," she said to Clancy who was sprawled across the bed looking bored and not caring in the least what it was she supposedly knew.

What she didn't explain to the dog whose eyes were fluttering shut was that she'd been absolutely convinced that something otherworldly was happening to Lorna. There was nothing mental about the things she'd been seeing. Her thoughts after hearing Lorna's confession were one hundred and eighty degrees from crazy. The advantage she had over Lorna was her chosen profession. It gave her access to things most people never even thought about.

Mia's declaration that Lorna was psychic didn't shock her. The things Lorna shared with her last night were way too specific to be just dreams or a mind in the midst of fracturing. It was more like a story, and that had to have some basis in truth. The only one person she knew who could make sense of what was happening had been Mia, and she'd been right.

As Renee hoped, Mia put the visions into perspective, and now she had some ideas to share with Lorna. What Lorna would think of her altered reality was anybody's guess. She deserved to know and understand. It was bound to make her feel better. Renee thought it was pretty cool.

All that aside, what she hadn't expected was the detour into her own life. She'd called looking for help with what was troubling

Lorna. Her problems didn't figure into the mix. Hers were of the real world, bad luck variety.

Mia always had different ideas no matter what she threw her way. This morning was no different. She'd zeroed in on Renee's current situation in a heartbeat, and the weird thing was, Renee hadn't shared any of it with her. In fact, she hadn't called anyone to tell them of her misfortune. The only ones she even talked to about it were her mother, Lorna, and Jeremy. Outside of Mom, she wouldn't have said a word to Lorna and Jeremy if it weren't for the fact she was in the same house with them.

Of course, the fire made the local Seattle news, and even if her name wasn't mentioned, her shop was specialized enough that those who knew her well would pick up on it immediately. It was also stupid of her not to realize her friends might try to come by. Toss in some extra skills like Mia possessed, and she had no secrets. By now, she suspected her Seattle inner circle all realized she was displaced and why.

That wasn't the part that surprised her when she really thought about it. No, what caught her off guard were the cautionary words with respect to her heart. Love was near, or so Mia promised her, and just hearing the words sent a little thrill through her body. It was exciting to dream love could happen for her. She'd been alone a long time now.

It was the warning that love found could easily be love lost that put a chill into the prediction. That part was not so exciting. *The Lord giveth, the Lord taketh away.* Story of her life.

For the time being, she wasn't going to dwell on herself. What did it really matter anyway? In the big scheme of things, her love life was a minor issue. At a personal level, getting her home and business repaired was priority one. She had to have a place to live and make a living. It wasn't cool to live off someone else's goodwill too long.

Despite the warnings about her love life, the rest of what Mia told her was pretty sweet. She couldn't wait to grab her computer and do some digging. Hopefully, there was an Internet connection now that Lorna was around. Bea hadn't been into technology at all.

There'd never been a television in the house, let alone a computer. Hopefully, Lorna was more technology savvy.

She dug through the meager clothes she had left here on previous visits and sighed. Not much to choose from. A trip into town to hit the local thrift shop was most definitely in order. With her source of income kaput, the thrift store was her best bet for adding to her non-existent wardrobe. Honestly, she didn't mind. Going to the secondhand stores was sort of like gold mining. Most of what she came across was crap. Then, when she least expected it, kaboom, a gold nugget.

For today, she'd have to be content with a very old pair of jeans and a University of Washington sweatshirt. As it turned out, there was a good reason she left a few clothes here between visits. She always thought it was because of walks on the beach, random rainstorms, and other unexpected reasons to need a change of clothes. Seemed to be more a case of the universe keeping a few clothes on her back when tragedy came calling.

A comb through her wet hair, and she was ready to face the day. Clancy, on the other hand, was still snoring softly in the middle of her bed. The dog was a real ball of fire this morning.

"Seriously," she said as she ran a hand over his head. His fine black hair was soft and shiny. "What kind of guard dog are you anyway? You snore so loud an earthquake would be quieter."

He raised his head, his dark eyes blinking. The expression on his face seemed to say, "What?"

She laughed, gave him one more pet, then walked to the door and opened it. "Come on." She waved her arm in the direction of the hallway. "Rise and shine, handsome. Another day awaits us. Dragons to slay, demons to defeat, breakfast to be eaten."

As if he'd been up and perky all along, he leaped off the bed and trotted out in the hall. His nails were a brisk click, click, click against the floor as he trotted toward the kitchen.

"Show off." She followed, laughing.

Chapter Eleven

Jeremy was hanging over Lorna's shoulder as absorbed in the search as she was when Renee walked into the kitchen. She glanced up and smiled. A second later, she was laughing as Clancy draped himself across her lap, waiting, apparently, for the petting he believed his due. The dog was a crack-up.

All in all, it was turning into a good morning. By the time she'd finished telling Jeremy her theory on the strange doings around here, instead of thinking her crazy, he'd been intrigued. The feeling of lightness his belief in her instilled was astonishing. She hadn't realized how important it was to have him believe her, particularly when she had a hard time believing it herself.

It was nice to have a brother who had her back. She had the same sense about Renee even though their time together had been short. There was just something about her that radiated trust and honesty. That was something she needed in her life. The breakup with Anna had been traumatic enough just on the face of it, but throw in the fact that she discovered Anna had been lying to her for months, and truth was something she sorely needed in her life. She had the sense that regardless of what was going on, Renee would give her that.

"Good morning," she said to Renee, really looking up this time and telling herself not to stare. It wasn't that Renee came in looking like a model, but there was something about her casual clothes and long shiny hair that made Lorna want to drink her in.

She was lovely in a way Anna never had been, and it struck her how snarky that sounded. Still, it didn't make it any less true. There seemed to be a light around Renee. She almost laughed at that, thinking that perhaps Renee was rubbing off on her, and she was now seeing auras. Could be that she just wanted to see a light around her. It made her even more dazzling and, frankly, a little intoxicating. Even with everything going on around her, Renee was a distraction she found thrilling though she'd keep that to herself.

"Good morning," Renee said. "You two are up early."

Jeremy laughed as he looked up at Renee. "Definitely up early for me. Big sis here didn't really go to bed."

Renee looked surprised. "I saw you head off to bed. What got you back up, and why on earth would you stay up all night?"

Lorna leaned back in her chair. "I had some ideas that I wanted to start digging into, and no matter how hard I tried I couldn't switch my brain off. Let's just say I came up with some interesting shit."

Renee poured a cup of coffee from the fresh pot Jeremy made, though she didn't know why he'd dumped out the stuff she'd made about three a.m. Maybe it was a little strong, but she didn't have a problem with it. It was great for keeping her wide-awake. No sissy coffee in her kitchen.

"Good," Renee said after taking a sip.

"I'll take credit for that," Jeremy said as he held up his mug in a mock toast. "Big sister here seems to think that black sludge is fit to drink. I respectfully disagree. We're in Western Washington, the home of awesome coffee, and I refuse to drink black, burned goop."

Renee returned the mock toast. "Amen. I'm spoiled living in Seattle. We certainly don't lack for fantastic coffee. And in case you're wondering, I don't do sludge either, thank you. So, sorry, Lorna, and thank you, Jeremy."

She just rolled her eyes and took a slug from the cup that had been sitting in front of her for hours. It was cold and gave her the expected jolt. In her opinion, perfect for the job. "You two are coffee snobs."

Renee shrugged. "No argument there. So tell me what you've been looking at."

A shot of excitement went through Lorna. A price was going to be paid later for not sleeping, but it was worth it. She always felt better when she was armed with information. "Great shit. I was able to dig up a bona fide mystery. It's about the family who built this house. They had one child, a daughter, who died under mysterious circumstances."

"As a child?" Renee asked. "Lots of kids didn't make it past a couple of years back then."

Lorna shook her head. "In this case, she was a young woman, healthy and attractive. With wealthy parents, she had the world in front of her."

"Interesting." Renee leaned back in her chair and sipped her coffee.

It was fun sharing what she'd found. "Gets better. Her death is just part of the mystery. One day, she's alive and well; the next, six feet under.

"You're thinking it was some kind of an accident?"

That was the last thing she thought when she'd read through all the old records. "No, I don't think it was an accident. There would have been more in the records of the day if it had been."

"That leaves suicide or murder."

"My first thought too. Then I narrowed it down a little more. If it was murder, once again, we should be able to find more in old newspapers, except I didn't find a single thing. Like I said earlier, it was as if one day she was here, and the next day she wasn't."

Renee set her mug on the table and caught Lorna's eyes. "It had to have been suicide."

"My thoughts exactly. Lots of veiled references in what I could dig up online, but nothing that came right out and said it. Seems a little too sterile for my liking. I'm convinced there's a story in there. You know, like a really rich and powerful family that could bury the embarrassment of a suicide."

"It occurs to me that if she did take her own life, maybe she's the one trying to get through to you."

Lorna was feeling great. For the first time since this all began, she wasn't alone. Renee appeared to be in total sync with her.

"Again, you're on the same page with me. I'm thinking maybe something like that could explain what I've been seeing. She could be sad and looking for forgiveness or something along those lines."

Renee nodded, a slight smile pulling up the corners of her mouth. "I agree, and if you promise not to laugh, I'll tell you why."

Lorna couldn't imagine what Renee could tell her that would make her laugh. In her opinion, none of this was a laughing matter. A young beautiful woman taking her life was a tragedy no matter how many years ago it might have happened. If any of what she'd seen in her visions helped push her to take her life, it made her all the more sad. "Cross my heart." She used her index finger to trace an "x" across her left breast.

Renee leaned back in her chair and turned serious. "I don't know how much of what I do professionally my mother might have shared with you."

Lorna shook her head. Jolene hadn't mentioned her much at all and certainly hadn't gone into detail about her business. Her memories of Renee were vague recollections of a girl about her own age who was pretty though quiet and reserved. Until she showed up with Clancy, she didn't even know she had a dog, let alone what she did for a living. The only unique fact she had was what Renee had shared last night about her ability to see auras.

"Nothing really. Just said you have a store in Seattle. She never said what kind of store."

"That's it in a nutshell. I own a building in Pioneer Square. I live upstairs, and the store is downstairs. Great view, wonderful walk-up traffic, and all things considered, pretty successful. The important part of the whole story is that my store is—was—rather specialized."

"Specialized, as in…?"

"As in mind, body, soul specialized. I carry all the things regular bookstores will barely touch and a whole array of alternative medicine. My herbal mixtures are well known throughout the region. I have some very unique skills and a very unique client base."

"So witchcraft and voodoo kind of stuff." She almost said *crap* and caught herself before the word fell out of her mouth. She didn't put much stock into shit like that. Never had and never would. She just didn't believe.

On the other hand, she didn't believe in visions until she came here. So either she needed to open her mind or find a really good psychiatrist. The way things had been going lately, opening her mind seemed like a much better alternative.

Renee didn't seem to be offended by her comment even though it really was awfully close to being snarky. Her voice was the same gentle melody that was growing on her more every moment she spent with her. "Not exactly. Voodoo isn't something I've ever delved into. I'm much more on the natural side of things. No dark magic, if you will. That doesn't mean I discount the theories behind alternative belief systems like Wiccan for example. Keep in mind, it was a form of pagan religion in years gone by, and there's a great deal of merit in some of their practices. There's a lot of healing that can be accomplished through nature. In my practice, I try to incorporate what's good and effective from all sources and bring them together."

"A sort of naturalist."

"In a sense, yes, but because of my unique inventory, all kinds come to me. I don't judge their belief systems or monitor what they do; I simply provide products that are natural and healing. I've made friends with witches and voodoo priests, Wiccans, and folks who are just tired of working with traditional medicine. Regardless of their beliefs, they're people like you and me."

She understood, sort of. Given the injuries, strains, and sprains suffered over the course of her years as a triathlete, she did understand that often it wasn't pills and surgery needed but bodywork and a belief in self-healing. Still, she wasn't so sure about a so-called natural healer. There was definitely room on her plate for a good old-fashioned doctor.

"So what does that have to do with anything here?"

"Here's the deal. One of my regular customers has become a pretty good friend. Out of the hundreds of people I know who claim to have the gift of sight, she's the only one I'm acquainted with who really does. I called her and told her what you'd seen. She gave me some advice."

Okay, now Lorna was intrigued. Her non-belief in things that go bump in the night was slipping even more, which was perhaps a good thing. If there was merit to the idea, it kept her sanity intact. Insanity was a nuisance that simply didn't work for her. Paranormal was weird but a better alternative.

Besides, she was totally curious now. "What did she say?"

"Long story short, my friend Mia thinks this house is haunted. Not in the creepy, try to chase us away kind of haunting. Based on the things I shared with her, she believes there's a spirit lingering because it needs something from us."

A shudder ran through her. "From me, you mean."

Renee nodded. "Yeah, from you."

"Why?" She didn't add that she was already inching toward that same conclusion. She definitely wasn't sure she believed her so-proclaimed psychic friend could shed any light on her predicament. In the alternative, what did it hurt to listen to a different point of view?

Renee shrugged. "She didn't say, and I doubt she knows. It was just an opinion based upon the visions."

"You know," Jeremy broke in. and Lorna realized she'd forgotten he was still in the room because she'd been so focused on Renee. "It all makes sense in a really odd way. Think about it, Lorna, you were sane, relatively speaking anyway, before you left Spokane. You get over here and all of a sudden, you're seeing visions. Now if the visions were random kinds of things, I'd be inclined to think you've tipped over the edge, if you catch my drift. But what you're seeing has too much of a pattern to it. It's more like a movie being screened just for you."

"I think what your brother is trying to say in a roundabout way is you could be psychic," Renee said with a gentle smile.

Lorna rolled her eyes even as she told herself not to. She was on board with the whole paranormal thing until right now. "I'm *not* psychic. That's something people want to believe when nothing else makes sense. I'll grant you that I'm leaning toward believing a fair amount of this stuff, but I'm afraid I'm not so inclined toward some latent psychic ability."

Renee put a hand on her arm. It was warm and friendly. "But you'll consider that there could be a ghost trying to contact you?"

Actually, the thought gave her the creeps. It also made her oddly curious. Could there really be such a thing as a ghost roaming the house, the ocean shore, and the grounds? Given what she'd been seeing lately?

Yeah.

❖

Jeremy took a fresh cup of coffee outside. The wind was blowing hard enough to pelt him with damp leaves. The sky was dark, the air carrying the scent of the ocean. Lorna and Renee were still debating the hows and whys of what was happening. The possibility of it being a ghost, and the idea that Lorna might actually be a psychic, albeit a reluctant one. Renee was holding steady with the contention that's exactly what it was while Lorna was putting up mild resistance. His money was on Renee wearing her down.

It was all pretty out there in his opinion, and at the same time, felt pretty darned real. He'd never much thought about anything supernatural before. Just wasn't his thing. Still, he had to wonder if something was happening here. Never before had he been in a place that *felt* like this. It was as if they weren't alone.

The story of the house and the untimely death of the original owner's daughter sure had the feel of an unresolved tragedy. Maybe she was still hanging around waiting for something…or someone… to set her free. If the reality ghost shows were to be believed, it wouldn't be the first spirit to hang around a house.

Lorna seemed an unlikely savior. She was strong and wonderful and grounded in the here and now. The stoic realism that was so Lorna was, in his opinion, one of the things that came between her and Anna. He believed that Anna ultimately realized she needed a woman more spontaneous and open. Lorna hadn't been able to give that to her, and so Anna, in an age-old story, turned to another. That really sucked. Lorna didn't deserve to be dumped like she didn't matter. Nobody did. He hated to see his sister in pain, particularly when he knew there was little he could do to help her. It was horrible to be that powerless to ease a loved one's suffering.

When she'd decided to move all the way over here, he'd been incredibly sad. Now that he was here too, he understood the potential it had to help heal her heart. This was a special place, potential ghost and all. The moment he drove up, he felt it. He'd probably sensed it even as a kid. Her decision to come here was the right one, and well, Renee's presence certainly didn't hurt either. He had a good feeling about her. He hoped Lorna did too.

The only thing that would make things better was Merry. He wished she were here. Jeremy stood staring out at the ocean and sipping his quickly cooling coffee. The sound of the ocean in the distance, the faint smell of the water in the air, made him smile. Last night's storm clouds were fading, and the sun was beginning to peak through. It was going to be a beautiful day. He'd have to tell Lorna he was going back to Spokane. She wasn't going to be happy with his quick turnaround. He didn't see that he had a choice. He had to get back to Merry. Besides, with Renee here, now it wasn't like he'd be leaving her alone.

He was lost in his thoughts when the sound of an approaching vehicle made him turn around. The car looked familiar, though it was too far away to make out clearly. As it grew closer, his heart began to beat, and he smiled.

Merry.

He had no clue why she was here, not that it mattered. He didn't care why. That she was here made his heart light. He wasn't going to have to wait another six hours or so while he drove across state to see her. She had come to him. Everything was right with his world.

Well, almost everything. Despite the joy seeing Merry gave him, it didn't change the fact that something funky was going on with Lorna. She wasn't the kind of person who was inclined to see things, and yet he was convinced that she was. No question she was understandably upset over her breakup; anyone with half a heart would be. That didn't mean she was slipping into the world of hallucinations. If anything, she seemed more grounded and like herself than he'd seen since it all went down. That her spirit was coming back made him smile. This place was good for her.

And maybe a little bad.

If she was a bit psychic how, bad could it be? As long as she didn't run around telling people it was bound to be okay. He believed her, and obviously Renee did too. Others might not be so understanding or kind.

Still, in the big picture, good was winning out, and the bad, well, they'd figure that out together. After all, isn't that what families do? Now they were about to have a bigger family—his baby, and if Merry would have him, a wife. It had been a long time since he'd felt this fine. He wanted to hold on to the feeling.

Merry got out of the car, and his good spirits fell, replaced by cold fear. She was pale, and beneath her eyes the skin looked as though it had been dusted with ash. Pregnant women glowed; he'd heart it a hundred times if he'd heard it once. She wasn't glowing, far from it. The sight sent a knot of dread into the pit of his stomach.

Jeremy sprinted over to her and laid a hand gently on her arm. Just the simple act of touching her made him feel at least a little better. "What's wrong?"

Her pale face tipped up to his, and her smile thawed the ice in his veins. "Not a thing now that I see your mug." She got up on her toes and kissed him. "God, I've missed you."

The feel of her warm lips against his sent any lingering worrisome thoughts fleeing. Bottom line, she was here, she was his, and they were having a baby. Whatever else was happening around them was background noise. As long as they were together, everything was perfect. Corny but true.

"You're awfully pale," he said when they drew apart at last. He held her face between his hands. "Are you sure you're okay?"

She nodded and took one of his hands to hold in hers. She leaned close into him. "A bit of nausea now and again. That's all. The doctor says it should pass sometime between now and the end of the first trimester. I hope it's sooner than that, but even if it lasts that long, I'm still going to be fine. It's just part of the deal."

Despite the sound of conviction in her voice, he wasn't convinced. The paleness to her skin really bothered him. "And the baby?"

She hugged him even tighter and laughed lightly. "Our baby is fine too. Trust me, big boy, we're both just dandy." Her gaze swung past his face and to the house. "This is Lorna's new digs? Wow. Talk about stepping up her game."

"Yeah, pretty smoking, isn't it? Aunt Bea really knew how to live."

"If the inside is anything close to the outside, it's got to be magnificent. She hit the jackpot here. Must be nice to be the favorite niece. I'm pretty sure none of my family likes me this much! And apparently, Aunt Bea didn't like you that much."

He laughed. "Apparently not, but hey, who says we can't mooch off my sister?"

The house and grounds really were something It was all magnificent in more ways than one. A million-dollar view...literally, an incredible old house, and he was beginning to believe, a century-old murder mystery.

That was all stuff he could share with her later. Right now, what he really wanted to know was why she'd driven all the way across the state—by herself—to come here. She insisted nothing was wrong, but he wasn't sure she was coming clean with him.

Again, he asked, "What's wrong?" He looked down into her eyes.

The look on her face was a little sheepish. "Physically, I'm feeling not too bad, considering."

"I get that. What's the but you're not telling me?"

She took in a big breath and let it out slowly. "But, the thing is...I sort of quit my job."

Of all the things he expected to come out of her mouth that was about the last thing he thought he'd hear. She had worked long and hard to put herself through law school, and then after clerking for a federal judge for two years, landed an associate position at one of oldest firms in the city. She was on the fast track for becoming its latest young partner. Merry was a bright star in the Spokane legal community. He always thought that one day she'd be sitting on the federal bench. Maybe that was his vision more than hers.

The news took him so much by surprise the only thing he could think to ask was, "Why?"

The sheepish look on her face grew even deeper. Her smile was rueful, her pale cheeks taking on a tinge of pink. "As it turns out, I hate practicing law."

For a second, he was so stunned he did and said nothing. Then he burst out laughing. "Oh Lord," he sputtered. "This is truly priceless."

Now hurt clouded her face. Her lips pulled down into a frown. "It's not funny. It's horrible really. My parents are going to kill me. I'm going to be the black sheep of the family. All their big dreams about a barrister daughter just went up in smoke and I don't have a clue how to tell them."

Her timing was perfect, not to mention funny, even if she didn't realize it yet. She was in for a surprise too. "Oh, baby, we are a pair to draw to." He kissed the top of her head.

Her eyes narrowed. "Really? Why?"

He pulled her close and wrapped his arms around her, loving the way she felt pressed tight against his body. "You aren't going to be the only one your parents kill. You see, beautiful, our bouncing baby girl or boy currently has two unemployed parents because I quit my job too."

At first, her reaction seemed to be stunned silence, and then she burst out laughing. "Good grief, Jeremy, we are seriously messed up, you know that, right?"

"Maybe so, but I happen to think it's messed up in a really great way. So what do you say we go break this news to the others?"

She stood on her tip toes and kissed him on the cheek. "Which news do you mean? That we're having a baby or we're both unemployed?"

Chapter Twelve

Renee couldn't believe how fast the day went. She and Lorna had left Jeremy and his girlfriend, Merry, at the house to discuss the details of their impending life changes while they took a drive to Seattle. First, because she had a meeting with the insurance agent at the store, and second, so they could go to the Seattle Public Library. Places to go. People to see.

Stop number one was her depressingly smoke-infused building. If Lorna hadn't been along, she'd have been terribly sad at the sight of the boarded up windows and the yellow caution tape. Throw in the strong lingering scent of smoke, and it was enough to make her want to throw up. Her life was in front of her all broken and burned. It was not a pretty sight.

The charred exterior bricks that just days ago were a beautiful shade of red were now blackened. The place had been her anchor since she declared her independence, and now her anchor was gone, or if not gone, seriously crippled.

But there was Lorna, and the fact was, she liked her a lot. Just being around her made Renee feel lighter and happier. Not just her either. The draw to Lorna appeared to be contagious because Clancy seemed to adore her too. Renee had one truism that stood her well through the years: if all else fails, trust the dog. And Clancy hadn't steered her wrong yet. If he loved Lorna, then her trust in Lorna was not misplaced.

Fortified by Lorna's company, they parked at the rear of the building and walked around front to meet with the adjuster from the insurance company. He turned out to be a serious young man with short hair and a neatly trimmed beard named Stan Snowden. He had all her pertinent policy information on the newest version of a popular tablet that fascinated Lorna. Once she was able to tear Stan away from showing the intrigued Lorna all the tricks of the tablet, they quickly reviewed the policy highlights. Next was the hard part: a tour of the mess that had once comprised her home and business.

It was a mess too. Between the fire, the firefighters, and the arson investigators, it was a ghost of what it once was. It was hard to envision that a resurrection could even become a possibility.

Stan said little as they picked their way through the odorous stew of charred wood, broken glass, and melted plastic. She followed his lead and said nothing. What was there to say? It was all gone, and she was left with a pile of damp ash. So much for the life adventure she'd so carefully carved out for herself after the divorce. Best laid plans and all that.

After Stan looked things over, asked a few more pointed questions, and wrapped up all his notes, he politely told her the insurance company would be in touch soon.

Soon, of course, being relative and contingent upon the final story from the fire investigator's report. It was a polite way of saying they had to first figure out if she torched her own building. If there was no finding of arson, the insurance company would finish up the claim and pay out the policy limits. That little tidbit meant what she already knew in her heart. Her home and place of business were a total loss.

Once that determination came down, she'd have a difficult decision to make. Either rebuild everything or sell the ruins to a developer and move on. Either way she went, it wasn't going to be easy. It was a decision to be made in the not too distant future but not today. Far too many variables involved for her to make any kind of decision right now. There was time to weigh out the good, the bad, and undoubtedly, the ugly.

She let out a sigh when Stan drove away through congested Seattle traffic. Not getting how difficult this visit would be was a little naïve on her part. She felt drained and had no problem letting Lorna drive them away from the ruins.

Now she leaned back in the chair and stretched her arms over her head. After leaving her burned out shell of a life, they'd settled in at the Seattle Public Library. It did wonders for her sour mood. Amazing what hours in comfortable silence and poring over books and historical records could do for a person. Sometimes it was the simple things that made life pleasant. Simple things and an intriguing companion, that is.

It had taken them a while to locate what they needed, but once they did, it was like winning a jackpot in Vegas. Not that she'd actually ever won a jackpot…or been to Vegas.

The history of the house and its inhabitants began to unfold for them like a really good movie. A mystery movie that is, because in some areas they were able to uncover a great deal of detail. Yet, in others, it was strangely silent. She was dying to know why. She loved mysteries.

Like most stories, this one started with a single visionary person. In this case, a man named John McCafferty. A big deal in his day, he was wealthy in a Bill Gates kind of way. The house he built on the shores of the Pacific Ocean was state-of-the-art for its time, and he was understandably proud of it. Numerous articles had been written and grainy black-and-white photographs preserved that depicted a tall, handsome man with serious eyes. The location he chose for his own personal Valhalla might have been isolated, but he certainly wasn't keeping it to himself.

He gave lavish parties with notable guests: the governor, senators, entertainers, and the who's who of the Pacific Northwest. Everyone who was anybody showed up on the doorstep of the house that now belonged to Lorna. It was pretty darned impressive.

What really caught her interest was that despite the fact he managed to get both himself and his masterpiece mentioned on numerous occasions, only passing mention of his wife and only child, a daughter named Tiana, was found in the mountain of records. Even less was reported on Tiana's untimely death before her twenty-first birthday. A brief obituary with bare-bones biographical information was all. Nothing extra, no words of sorrow about the loss of a beloved daughter even though she was young and on the verge of a life in society. No follow-on articles detailing the brief life of a tycoon's only child. Given her father's standing in the State of Washington, there should have been more. Today, it would have made the front page online and in print. Things had not changed that dramatically in the intervening years.

"What do you think?" she asked Lorna. "Get the feeling something was rotten in Denmark?"

Lorna nodded her head slowly as she tapped an open book. "No shit. Daddy sounds like the stereotypical nineteenth century rich guy in a society that worshiped men. It was all about him all day, every day. Did I mention that kind of crap pisses me off?"

"Indeed. I picked that up too. Could be wrong, but don't think I'd have cared much for the man. Quite a bit more self-involved than I find attractive, though I suppose it was one of the traits that helped to make him so terribly rich. Things haven't changed much in that respect. It takes a certain amount of cold-blooded self-interest to climb that far up to the top."

"In other words, a nice way of saying he was a narcissist?"

It was her turn to nod. "I bet a good shrink would confirm that diagnosis in a heartbeat. In the big picture, he doesn't figure in as much for me. It's the daughter that has me bothered. Something wasn't right with Tiana's death. Too many holes and way too much silence if you catch my drift. These papers—"she tapped the stack of newspaper reproductions spread out on the table—"don't tell us much of anything beyond the fact that she was a lovely and available young woman. Why wouldn't there be more about her death?"

Lorna raised an eyebrow. "Yeah, I definitely catch your drift. Everything we came across was lightweight. More than a little lacking in substance."

True story there, and it wasn't just lacking in substance; it was more like non-existent information. It wasn't right on any level as far as she was concerned. "Inquiring minds would like to know what happened to Tiana. How and why did she die? You'd think if she was sick or had some terminal disease that somewhere in the stories about her father there'd be at least a passing mention."

Lorna nodded, her lips pressed tight together. "Yeah, you would think that wouldn't you? From everything I found in the old business journals, he liked to talk about one thing only and that was himself. That obituary he put in the paper for her was pathetic."

"It makes me sad," Renee said.

Lorna nodded. "Makes me sad too."

Renee reached over and covered Lorna's hand with her own. They might have hit the proverbial brick wall when it came to discovering the secrets of the house, but they were further ahead than they'd been when they left this morning. They had names, they had dates, and they had a little less mystery.

"At least we have something. It's got to be Tiana you're seeing, and now all we have to do is find out who the other woman was. I really think that's our job. That's what we're being told." It came to her in a flash of understanding. A complicated puzzle that suddenly had the pieces beginning to come together. If they could figure out the who, then they could figure out the why.

Lorna rubbed her eyes with the heels of her hands and said in a voice that sounded as tired as Renee felt, "You mean I have to find out. I'm the only one seeing this shit."

Renee laughed even though Lorna's tone was darkly serious. It was true. Beyond her natural ability to detect auras, she had squat. Lorna was the one the women chose to visit, and she was the one who ultimately had to figure out what they wanted. All she could do was be right behind Lorna with support and encouragement.

"I'm afraid so. You're the one the story's being played out for, but I'm the one who believes you're not crazy and really are being visited by spirits. The women want or need something from you, and all we have to do it figure it out. We can do it together, Lorna, we really can."

"I'm not so sure." Her gaze settled on their touching hands. She didn't pull away.

Renee squeezed gently. She loved the way her hand fit with Lorna's and the warmth of skin against skin. "We'll figure this out. Together. I promise."

"I don't understand, Renee. You don't really even know me. Why are you so willing to hang in there with a woman who could be having a mental breakdown?"

She looked at Lorna's bent head and smiled. "Funny thing about that. I feel like I've known you for a long time, and if you think about it, we really have. We met as children."

"That was a long time ago. We're not those little girls anymore. We're different people now."

"You really think so? I personally think we're much the same as we were back then. Yes, we've grown up and we're mature and responsible women now. Our hearts? Well, those are the same hearts of the little girls we were all those years ago. And for the record, you're not having any kind of breakdown."

Lorna finally looked up, her eyes a little brighter. "You are such a breath of fresh air."

Renee put an arm to her nose and then grimaced. Her shirt reeked. "After going through my place, I'd say a breath of stale smoky air."

This time Lorna laughed. "See, that's what I mean. You face tragedy and come out making jokes. I'd have been crying in my beer."

"Oh," Renee said on a sigh, forgetting all about her smoke-drenched shirt. "Beer sounds good."

"Come on." Lorna pulled her hand away, and with a snap closed the latest book they'd been perusing. "Let's call it a day and go find a nice pub."

Renee made a tidy stack of the notes she'd made and grinned. "You're on."

❖

Darkness flowed over bluffs, and the Watcher stepped into it with the ease gained by centuries of practice. Wind whipped around his body, but he didn't feel the cold or the damp ocean air. None of it touched him. It had been millenniums since the world of humans had been his to experience. Like so much else, the right had been stripped from him on the day of his fall. He'd like to believe that had he known the ultimate consequences of his actions he would have done things differently. In his heart he felt the lie. The temptations before him had been too great. He would not have changed a thing.

Now, he stared at the house and felt its emptiness in his heart. Though three still remained inside the sturdy walls, the old woman, the man, and the new woman who carried the child, they meant little to him. Lost souls did not, could not, touch them.

It was the one they called Lorna he searched for. She was the key and the savior. Not just for them but for him as well. Her absence at this critical time was alarming. Keeping the evil one at bay was taking every ounce of power he still possessed. When she was there, his job was easier.

The evil forces that worked against him took back strength once she left the house. Without her heartbeat to keep them subdued, the darkness stretched and reached out invisible fingers looking to take purchase. It was not good. *He* carried darkness in his soul during life, and in death became one with it. The Watcher could not allow him to win again.

He crossed the grass and stopped when he was next to the house. He peered into the windows searching for any sign of the spirit that troubled his soul. The reflections that gleamed back at him were of trees and a wide expanse of lawn. Of night sky, endless stars, and a round, buttery moon. His own visage was part of the reflection and nothing else. No ghostly apparition to give substance to his sense of unease.

Icy wind whipped around him, the tendrils of cold snaking down his back. It was not the air coming off the turbulent ocean, rather something far more frightening. It pulled at him as if knowing he could nothing without her, taunting his impotence.

With concentration, he blotted out everything around him and brought his own power to center. The best he could do alone was to gather as much strength as he could and push back. Around the edges of his being, he felt the pressure as the other returned the push, upping the ante by prodding and pinching. The evil one wanted in so that he could destroy everything once more. Death hadn't lessened his need to control and to wipe out anything and everyone he couldn't.

It would not happen. He would not allow it. No. Not again. Not ever again. This time it would all end and the evil would be forever banished from this beautiful place.

Still, he worried even as he felt the other relinquish and shift again into the expectant background. It had taken everything he possessed to give chase to the darkness. Would he be able to do the same again tomorrow? The next night? How long before the strength that had been with him since his fall finally failed him? He sighed, knowing that the only thing he could do was try.

Inside the house, a light came on glowing bright and giving him a clear view of the people who walked into the room. A shiver ran through him as he studied them. Where a moment ago there had been nothing, now a shimmer of dark light began to grow around the man who gazed upon the young woman with clear adoration. The same man he thought had no hold on this place. Dread filled him as he considered why.

Time was growing shorter with each passing moment. He'd seen it happen before. The light would grow deeper, more intense, and he would lose his hold on those within the house until it slipped through his fingers like water. In the end, his quest failed.

He trembled and shook his head back and forth. Not again. He clenched his hand as if to stop anything from falling between his fingers.

He would not allow the worst to happen. Regardless of what befell him, he would bring them home as they deserved. She would help. She would return to the house and would see; would understand.

She had to.

❖

A fire crackled in the big fireplace. His long legs stretched out on the ottoman, Jeremy leaned back in the chair and let the warmth spread throughout his body. Before retiring for the night, Jolene had fixed them a wonderful dinner, and he'd eaten like he was a teenager again. Now the big meal had him relaxed and comfortable. A guy could get used to home-cooked meals, warm fires, and a beautiful woman at his side. No question about it.

Jolene bid them good night and headed down the hall in the opposite direction. It was just the two of them. For a long time, he sat with Merry and just talked. The tension of recent weeks disappeared as if it had never been there at all. They spoke about everything from the baby to plans of the future. Talking like this was a breath of fresh air.

Even so, he had to summon the courage to bring up marriage. It scared him to think that he could very easily frighten her away again. The fear was so deep and strong it made his stomach roll and that great dinner threatened to make its return.

"Merry?" Was that really his voice trembling?

"Yes, baby?" Her head was resting on his shoulder and her eyes were closed. It had been a while since they'd sat together like this and he'd seen her so relaxed.

"I need to ask you something."

"Sure."

"Ah, what would you think about us getting married?"

"Of course we're getting married." She didn't open her eyes.

"Of course we are?"

"Yes, Jeremy, we're getting married."

"I love you," he said as he kissed her head. "I really love you."

"Back atcha, big boy."

The urge to throw up disappeared, thank God, and he leaned his head against the sofa. When he noticed her breathing turned slow and easy, he gently eased her down and covered her up with a throw blanket from the back of the sofa. He moved over to one of the big chairs that flanked the fireplace and watched her as she slept.

That she'd conked out pretty early wasn't particularly surprising. It was a long drive from Spokane, and she was, after all, pregnant.

When his assistant Penny had been pregnant, the first couple of months, she'd been exhausted. There had been many naps on the sofa in his office. He figured there'd be lots of naps for Merry too.

The silence was pleasant and comfortable. Sitting here with the fire filling the room with flickering light and warmth, the love of his life resting peacefully, he didn't remember when he'd been so happy. He smiled and leaned his head back against the soft chair. All was right with his world.

Sort of.

At the edges of his vision, something flickered like a swarm of moths moving around in the darkest corner of a closet. Something was faintly disturbing about it. It didn't make sense. Here he was in an incredibly happy place, and by all conventional logic, it should trump anything else. He opened his eyes and scanned the room. Even as full of magic as it was sitting in this tranquil room with his one and only at his side, a disquieting sense of something not quite right nagged at him.

Ignore it. That's what made the most sense. Stretched out and relaxed in a sweet chair with the most beautiful woman in the world sleeping close by, a wise man would enjoy it. He took a deep breath, closed his eyes, and let the warmth in the room flow over him. The sounds of the logs popping and snapping as the flames licked the wood finally lulled him into drowsiness. Yeah, this was living in the moment and not letting anything else intrude.

Now he knew how Merry felt before she drifted off to sleep. Resting easily in the soft chair, his arms grew heavy and his breathing became slow and easy.

The moon was high and full, casting spikes of gold light across the thick grass. His back ached, and sweat trickled down his spine to soak into his shirt. He barely noticed. Again and again, he pounded the shovel into the hard earth, the vibrations shooting up his arms like thunder. With each thrust, the hole grew larger, deeper.

At last, he stood with his back straight and stared at the night sky. It was ready, as was he. With a mighty shove, he threw the shovel up to the grass and followed it out of the hole. He kicked the shovel out of the way. Around him, the night was eerily quiet; the only sound was his own labored breathing. His eyes, accustomed to the darkness, easily made out the cluster of bushes. He easily retraced his earlier path, and he was there in a heartbeat.

Even in death, she weighed little. He easily hoisted her small frame, tossing her body over one shoulder. With far less effort than it took to dig the grave, he carried her from the bushes to the edge of the hole. He shrugged and sent her lifeless body tumbling into the dirt six feet below. She landed with a thud on the damp earth.

For a long moment, he stared into the dark abyss. He couldn't help smiling. "You had it coming," he said into the silent night. "I warned you, and you did not listen. Are you listening now?"

Facedown in the cold damp earth, her black hair spread out around her head. The effect was odd in that it blended so completely with the dirt that it appeared she was headless. All he could make out in any detail was the unnatural angle of her arms and legs, and the pattern of her pale cotton dress. In the darkness, the blood didn't show. The only trace was on the fine cotton of his shirt. He'd have to burn it, which was a shame considering the price he'd paid to have it custom made.

From where he'd kicked it, he grabbed the handle of the shovel. Blisters had risen on his palms, and they stung when he wrapped his hand around the wooden handle. He ignored the pain. Soon enough, this would all be over. Things would be as they should once more.

With renewed energy, he leaned down and filled his shovel with rich dirt. The earthy smell rose into the air and it filled him with peace. With a heave, he threw the dirt into the hole. The first shovelful fell on her head. The sight renewed his resolve and he picked up steam. Within a few minutes, her body was covered, erasing her as if she'd never existed at all.

When it was all done and the sod he'd carefully pulled up had been replaced, he leaned on his shovel and said once more, "I warned you."

No more left to do, he turned and walked away without looking back. Nothing to see except a bit of dirt in his otherwise pristine lawn. By morning, even that would be washed away by the beautiful, cleansing rain. His heart was light, his conscious clear.

Jeremy's head snapped up and his eyes popped open. "What the fuck," he muttered under his breath and then quickly looked over at the sleeping Merry. She didn't stir.

He ran his hands over his face. That was one fucking weird dream. What he saw lingered as if it didn't want to leave him in peace. Since when did he start dreaming about a dead girl and the man who buried her?

Funny that it felt somehow right. That feeling didn't make any sense either. How could a dream about burying a woman feel okay in any universe? Sure as hell didn't in his. He might be a lot of things, but he wasn't that kind of guy. Must just be all the changes and surprises sending his sleeping brain into overdrive. Yeah, that was it.

He got up and put a log on the fire. Sparks flew from the fireplace like tiny fireflies, and the sweet scent of tamarack filled the air. Jeremy walked to the windows and stared out. The night was very black, the storm clouds heavy with rain blocking out any starlight and obscuring the moon. Oddly, it didn't depress him. Under different circumstances, it might. Not tonight, in spite of the disturbing dream.

At the featherlight touch of a hand on his shoulder, he smiled. While he didn't hear her move, it was obvious Merry had finished her nap and was up. "Hey, baby," he murmured.

He turned, intending to take her in his arms. The smile faded. It wasn't Merry whose hand rested on his shoulder. She still slept on the sofa.

No one was behind him.

CHAPTER THIRTEEN

Lorna giggled. *Giggled*! Obviously, she'd had way too much beer. But it wasn't her fault. Renee was the one who took her to the awesome microbrewery, and only being considerate, she drank the beer with genuine appreciation. It was, after all, the polite thing to do.

Now she was maybe just a little on the tipsy side. Usually she'd feel guilty for letting loose. Not tonight. No siree, she didn't feel even a tiny bit remorseful. They'd had a wonderful afternoon sampling the different brews, snacking on salmon bites, fresh clams, and cheddar biscuits. The tipsy part sort of snuck up on her and as she studied Renee changed her opinion. It had snuck up on both of them, in a good way that is.

It did create a bit of a problem though. How exactly were they going to get home? It would be ill-advised and frankly, just plain stupid to drive back to the house. As Aunt Bea would have said, they were up a creek without a paddle, between a rock and a hard place, all dressed up and nowhere to. The old sayings made her giggle... again. Good thing Jeremy wasn't here; he'd never let her live this one down.

Renee came to the rescue with her handy dandy cell phone and solved their no transportation problem. Half an hour later—time for one more brew—Willie showed up. He was a tall, dark-skinned man who smiled at them like they were naughty children. She didn't mind, considering they actually were being a bit naughty. She took an immediate liking to Willie and liked even more that he herded them into the backseat of a late model SUV. She thought he was going to drive them to a hotel and was pleasantly surprised when he headed out of Seattle. Strangely enough, he was driving in the exact direction of home. How did he know that's where she wanted to go? Was he psychic too?

"It's too far for you to drive us to my place," she protested, her arms on the back of his seat. He actually smelled pretty good, for a guy. Nice cologne.

He didn't flinch when she brought her face close to his neck to breathe his great scent. It was a testament to his good nature because she surely smelled like a distillery. Another plus in his column. "No worries, little Lorna. I plan to deliver you and my little pal, Renee, right to your front door. You'll sober up a lot better sleeping in your own bed than you would in some strange place."

Smart guy too. "You'll have to stay with us then."

He reached back and patted her hand. "Not necessary. My cousin Louie lives only about twenty miles from your place. I'll be staying there. He'd kick my ass if I got out his way and didn't come on by. It's a family thing you know."

She plopped back into her seat and turned to look at Renee. "You have great friends." She was jealous really. She couldn't think of a single friend of hers back in Spokane who would make this kind of drive at this time of night just because she'd sat around a bar getting loopy.

Renee nodded, her eyelids drooping. "I certainly do. You're a peach, Louie."

"Right back to you, my pretty." He laughed and kept his eyes on the dark highway.

Her shoulders touched Renee's as they leaned together in the backseat. They talked and laughed for what seemed like hours, though she suspected it was more like half an hour. Her eyes grew weary, and she leaned her head back. If she closed her eyes for just a minute, it would be okay. Renee's head was resting on her shoulder, the pressure warm and natural. The motion of the vehicle was as relaxing as grandma's rocking chair.

She woke up after Willie had stopped the car and reached around to tap her on the shoulder. "Ladies, we're here."

Slowly, her eyes opened. Her mouth was dry, and she was so tired she had no desire to move a single inch. What she really wanted to do was close her eyes again and go back to sleep. It didn't matter a bit that she was sitting in the car with her seatbelt still on. She was too tired to move.

Renee stirred next to her, and the movement propelled her into reluctant motion. If everyone else was leaving the car, she supposed she could work up enough energy to drag herself after them and into the house. A glance at her watch made her flinch. Three in the morning. Not exactly her typical evening. She couldn't remember the last time she'd been out that late...or would it be this early? The house was dark except for a lone light in the front room. Probably Jolene making sure they didn't come home to total blackness.

She took Renee's hand but looked over at Willie. "There's plenty of room. It's really late. You've already driven a long way, and I don't want you to have to drive any farther. Stay here and rest."

"Don't worry about me," he told her with a toothy smile. "First, I'm a night owl, and second, I'm gonna stop at my cousin's house. It's all good."

"Thank you, Willie. I can't tell you how much I appreciate this." Renee stood on her toes and kissed him on the cheek.

He winked at Lorna over Renee's head. "That's what friends are for. Nice meeting you. Take care of my little girlfriend here. She's a special one, my pretty Renee."

"Yes, she is and I promise to look after her. Thank you, Willie." Like Renee, she gave him a kiss and a hug. She hoped she'd get the chance to see him again. Sober next time. As he drove off, she slung an arm around Renee's shoulders and headed for the house.

Renee leaned into her. "Nice guy, huh?"

"Really nice guy. Can't believe he drove us all the way out here."

Then the obvious occurred to her. At some point, they were going to have to head back to Seattle to retrieve Renee's car. They'd left it in a parking garage not far from the brewery.

"Your car. We have to go back tomorrow and get your car. I can't believe we just left it."

"No, we don't. I left the keys with Willie along with the parking fees. He's going to grab it tomorrow and take it to his place. I'll pick it up next time I go into the city."

Relief made her relax. The idea of turning around and heading back to Seattle was not very appealing at the moment. "Again, what a great guy."

"Yes, he's been like a brother to me and I love him a ton. Now, however, I'm too tired to worry about anything else. I don't know about you, but I really need to make a date with my pillow."

"I am totally with you on that one."

The effect of the too much beer was wearing off, and exhaustion replaced the earlier euphoria. They made their way in the darkness to their respective bedrooms. At the door to Renee's room, they both paused. Renee's head tipped up until she was gazing into Lorna's eyes.

"Thank you," she said softly.

Again it struck her how lovely Renee's eyes were. "You're welcome. It was a nice day." She meant it, even if there might be a touch of hangover in her future.

"I mean for everything, not just today."

A lump formed in her throat. Renee was thanking her for opening her home to someone in need? It was the kind of thing she was raised to do. What was right was right. "No big deal."

Renee reached up and touched Lorna's cheek. "Yes, big deal. You have no idea how big."

Without giving herself a chance to think about it, she lowered her head and touched her lips to Renee's. The kiss started out as a quick thank you, but in a flash it changed into something far different. It was as if a spark flew between them to ignite a fire already laid and waiting.

Her heart was pounding when she pulled away. "I'm sorry," she muttered, though honestly, she didn't feel very sorry. Not sorry at all. In fact, she wanted much, much more.

A smile curved Renee's lips, and her eyes sparkled. A slight flush in her cheeks made her even prettier than she already was. "I'm not. Good night, sweet Lorna." She kissed her quick on the cheek and then she was gone, the door to her room closing softly, and leaving Lorna standing in the dark hallway wondering what the hell had just happened.

❖

"Damn it." Jeremy threw back the covers and shoved up to his feet. He was trying to get some sleep, and there they were, at it again. Their hushed whispers and soft laughs came through the walls almost if they were right here in the room with him, though he knew they thought no one would hear them. That's what they did night after night as soon as they thought he was asleep. They believed they were discreet enough with their sneaking around not to get caught by him.

Well, he heard them just as he had so many times before, and he'd had enough. He had told her and told her to stop her foolish behavior. Actually, it was beyond foolish. It was indecent and sinful. It wasn't God's will, and yet she defied him over and over. How she could act against all that was good and right was a mystery. What was wrong with her? He'd raised her better than that.

The blood that ran between them was strong. Pure. What she was doing tainted that perfection, and she was going to have to make it right. He could turn a cheek to what she had done already as long as it stopped tonight. She had to come back into the circle of righteousness before it tainted her so completely there would be no way to save her good name or her soul. His patience with her had come to an abrupt end.

His footsteps were sure and steady in the room so dark he couldn't see his hand in front of his face. The path was well known to him, and he didn't need light to find his way. Tonight this would be finished once and for all. He reached for the doorknob and wrenched open the bedroom door with a decisive snap.

In the hallway, he started in the direction of her room and stopped. The silence from that direction told a story. No one was there. He stood in the middle of the hallway listening. Where did they go? He squared his shoulders and peered into the blackness knowing he would have to find them. His fingers curled, his hands clenching into fists. The sound of voices, low and happy, came from outside; he was sure of it. He turned and walked with purpose down the long hallway.

Jeremy shook his head and stared. How the hell…he was standing on the large expanse of grass behind the house. Cold wind whipped at his body, and he shivered. His bare feet were ice-cold and damp, his chest bare. How in the world did he end up out here? Last thing he remembered, he'd been in bed, Merry warm and beautiful at his side. He'd fallen asleep happier than he'd been in weeks, his arm draped around her soft body.

In nothing but a pair of boxers, he began to shiver. "Jesus," he muttered as he turned and raced back to the house, slipping several times in the grass made wet by the latest rainstorm to have passed through. The last time he had done any sleepwalking he'd been about seven and he'd gotten only as far as the kitchen.

He'd been a bit of a sleepwalker in those days, along with having the craziest dreams night after night. It got so bad at one point the folks had taken him to several doctors who assured them he was fine and would probably grow out of it. He did, and like the sleepwalking, the dreams faded too. He rarely dreamt at all anymore. Until he came here that is.

A vague sense of dread came over him as he caught flashes of feelings brought up by uneasy sleep. Tinges of fury caught at his mind, and that was disturbing. He wasn't that kind of guy, and the intensity of the emotion was messed up. When he was a kid, even when the dreams were at their worst, as soon as he woke up, he was back to being himself. Light always banished the demons.

Inside the house, he returned quietly to his room. Merry still slept peacefully, and from all appearances, so did the rest of the household. He didn't recall hearing Lorna and Renee return home though he somehow knew they were here. He always knew when his sister was around.

He lay back against the pillow. The anger suffused in the dream lingered even as he tried to concentrate on happier thoughts. After several minutes of tossing and turning, he put one hand on Merry's arm. The feeling of her body, warm and solid, helped quiet his mind and body. Still, he lay staring at the shadows dancing on the ceiling for a long time.

❖

The face of the man who charged out the back door wasn't that of the man who visited this house in this time and place. The Watcher recognized the hard lines and cold eyes, and his heart fell. *He* was gaining too much strength far too quickly, and if she didn't act soon, he would triumph once again. It could not be allowed to happen, for he was dangerous. Death had not destroyed that part of him.

Weariness and discouragement bent his shoulders. Would this ever end, or would he be destined to live it over and over again? He'd made the promise so many years ago to set them free, and yet no matter who came or how hard he tried, he failed every time.

It wasn't fair and it wasn't right. In his fall, the fault lay on him. He'd made his mistakes, and the high cost was his alone to bear. He had reconciled with that truth a very long time ago. This was different. The injustice visited upon the two women wasn't just tragic; it was unforgiveable. They had done nothing wrong and deserved to be brought home. The task had been laid at his feet, and in the beginning he had been so full of his own bluster that he'd believed his path to redemption would be easy. Perhaps that's why it had been entrusted to him. In the intervening years, he'd come to understand humility. Now he wondered if he would ever be able to make it happen.

Tonight, as the man tromped angrily across the grass, he concentrated intensely. His own despair could not be allowed to deter him. Even if he failed yet again, he had to at least try. With every ounce of effort he possessed, he pushed. At first, he thought it was a useless effort, then the man stopped and stilled so completely it was almost as if he died on his feet. He waited, watching from his place in the shadows.

In the moonlight, the man's face changed. The angry, bitter façade that a moment before defined his facial features disappeared, and the gentle face of the younger man reappeared. The lines that spoke of age and anger smoothed out, and dark eyes turned blue once more. A middle-aged man had confronted the night. A young man awoke to it.

He silently watched as the man, his expression confused, turned toward the house and hurried inside. Once the door had shut and he was once again alone, he tipped his head up. Above him, the sky began to lose some of its darkness. Soon the stars would fade, the moon would set, and his time would be at an end. For now, he'd done all he could.

Chapter Fourteen

Renee woke up with a mouth full of cotton and a pounding at the back of her eyes so intense it was like someone was hitting them with a sledgehammer. What in the world possessed her to drink that much? Oh my, she remembered now. It was coffee chocolate beer recommended by the friendly server. It had sounded hideous and took some convincing to get her to try it. As it turned out, the brew tasted heavenly. Toss in Lorna's company, and it was a recipe for...well, this.

All things considered, she'd do it again. The trip to Seattle had started out crappy. How could it not, considering she had to spend several hours with an insurance adjuster at her charred up property? Not only were her worldly possessions for the most part burned, melted, or charred, but fighting with the insurance company about their value was a given. Didn't matter that she'd spent years faithfully paying her insurance premiums on time, battling for every dollar of benefits when it came time to actually use said insurance was on her upcoming agenda. It was one messed up system.

Thank the gods for Lorna. She was a calming influence during the whole day. The meeting with the adjuster turned out to be far more pleasant than she anticipated, and the trip to the library, pretty darned fun. By the time Lorna suggested beer, she was on board. It was her idea to swing into the neighborhood microbrewery. Her friend, Cliff Mason, not only owned it, he was the master brewer as well. Seemed like a good idea to wind down a little before they headed back. It had been a really full day.

Oh, she wound down all right. All the way down. The last time she remembered drinking that much was the day of her wedding, and that was a whole other story. She was drinking for a different reason that night, and it didn't involve a good time.

Truth was that last night turned out to be one of the best evenings she could recall. She laughed and talked as though she and Lorna had been lifelong best friends. The whole day had been comfortable camaraderie, and she didn't realize how much she needed it until it happened.

Maybe that's why she'd felt the irresistible urge to kiss Lorna once they'd gotten back here. Or maybe it was the lingering effects of the alcohol? She didn't think so. No, she kissed her because she wanted to. Lorna was intelligent, attractive, and sexy as all get-out. She'd thought so the minute she'd gotten here, but after their enjoyable evening together that almost felt like a date, her feelings ratcheted up a bunch.

The real question was did Lorna feel the same way about her? Renee had no illusions about herself. She was pretty in a run-of-the-mill kind of way. Most people seemed to like her well enough even after she bailed on her marriage and came out. Unlike Lorna, though, she had very little to call her own. Her home and her livelihood were gone. She had her car, a few clothes, and her dog. Lorna was a toned and accomplished athlete, only about a hundred and eighty degrees from Renee.

From what she observed, Lorna had it all. A successful career, a gorgeous home, family, and friends. If those weren't enough, she was training for Ironman, the pinnacle in the triathlon arena. She was amazing.

Renee didn't see that she had much to offer someone like Lorna, not that it changed much as far as her feelings were concerned. Reality had little to do with emotion. If she was attracted to her before their trip to the city, after last night, she was hot for her. She just didn't exactly know what to do about it.

Right now, the only thing she was going to do about anything was take a shower, swallow a couple of ibuprofen, and then hunt down a really big, hot cup of coffee. The rest, she'd sort out later. Easier to think when the hammer behind her eyes stopped pounding.

In the kitchen, her mother was pouring coffee into a go cup. Her head tilted and she studied Renee. "Not to be a harping mother, but, honey, you look like something the cat dragged in."

She sidled up next to her and poured a cup for herself. No puny little go cup for her, she went for the big ceramic mug. "Feel like it too. Where you going?" She pointed to the mug with the screw-on lid.

"Heading to town for groceries and to see the doc," she explained as she kissed Renee on the cheek.

Her heart thudded, and the beer-induced lethargy disappeared. "The doctor? What's wrong?" Her mother was the only family she had. Her father died when she was barely two, and she had no memories of him to fall back on. All she possessed to remind her she even had a father were the pictures her mother shared with her. Any hint of trouble where her mother was concerned made her insides roil. Not a great thing to happen, particularly after last night.

Her mother smiled, her eyes clear and honest. "Routine yearly checkup, worrywart. Not a single thing for you to be concerned about."

"You're sure?" Renee studied her face intently.

Her mother patted her cheek. "One hundred percent."

The confident words eased her worry at least a little, and she gave her mother a hug, thinking as she did so how thin she felt. Had she always been such a twig and she was just now noticing? Or was her mother's reassurance of good health a façade put on for her benefit? Mom would do something like that.

Then again, as Renee watched her through the window, energetic steps taking her to the car, she had to think, with relief, it was the former. Probably nothing more than overreaction on her part. She was tired, a tad hung over, and way out of her normal element. That's all it was, she hoped. Mom was fine, just like she said.

"Hey, sunshine."

Lorna's bright voice made her smile, and once again, she was acutely aware of her growing attraction. Each time she saw Lorna it seemed as though she was drawn to her a little more. How could she help it? She was such a unique and interesting person.

"Sleep well?" Kind of lame, but it was the best she could come up with under her rather foggy circumstances. With hands shaking a tiny bit, she poured a mug of the coffee and held it out. "Cup of coffee sound good?"

"Oh my God, you're an angel." Lorna now stood so close to Renee she could smell the fresh scent of soap on her skin.

Her hands shook a little more as she handed it to Lorna. Their fingers touched, and she'd swear there were sparks, something she didn't think she could ever tire of. Nobody else had affected her that way. She liked it.

A slow smile lit up Lorna's face. Her eyes seemed to sparkle. "You felt it too, didn't you? Don't deny it, because I can see it in your eyes."

No sense in trying for a lame denial. She felt it all the way to her toes. Instead of answering, though, she simply nodded. She couldn't say anything because she didn't trust herself to say something that wasn't dorky.

Lorna let out a long breath and then smiled. "To tell you the truth, Renee, I thought it was just me. I mean, after all, you were married to a guy so I figured I'm the last person you'd be interested in."

It was her turn to smile. "Obviously, Mom didn't share with you the reason why I got divorced. You're going to love it."

Lorna shook her head. "No, she didn't say a word and I didn't ask. Besides, what business is it of mine to pry into something as personal as the reason behind your divorce?"

Renee took her coffee and went to the table. She sat and looked up at Lorna. "Usually, that sentiment would be dead-on. In this case, I think you need to know that I left my husband for two reasons. First, because even though I loved him, it was the love between friends. The kind of love you share with a good buddy. Not exactly how you should feel about your spouse."

Lorna grimaced as she joined Renee at the table. "Ouch."

"Indeed. Now, the second reason for the divorce is more important, and it explains reason number one." She took a sip of her coffee and then looked up to meet Lorna's eyes. "I left my husband because I had to quit lying to everyone, including myself."

"Lying? I don't get that kind of vibe from you. You seem like a straight shooter."

"The truth is I spent a lot of years lying, and it took me right to the altar with someone I never should have married. I was pretending to be something I'm not: straight. Suffice it to say, I've known for a long time that men weren't for me, and I longed to come out. I was just too scared to make the leap, and then one day I said, 'screw it.' If I didn't do something I was going to implode."

Lorna's smile grew warmer, and she reached across the table to lay her hand against Renee's cheek. "I'm awfully glad you took that brave step."

She smiled back at her. "So am I. I'll tell you honestly, at the time, it sucked. I still feel horrible about hurting my husband, but I'd feel worse if it I had let the lie go on any longer. He deserved better than what he got from me."

Lorna came around the table. She brought her face to Renee's, her kiss so sweet it made her knees weak. Good thing she was already sitting down. She brought her arms up to wrap around Lorna's neck and let her fingers weave through her soft, damp hair. It was like being in heaven.

She almost tipped over in her chair at the same time Lorna jerked away when an angry male voice in the doorway roared, "What the fuck are you two doing?"

❖

White-hot fury ripped through Jeremy's body the second he stepped into the kitchen. The explosive anger that filled him was deeper than he'd ever experienced before. To see Lorna and Renee kissing ignited his rage like a crematorium furnace. It was all he could do not to run in, grab Lorna by the hair, and tear her away. What they were doing wasn't right, and he refused to stand by silently and watch her disgrace herself in such a way. It had to stop this instant. People were already talking in low whispers about the two of them and it was horrifying. He was not about to allow his family to live under a cloud of shame and embarrassment.

"Jeremy," Lorna said in a loud, sharp voice that broke through the red haze of resentment and made him whip his head around. Her cheeks were crimson, her eyes wounded.

The sight of her misplaced hurt feelings made him even angrier. "Do not speak to me in such a tone."

"Jeremy!"

This time her tone was full of surprised annoyance, and yet it was forceful enough to make it through the fog. His head felt thick and heavy, his vision a little blurry with everything just a touch out of focus. A tinge of nausea worked in his stomach, and all of a sudden, it kicked up in intensity to double him over, his arms crossed over his stomach. He peered up at Lorna and wondered at the dark look on her face. She looked angry.

"What?" Man, his stomach hurt and his head…it felt like someone had coldcocked him. If he'd been out pounding down brews with the guys it would make sense. A peaceful night with the woman he loved should have resulted in feeling great.

Her expression morphed from anger to puzzlement. "What exactly was that about? Since when have you become the morality police?"

"What was what about? Got no idea what you mean. Morality police? Me?" Man, he needed to sit down. The fuzziness in his head was playing havoc with his equilibrium. It was either sit down or fall down, and he'd prefer the former.

"I mean your nasty question and rude expletive."

"Lorna, you're not making any sense. I haven't said a thing. I just got here. And you know as well as I do that I'm not into passing judgment on anyone. Not my style or my inclination."

Lorna and Renee shared a glance. He didn't get the look that passed between them. Not the glance. Not Lorna's question. All he really knew was that he felt like crap, and the only thing he could figure was he must have picked up a flu bug somewhere along the line.

Lorna pulled out a chair and pushed him into it. "Sit down. You're about ready to drop like a sack of rocks, and I don't want to be the one to pick your big butt off the floor."

He'd take exception to the big butt remark if he felt better. "Thanks." He laid his head on his arms and closed his eyes. The nausea in his stomach eased a little, but only a little.

"Okay, bro, what we're wondering about is why you came through the door like a bull yelling me and Renee. Seriously, what was that about? Despite what I might say to you, it really isn't like you to be a jackass."

"I wouldn't do that, Lorna. Why would I?"

"Because we were kissing and apparently that's a problem for you."

That was messed up, and it still didn't make sense. "So? I'll repeat myself. I don't know what you're talking about." Except in the back of his mind, something nagged at him, telling him he did know. The hint of a foreign emotion that didn't leave him feeling good tugged at him in a way that was distinctly uncomfortable.

Especially after what happened last night in the rain. He didn't intend to tell her that though. He didn't intend to tell anyone. It was way too creepy and the kind of thing that didn't need to be shared.

"It wasn't just what you said," she told him in a soft voice as she came over and put a hand on his head. "It was also your face. It was you, but it wasn't. It was almost as if you had on one of those clear plastic masks. Freaky, if you know what I mean."

As she'd related the brief encounter, a hazy memory was jogged. The sick feeling in his stomach grew stronger. He did remember, though it was as if it had happened from a distance and he'd been an observer. Now, however, as he let the thoughts settle in, the lingering feelings of outrage rolled back in, and vague, disturbing emotions rapped at his consciousness.

This was fucked up and he didn't like it. He wasn't that kind of man: the one who was holier-than-thou and hated anything that was out of the mainstream. One of the things he loved about Lorna was her independence and the way she stood up for herself. She didn't let society tromp her down or people with small minds diminish her. For as long as he could remember, she was a role model to him and he would never, ever berate her. Certainly not for kissing a woman she was attracted to. If anything, that would make him happy because he'd know she was ready to move beyond the hurt Anna caused her.

So why did he now barge in here and act like a small-minded moron? He wanted to say that Lorna was been wrong and he hadn't charged through the door like an angry bull, spewing ugly things as he did. If he could, he would deny it all, except deep in his heart, he believed her. There had been a brief time between the stairway and finding himself in the kitchen that he couldn't clearly remember. One minute, he was stepping off the last step and the next, Lorna and Renee were looking at him like he had the plague.

The only question he had was what happened in those few minutes? He didn't know and didn't like what he was hearing. Apparently, Lorna wasn't the only one in the family reacting to this place.

"It's this house," Renee said firmly, as if it were obvious. "It's got you in its grip too. Come on, you guys. There's something here. You can't deny it, especially after what just happened. We have to find out is what it is. Personally, I believe it's trying to reach both of you. How cool is that?"

He looked at Lorna and opened his mouth to say that was a crock. He closed his lips without saying a word and nodded ad. "You know, I hate to say it because I'm really not into that woo woo stuff, but I think Renee's right. I don't know about the cool part, but the reaching out to us might have some merit. I had a little incident last night that wasn't me either. I'm pretty confident I'm not crazy in the strictly legal sense, so it's got to be a ghost or an evil spirit."

From behind him, Merry sidled up close and put her arms around him. She pressed a kiss against his hot neck. "What have I missed?"

Lorna chuckled and pointed to the sole unoccupied chair at the table. "You might want to sit down. This is going to take a while."

CHAPTER FIFTEEN

When they finished bringing Merry up to date, Lorna dumped her cold coffee down the sink and refilled her mug with the fresh pot Renee had made during the course of the tale. It wasn't quite as good as her version of the stuff that only grew better and thicker with time on the warmer, but it would have to do.

"So there you have it," Lorna concluded. "Either we have a ghost or we're all going nuts, to put it in technical terms."

Merry smiled, her face lighting up. She turned her bright eyes on Jeremy. "A ghost, how sweet is that? I love those reality shows about chasing ghosts."

Jeremy frowned. "Mer, I hate to burst your bubble, but I don't think it's cool at all. Especially uncool when it turns you into a world-class asshole. Don't get me wrong. I have my moments. This wouldn't be one of them."

She patted his arm, her smile still bright. "Don't worry, baby. We'll figure this out. I mean, after all, it sounds like Lorna and Renee have a pretty good start. We know the names of the family members, we have a mysterious disappearance, an untimely death of a young woman, and a big old house that's trying to talk to us. This is so intriguing we might have to all collaborate and write a book when we have the mystery figured out or call in the ghost guys from TV. What do you think about our own reality show?"

Jeremy shook his head and hugged Merry. "No reality show, and we're definitely not calling in the ghost guys. This is something we have to do, and I'm thinking we keep it to ourselves."

"I'm on board with that," Lorna told him and Renee nodded.

Lorna did appreciate Merry's take on the whole thing. The way Merry told the tale didn't make it sound quite as crazy as it did inside Lorna's head. Of course, Merry wasn't the one seeing visions at all hours of the day and night. It was pretty weird when it was happening to her regardless of how rational Merry made it sound.

She'd actually been giving the visions a great deal of thought especially since yesterday afternoon's fact-finding mission. "I think it has something to do with the relationship between the two women."

"What relationship?" Merry asked.

Lorna considered the first vision she'd had as well as the one that hit her while on the beach. What she'd seen was much more than a simple physical relationship. She didn't have to be a licensed professional to know love when she saw it, even if it was happening in a paranormal realm. What she knew was that the two women weren't having sex as much as they were making love. There was deep emotion in what passed between them. That couldn't be faked.

At the same time, the man she'd seen dragging who she now believed was Tiana away was as full of rage as the women had been filled with love for each other. It had to be John McCafferty, the man who'd built the house. The pictures they'd come across yesterday were grainy and his features blurred. Her visions were the opposite. His face had been clear enough to see the frown lines around his mouth and the deep creases at his eyes. It was not the face of a happy man. The lines in his face were not from smiling.

She turned again to Merry's question. "Tiana was in love with another woman. Given where this house is located, she wouldn't come into casual contact with very many people. Either someone came for extended stays, or the woman she loved was someone from nearby. I'm banking on the latter, which means her love was more than likely from the Makah Tribe."

Merry's eyebrows went up. "Oh, that had to fry her daddy's ass. The nineteenth century wasn't exactly the age of enlightenment, especially when it came to women. Why the Makah tribe? Couldn't it be someone from town?"

Lorna shook her head. "The woman I see when this thing happens to me has darker skin and I just have a sense she's Native American."

Renee nodded. "Yeah, I'm thinking you hit that one right on the head. Daddy couldn't have liked that in any way, shape, or form. Gotta think he was pissed to high heaven that his little girl liked girls. Toss in falling in love with an Indian, and he's probably still rolling over in his grave."

Lorna looked over at the sheet of paper Renee was doodling on. She had a kind of spreadsheet going that listed the cast of characters as they knew them to be. Tiana, her father, her lover. In the middle was the house.

"So." Renee tapped her pencil on the paper. "Let's try and figure out what this all means. Lorna, how about you and I take on the two women?"

She liked that idea for more reasons than one. The women intrigued her, but more than that, it meant she and Renee would spend more time together. That appealed to her on several levels. Their day together in Seattle had been wonderful. Best time she'd had in months.

Nodding, she smiled over at Renee. "Sounds good."

"You want us to take on the old man?" Jeremy asked, leaning close to Renee to study her intricate notes.

Renee tapped her pencil on the paper. She looked up at Jeremy. "He seems to like you, so I think it's the best place for you two to start. You might as well take on the ass headfirst."

"I don't know about liking me," Jeremy said with a frown. "If he's the one getting inside my head, he's a bitter guy. Even though I don't remember what happened afterward, I feel dirty when it's all over."

Merry kissed the side of his head. "Not to worry, my handsome man. I'm on your side, and now that I know what the bastard is up to, I'll be on the lookout for any hint of intrusion. Nobody touches my man and gets away with it."

He laughed. "That's all well and good, my pretty one, but what exactly do you think you can do if he grabs my body again?"

"Easy. I'll just kiss you so hard the old bat will be forced to leave. I have a hunch I'm not the kind of woman he'd like. He'll hightail it and run when I lock lips with you, especially if I throw in a little tongue." She laughed and proceeded to demonstrate what she meant.

Jeremy's smile warmed Lorna's heart. He loved Merry deeply, and that made her incredibly happy. They were good together, and the word forever popped into her head every time she saw them like this. She wished them every happiness and was envious all at the same time. She wanted to believe that same kind of kinship was in her future though she didn't hold out much hope. So far, she'd pretty well sucked at the forever thing.

"I like this plan." Her gaze met Renee's. What she saw in her eyes made her heart beat faster. A glimmer of something close to hope happened when those eyes met hers.

Did she dare let herself hope? Or was she setting herself up for failure yet again? There was a time she'd believed what she and Anna had together was the stuff forevers were made of. How wrong had she been on that count? Hopefully, she had a better grasp on it now.

She stood and smacked both hands on the table. "All right then, ladies and gentleman, let's get cracking and figure out this mystery."

❖

When Jolene came in through the back door with three green grocery bags in her hands, they were all still sitting at the table. Jeremy jumped up and ran over to take them from her.

"Thanks," Jolene said with a smile, patting him on the cheek when her hands were free. "So very nice to have a handsome man carry my groceries inside. It's been a very long time since I've enjoyed that kind of luxury."

He laughed as he put them on the counter. "Any time, Jolene. Do you have more in the car?"

"Yes, if you don't mind."

"Be back in a flash." He trotted out the back door toward her car.

She actually had a lot more in the trunk. Apparently, she was anticipating the continued stay by all of them, and he was okay with the idea. Given his and Merry's current unemployed status and the freaky things going on around here, he was more than willing to make camp a little longer than he'd intended to. Besides, it was beginning to feel like they were a big family. It had been just the two of them for so long; it was quite nice to be part of something bigger.

Besides, truth was he wanted to know exactly what was happening here. He hesitated to say haunted house, but only briefly. If there was ever a series of events designed to make a believer out of him, this was it.

When the last bag was on the counter, he had a thought. "Hey, Jolene, you've lived around here for years, right?"

She smiled and nodded. "Indeed I have. I've lived on the coast all my life so that's quite a few years."

"Great. Then maybe you can point us in the right direction. We're trying to find out more about the original family that lived in this house as well as a young Makah woman. Where would we go to dig out historical records? Renee and Lorna found some info when they were in Seattle yesterday, but we're looking for the kind of info you typically find locally. The people talk kind of stuff."

"Oh," she said as she began to pull items out of the bags. "That's an easy one. Go into the library in town and ask for Lettie. She runs the historical room. They have impressive records on the area including the history of this place. For the young Makah, head over to Neah Bay and ask for Alden Swan. He's a tribal historian, and if anyone can give you a wonderful recollection on elders, he's the one. Nice man too. I've known him for years. I'll admit I actually had a crush on him once upon a time."

Renee laughed. "Mom! Really? I never knew."

Jolene shrugged. "I might be your mom, but I'm also a woman, and I had needs back in the day. Not so much these days though." She laughed as she continued to pull items from the numerous grocery bags.

With a finger stuck in each ear, Renee chanted, "La la la, too much information, mother."

Jolene said, "Out with all of you. I have work to do, and you all have homework to do."

Jeremy was ready. He wanted to know more and to understand what could possibly have happened here to leave souls lingering for such a long time. He also wanted some alone time with Merry. The chance to play private detective had a certain macho appeal to it, and she was the perfect partner. Watson and Holmes.

In town, they headed to the library. At the intake counter, he stopped and asked for Lettie. It was a toss-up what surprised him the most, her pierced nose or the fact that she was not even thirty. The name Lettie conjured up the image of an older woman with gray hair and blazers. Not for this Lettie. She was six feet tall wearing skinny jeans and a flowing blue top. Her black hair reached her waist and a red stone glittered in her nose.

She smiled as she walked toward them. "Hi, I'm Lettie. How can I help you?"

"I'm Jeremy," he told her. "And this is Merry. We're staying with my sister out at the old McCafferty place."

"Oh God, I love that house. It's such a jewel of our area. I haven't met the new owner yet, although Bea and I were great friends."

"She was my great-aunt."

Her smile grew. "Oh my God, you're that Jeremy. I'm so glad to meet you. It's your sister who owns the house now, right?"

"You keep up with things, don't you?"

"Oh, honey, this is a small town. Everybody knows everybody, and everybody knows what everybody is doing. If you're gonna be around here you might as well get used to it. Now, what can I help you with?"

He and Merry explained what they were looking for. A gleam came into Lettie's eyes as they talked. She might be young, but she loved her job.

"Come on back here." She led them to a small room off the main reading room. Inside were shelves full of books and ledgers. It was hard to say what else because there was simply so much.

• 150 •

"I need your bags, please," she said to them and held out her hand. "We only allow paper and pencils in here because much of what we have are the actual historical records.

Merry pulled a notebook out of her bag and then looked up at Lettie. "I don't have a pencil."

"No worries. I have some you can use."

Lettie buzzed around the room pulling books for them and then made a pile on one of the tables. She handed Merry three pencils. "This should get you started."

He was happy to take his notes in pencil just as long as they could make notes. He wasn't one of those people with total recall. He needed to write stuff down.

There was something very intimate and permanent about doing this together with Merry. He'd felt connected to her before. Now, with the baby and the mystery-solving mission, it was like they were already a family. He liked it.

Besides, here in the library, the edge of angriness that had been with him since last night was gone. He felt much lighter and his head clearer. More like himself. He was beginning to think Renee hit on something when she said the house was trying to reach out and touch them. Out here, the touch was gone and the difference was immediately noticeable.

His feeling of euphoria lasted until he turned the page of the book he in front of him. The face that stared out from the full-page black-and-white photo, made his blood turn cold. A roar began in his ears, and fog clouded his vision. Anger boiled up inside him, deep and consuming just as it had earlier this morning...at the house.

"Jeremy? Jeremy!"

He blinked and looked up. Merry had hold of his shoulders and was shaking him, her face close to his. Concern rang through her words and shone deep in her pretty eyes. The roar in his ears faded, the fog receded, and the historical room came back into clear focus. Tables, chairs, bookcases filled with books, journals, and boxes. His vision cleared, though his heart still pounded, and the disturbing emotions lingered like a bad cold that wouldn't go away.

"What happened?" she asked as she cupped his face in her hands. "One minute you were here and the next it's as if you were in another world. You checked out on me. I've never seen you do anything like that before. I've never seen your face look so angry."

He thought about the strange fugue-like state he'd been in and decided she was right. It was the same inside his head. One minute, there, the next, inside some vortex that wrapped him in a cocoon that was ugly and mean. The feeling of wanting to hurt somebody was overpowering. So much so it made him sick to his stomach.

"This guy." He tapped the picture of John McCafferty. "He wasn't right in his lifetime and still isn't. Now it's like he's trying to worm his way inside of me and morph me into him. I hear thoughts that aren't mine and have feelings that are so outside of anything I've ever experienced. It scares the living bejesus out of me."

"Why do you think it's him?"

Good question. There really wasn't anything concrete that let him know it was McCafferty. It was simply an unshakeable feeling that it was that man whose body had long since turned to dust. His spirit was another story altogether. Jeremy had the sense it hadn't gone anywhere.

"Intuition is the best explanation I've got for you."

Merry rubbed one hand across her stomach, the gesture heartwarming in its protectiveness. It helped to bring him firmly back into the present. He loved the fact that even so early on in her pregnancy, she was guarding their child. She was going to be a great mom.

"This craziness has me worried, Jeremy. Something isn't right about all of it. It's bad enough Lorna is being tortured by visions, but now you seem to be catching it too. At least the visions she has aren't filled with bitterness and anger. I don't think I really understand what is happening. I do know I don't like it. I'm positive I hate what it's doing to you."

He would argue with her except everything she said was true. He didn't like the way it felt any better than she did. In fact, it probably felt a whole lot worse than what it looked like on the outside. Each time it hit him, he felt creepy in a lock-him-in-a-psych-ward kind of way. He didn't exactly know what to do about it though. It wasn't like he had any control over when it came and went. At first, he thought it was limited to the house. Now he knew better.

He started to close the books and stack them in a tidy pile. "Let's take what we've found back to Lorna. See what she and Renee have come across. We can all put our heads together to see what we can figure out, at least for the time being. Then maybe you and I can think about heading home, take a break from this—whatever this is." He waved his hand over the stacks of books.

She kissed him on the top of the head and then helped him pull all their scattered notes together. "Great idea. I think you're in need of some fresh air anyway."

They carried the books back to the counter at the front of the room. Lettie was bent over her computer, her nails clicking away at the keys. She looked up and smiled. "You guys need more?"

Merry shook her head. "You gave us plenty."

"I just got started."

Jeremy set down the stack he was carrying. "Appreciate it, Lettie, but for now I think we're good."

"Happy to help. You need anything else, come on by. We might be a small library, but we're mighty."

"Thanks, Lettie." Merry touched her arm before handing over the loaned pencils and retrieving her bag. "It was wonderful meeting you."

"Same to you."

The minute he handed everything back to Lettie, the heaviness that had fallen over him disappeared. The house, the books, the picture, it all combined to set him on edge, and he resented it. He was in a good place, and he didn't appreciate some narrow-minded old guy screwing with his buzz. He held Merry's hand as they left the library, his back straight, his head held high.

The old bigot could just go to hell.

Chapter Sixteen

A lden Swan wasn't what Lorna was expecting, not that she really knew what to anticipate from the tribal elder and keeper of the historical records. He was about her height with blue eyes and jet-black hair. At about fifty, he had the lean build of a lifelong runner.

"Hello, hello," he said as he approached them with hand extended.

Lorna met his outstretched hand with hers and liked the firm handshake. "Thank you so much for giving us a little time. I'm Lorna Dutton and this Renee Austin."

"Lovely to meet you both." He ushered them into his office at the tribal center.

Each time she came into Neah Bay, it took her breath away. Lorna totally understood what brought Bea to this area. Having been born and raised in Eastern Washington, this coastal lifestyle was much different from the distinct four seasons on the other side of the mountains. By all rights, this damp, coastal town should feel as foreign to her as if she'd traveled to a faraway country. On the contrary, it felt much more like she was coming home.

Now, sitting beside Renee and across from Alden, his battered but lovely wooden desk between them, it was as if they were all old friends. She liked the feeling. It made all the sadness and heartbreak of Anna fade into the background a lot more.

"So tell me what I can help you with, or maybe I should tell you what I think I can help you with." His eyes were sharp, and there was a tiny smile on his lips.

Lorna cocked her head and looked first at Renee then back to Alden. "You know what we're looking for?"

A sad look flashed briefly across his face as he nodded. "You're searching for the truth."

"Actually," Renee began before Lorna could answer. 'We're searching for a name."

He nodded again, his hands clasped on the top of his desk. "Same thing really. Her name and the truth are tied together. You can't have one without the other."

"How do you know we're looking for a woman?"

"I'm a wise man."

"All right, I'll buy that. So tell me what's her name?"

"Catherine Swan."

Lorna looked at Renee who had the same expression of surprise on her face that she more than likely had on hers. She scooted to the edge of her chair, perched like a cat about to leap. "You're related?" Funny how this world kept getting smaller and smaller.

He nodded, a thoughtful look on his face. "Yes, she was my great-aunt, my great-grandfather's sister. A gentle and beautiful woman who tragically went missing over a hundred years ago. Not a sign has been found since the day she disappeared."

"She was Tiana McCafferty's friend." She wasn't asking him a question this time because she knew that much of the truth. She'd seen it with her own eyes.

Surprising her again, this time he shook his head. "She was much more than Tiana's friend. She was her heart. Stories the elders handed down year after year tell of their love affair and how death could not break their devotion to each other. They are both gone, but their bond survives even to this day."

Shivers raced up Lorna's arms and tears pricked at the back of her eyes. She felt the truth of his words deep in her soul. She'd not only witnessed their love, she'd felt it. "Even from the grave, they still love each other," she blurted without thinking.

Renee reached over and took her hand. The warmth of her touch was reassuring, grounding in a way she needed. "I'm not crazy," she hurried to add, then smiled. "At least I don't think so."

"She's not crazy," Renee confirmed and patted her hand. "But she is having visions involving Catherine and Tiana. Not anything you might be able to help her with, would it?"

Alden leaned back in his chair and studied her for a long minute. "Ah, so you're the one." It wasn't a question.

Not exactly sure what he was getting at, she confirmed the basic truth, "Well, yeah, I'm Bea's niece if that's what you mean."

"No," he said the word slowly, his fingers now tapping on the desktop. "Your coming to the house on the bluff has been spoken of for a great many years. Both you and the Watcher, for you alone are the one he can touch. And you alone will right the wrong done so long ago."

He seemed so rational when they first got here. Now he was talking about prophecies and beings. Didn't sound very rational now. She'd play along for a minute, but only a minute. "The Watcher? What is that?"

He was nonplussed by the obvious skepticism in her voice. "Not what but rather who."

Breathe, she told herself. "Okay, who is this watcher guy and what does he have to do with me?"

Alden stood. "Come, let us walk down to Lily's coffee shop, order some good coffee, and I will tell you of the legend of the woman savior and the Watcher."

The coffee was good and Lorna settled back in the chair. Alden's voice was mesmerizing as he began to tell them of the Watcher.

"Many think the Watcher is one of the spirits of our tribe, but he is not. He was once an angel sent to earth by God."

"Seriously?" Lorna was having a more difficult time grasping the concept of an angel on earth than she did ghosts in her house.

"I am most serious. The Watchers were sent to earth by God to watch over the humans, but somewhere along the line they failed the Lord and lost their place in heaven. The Watchers were condemned to roam the earth trying to redeem themselves and earn a place in heaven again."

"What does this Watcher guy have to do with us?"

"Everything. He has been watching over Catherine since the day she left this world, and he's been waiting for you to help him bring her home."

Lorna wasn't quite sure what to make of this. "How could you possibly know any of this?" Renee reached over and took Lorna's hand. She was glad to feel the warmth and reassurance of that simple touch.

Alden leaned across the table and placed a hand on her arm. His blue eyes were steady on her face. "We all have our own gifts. Mine is this. Open your heart and your mind, Lorna Dutton. Let Catherine come to you. Let the Watcher guide you, and when you do, you will be the one to set the universe right once more."

❖

The Watcher frowned and crossed his arms across his chest. Dusk was settling in, and they had not yet returned. It was good that they were all out because at last they seemed to understand the importance of the task before them. Still, he was unsettled by their lengthening absence. Giving the other one time to gather strength was not good. It was important to hold him back as long as possible.

The setting sun sent long shadows across the expanse of grass. From his place in the shadows, he watched the house as he had on many other nights. At first, he could not understand what was bothering him so greatly beyond the fervent wish for the women to return. Then he realized what it was: the entire house was dark.

The older woman, the one always here, was not inside. Unease rippled through him as though a cold wind had blown in. She was a woman of habits rarely broken. For the many nights he'd stood in this spot waiting for the one who would come, he'd watched the lights in the house come on. The woman would work in the kitchen making meals and cleaning. Her spirit was clear, clean, and consistent.

Now, with a sickening realization that he could no longer sense her presence, his fear grew. Her spirit, always so strong, was gone from the confines of the home's walls. He closed his eyes and concentrated. Weakly, he felt the thread of her, but it came from far away. He wanted to reach out and touch her. It would do him no good. He lived in the shadow world, and only a very few could move between them. The older woman was not one of them.

Inside the house, something else made his unease skyrocket. *He* was growing stronger. That worried him immensely. Especially now when there was no one inside to keep him in check. Had he done something again? Had he hurt yet another?

It could not happen again. Though he sought redemption for his own soul, he would gladly forfeit any right to return to heaven if he could banish the evil one. So many years and so much heartache had resulted from the man's walk on the earth. Even now, when he no longer existed in the world of the living, his being infected the world around him. It wasn't right, and it was up to him to stop him once and for all.

The problem was he couldn't do it alone. He needed her and he needed her now. Time was slipping away faster and faster with no way to halt it. Soon, it would be too late for all of them.

The darkened windows of the house seemed to mock him. The blankness of the glass reflected back his own isolation. As he gazed at them, a face appeared and stared back at him. One second it was there, and the next it was gone. His heart lurched at the sight. He wanted to scream at the top of his lungs.

His worst fears had been realized. There was no longer a question of how long they had to make things right. They were out of time. *He* was back.

❖

"Well, that's odd," Renee said as they pulled into the driveway. "I wonder where Mom went. She had her doctor's appointment this morning and said she was going to pick up groceries on the way home. I don't think she mentioned going anywhere else?"

Lorna shrugged. "Maybe she ran back into town for something she forgot at the grocery store?"

It was a possibility though not a very strong one. "Maybe, but I doubt it. You want to talk about someone with compulsive habits and you'll be talking about my mother. Mom is one of those people who make lists for everything. Trust me, if it wasn't on her list, she didn't buy it and she didn't need it. Besides, she's always been quite firm about dinner time. She should be in whipping up something by now and watching the clock to make sure we're back on time. Even at our age she would ground us if we show up late to her dinner."

"She has a cell, doesn't she?"

Renee nodded. "Reluctantly, yes. She fought me a little on that one, but I shoved her into the twenty-first century kicking and screaming." She pulled out her own phone and called as they were walking in through the back door to the mud room. No great smells of cooking food wafted through the open door to the kitchen.

They looked at each other when the strains of a familiar song could be heard coming from the other side of said door. Her stomach lurched. It was her mother's ringtone. Her uneasiness turned to fear. Something was very wrong.

"Mom!" She raced into the kitchen.

Lorna followed her in and flicked the light switch, bathing the kitchen in a warm glow. It was empty except for the phone on the counter still trilling her mother's favorite song. She stood staring at the phone while Lorna walked out of the kitchen. She came back moments later. "Unless she's upstairs, nothing."

A sound at the back door made Renee whirl around. It was Clancy. She opened the door and he came quickly in, his body language tense. "What, buddy? What is it?"

He jumped on her, something he rarely did, and then raced back to the door. When she didn't follow, he ran back to her and jumped up again hitting her hard before running back to the door.

She didn't know what had gotten into him. He knew better than to jump on her or anyone else for that matter. The only explanation was he was probably picking up on her panic.

"I think he wants us to follow him," Lorna said as she watched Clancy repeat the process a third time.

It was stupid on her part not to pick up on Clancy's attempts to make her understand. Of course he wanted her to follow him. He was a smart guy and she was the dumb human who failed to translate his very clear message. He didn't usually act this way, and now that she realized he was trying to communicate, it scared her. First her mom was MIA and now Clancy was fretting about something. She had a bad feeling.

"All right, Clancy," Renee told him as she followed him back to the door. "Show me."

He proceeded to do just that. The second she opened the door for him, he raced out and across the grass, stopping only long enough to look back at her, presumably to make sure she was following. He'd had enough trouble getting her to understand in the first place, and apparently, he wasn't taking any chances she'd go stupid on him again. At the bluff, he began to skitter his way down.

"Clancy!" Going down that steep incline in the dark was dangerous, and she didn't want him to get hurt. While she'd raced out of the house without considering the fact it was dark outside, Lorna, thank goodness, had thought to bring a flashlight. It would help her, but it wouldn't help her dog.

"Look," Lorna said as she shone the light down. The illumination was enough to catch Clancy as he continued to make his way down the slope. "There's something down there."

Though too far below to catch much of the light, she saw what had caught Lorna's attention. Something was there, and Clancy was heading straight for it. She squinted and tried to make out more detail. Could it be? Renee's heart was pounding as she started to follow her dog, her feet slipping and sliding on the loose rocks.

"Careful," Lorna said as she followed close on her heels, making sure to stay close enough to give Renee enough light to keep from losing her footing completely. Rocks were kicked loose and skittering down the hill. She kept stumbling and catching herself with her hands that were now scraped up from the rough ground.

As they closed in on the spot where Clancy stopped, his whining filled the night air. Clearly, he was upset, and she felt bad it had taken her so long to understand him. When she saw why he was so distressed, her heart nearly stopped. At the base of the bluff, her mother lay in a motionless heap, her skin a scary shade of white in the glow of the flashlight.

"Oh my God," she murmured as she fell to her knees, heedless of the rocks that cut through the fabric of her jeans. "Mama." She touched her face, alarmed by the coolness of her skin. "Mama."

Lorna kneeled beside her and took hold of her mother's wrist. "She's got a pulse." As she pulled her phone from her pocket, she told Renee. "I'm calling 911."

Renee heard her, but it didn't register. Nothing did except for the fact her mother was hurt, and badly by the look of things. How could this have happened? Why did it happen? She'd lived here for decades and knew the landscape like the back of her hand. She was aware of all the danger spots and how treacherous this bluff could be in the dark. There was no way she'd be wandering out here at night. Definitely not wandering around out here by herself. Renee was certain of that.

"Renee," Lorna said as she held her hand over the phone. "Put your sweater over her. Let's try to keep her as warm as we can while we wait for emergency services."

Lorna was right. They needed to keep her body temperature up as much as they could until help arrived. Quickly, she pulled her arms out of the soft sweater and carefully wrapped it around her mother's torso and shoulders, tucking it underneath. She put her hands on either side of her head intending to hold her head up until help came, but Lorna's single sharp word stopped her.

"Don't."

She looked up, confused and a little angry. "Why? I want to get her head off the cold ground. Her hair is wet; she's got to be cold."

Lorna shook her head vehemently. "We don't know what kind of injury she has. If she's hurt her neck and you move her head, it could make things so much worse. The EMTs will be here before you know it, and they have all the right equipment to make sure she's stabilized."

Her heart sank at the thought of what she might have done to her mother if Lorna hadn't stopped her. "I don't want to hurt her," she said with tears in her eyes.

Lorna put an arm around her and squeezed. "Of course you don't, and you've done what you can to keep her safe. Help will be here soon, and she'll be where they can make sure she's fine. Keep hold of her head just like you're doing now and just keep her still. It's the best thing you can do for her at the moment. "

That wasn't a problem for her. She was seated on the sand, one leg bent, the other straight out. She had her hands on either side of her mother's head and her elbows rested on her legs. If she had to, she could stay this way all night. Anything to make sure Mom was going to be okay.

It seemed to Renee it took the emergency people hours to show up. Not because her arms hurt or she was upset that by sitting on the sand she was getting soaked to the skin. It was the worry that made it seem like forever before help arrived. In reality, it was less than thirty minutes. Had they not lived so far out, the response time would have been quicker. There were disadvantages to the beautiful solitude this place offered.

The emergency crew navigated the bluff with impressive skill and speed. The beefy EMT with hands the size of plates, told her she'd done exactly the right thing and had her continue to hold until he had a cervical collar in place. Her fear that something was terribly wrong must have shown on her face because he gave her a pat on the back when they were done and told her it was a just in case thing and not to worry. She did anyway.

The crew checked her mother from head to toe before moving her as a team from the ground to the litter they'd brought down the hill. Through it all, she never made a sound or opened her eyes. Before they picked up the litter to carry her to the waiting ambulance, Clancy licked her cheek. Only then did she make a sound, a small moan. Renee didn't think a moan could ever sound so fantastic and there was no way she could stop the tears that trickled down her cheeks

Renee followed them up the hill, Lorna and Clancy right behind. It was trickier ascending in the darkness. Her feet slipped, and many times, she stumbled, catching herself before tumbling back down. The emergency crew didn't need a second victim. Like her earlier descent, it seemed like it took forever before they finally made it to the top of the bluff. The grass beneath her feet was a relief in more ways than one.

The lights of the ambulance cut through the night in flashes of color, a beacon that drew them all toward it. She hurried, her heart pounding and tears still pricking at the back of her eyes. None of this made any sense. She still didn't understand how she'd ended up at the bottom of the bluff. Mom didn't do crazy things, and coming out here in the dark was crazy.

As they were loading her mother into the ambulance, Lorna held her hand. The gesture was simple and yet it meant a great deal to Renee. The comfort of her touch was incredible. If not for Lorna, Renee would be falling apart. She could deal with losing her home and her business. Those were mere things, and things could always be replaced. Not so when it came to family. Even the thought of losing her mother made her want to scream.

"Go," Lorna whispered in her ear. "She needs you at her side."

She was torn. On one hand, she wanted to run to her side and hold her tight. On the other, she was afraid of what might happen. "I'm scared."

"It'll be fine. She's in good hands." Lorna placed a kiss on the top of her head. "Go. I feel it here." She tapped her heart. "It's going to be all right."

After squeezing Lorna's hand once, she reluctantly let go and climbed into the ambulance to sit beside her mother. The EMT shut the doors once she was in and seated. As the ambulance drove away, she watched out the small rear windows. Lorna, with Clancy at her side, gave her a wave. Her eyes stayed on Lorna and Clancy until they faded, swallowed up by the darkness.

She'd never felt so alone.

CHAPTER SEVENTEEN

Jeremy didn't think too much about the ambulance that passed them on the highway with its lights flashing and siren blaring, at least not until they got back to Lorna's house. The big old place that as of late was home to a party of five was almost empty. Only Lorna waited inside. Well, Lorna and Clancy, who sat like a statue in the front window staring out. He gave them little more than a sideways glance as he and Merry walked in the front door. It was pretty clear right from the second they stepped inside that something was terribly wrong.

They found Lorna sitting at the kitchen table with a steaming mug of coffee in one hand and her cell phone in the other. She stared at the phone as though by watching it intently, she could will it to ring. It wasn't working; the phone was silent.

"What's happened?" The tension in the room was so intense he didn't even bother with a hello. Neither did Merry. They both stood and waited.

"You better sit down," she told them without taking her eyes off the cell phone.

They sat.

By the time she finished filling them in on Jolene's accident, he was sick to his stomach. He'd been feeling better after the incident in the library, at least until he'd stepped foot back in the house. Now he ached all over, like someone had taken a baseball bat to his body.

He ran his hands through his hair and tried to think what they could do to help. This feeling of helplessness was horrible. There had to be something they could do, but he was coming up blank. As they sat there in silence, Merry's cell rang, and all three of them jumped. She glanced at the number and frowned.

"I need to take this." She walked out of the kitchen to talk in privacy.

He didn't give much thought to Merry's caller. His thoughts were on Jolene. She was such a wonderful woman, and the thought of her being hurt made him sad. They had to figure out some way to help.

"This sucks," he said to Lorna.

She nodded, her eyes looking tired. "Yeah, big time."

When Merry walked back in holding the cell phone in her hand, her face was clouded. She'd been full of energy all day and they'd had fun together. It was like the old days and as if the recent tension between never existed at all. Her expression now brought back the anxiety he'd hoped was gone.

"What?" He was almost afraid to ask, the way things were going since they'd gotten back here.

She cocked her head and met his eyes. "That was Lexie."

Inwardly, Jeremy groaned. Lexie was a straight up flake. Why Merry lived with her was something he'd never been able to understand. Granted, Merry and Lexie had been friends since childhood. It didn't change the fact that Lexie was weird. It also didn't change the fact that the bond between them didn't seem to be breakable no matter what dumbass thing Lexie did. And there were plenty.

He tried not to let the irritation sound in his voice, even if the last thing they needed right now was a Lexie crisis. "What did she do this time?"

Merry blew out her cheeks and looked at the ceiling. "She moved out."

Okay, now that wasn't what he expected, and in the big picture, it was not bad. In fact, in his opinion, it was a good thing. Not having Lexie in her day-to-day world was bound to make Merry's life a great deal easier. By the expression on her face, however, she didn't share his sentiments.

"That's good, Merry. You don't need her drama, especially now."

She shook her head. "No, Jeremy, you don't understand. This is definitely not good. I can't afford the rent by myself, and it's due in a week. I'm screwed." Tears welled in her eyes and spilled down her cheeks.

He didn't hesitate. He stood and pulled her into his arms, kissing away the tears. Her body trembled, and he smoothed her hair with one hand. "No, baby, you are most definitely not screwed. The solution is very simple. You'll move in with me."

She started to cry. "That's a horrible idea."

He held her at arm's length. Despite being a big, tough guy, her words hurt his feelings. "What?" After everything between them, the last thing he expected to hear from her was that living with him would be a terrible thing. They were going to be parents together. "I love you, Merry, and have loved you for a long time. This baby of ours is incredible and just makes me love you even more if that's even possible."

She sniffled. "It's not that. I love you too, and I love that we're having a baby together."

He didn't think his feelings could be hurt more, but he was wrong. What she said made it even worse. "Then what is it? Why won't you live with me?"

She gazed at him with watery eyes and sniffed. "I don't mean to hurt your feelings, but I hate your apartment and you live in an awful area. I'm not living there, and I'm not having a baby there."

The pressure disappeared in a heartbeat, and he began to laugh as he pulled her close again. His joy came rolling back in. "Okay, gorgeous, not a problem. We'll live wherever you want. You just pick the place and we're there."

"We don't have time," she wailed.

He hugged her even closer. He had to think there were some hormones at work here. Merry was not an emotional woman, not like the one he currently held in his arms. "We'll make time. I promise."

Lorna laughed lightly. "Merry's right you know, Jeremy. Your apartment stinks, and honestly, why you decided to live in that area, I'll never know. Might be okay for you, and I'm using the word okay loosely. It's absolutely no place for Merry and the baby. This"—she waved her arms around—"is the perfect place for you to have a baby."

He stared at her, not quite catching her drift. "Here?"

"Here?" Merry repeated.

Lorna smiled at them like they were small children. "Did you or did you not both tell me you're currently unemployed?"

"Yeah," he admitted. "We did."

"Well, then," she declared. "I can use help. Merry, you have some seriously mad skills that I can use, and while I can't pay you what you're accustomed to earning, I can nonetheless pay you a small salary. Jeremy, you're on your own for employment, but knowing you like I do, I'm confident you'll find something. In the meantime, there's plenty of handyman things you can help me with around here. Think about it. It's a win-win for all three of us."

"I don't know," he said. He'd always lived in Spokane and had never given serious consideration to moving anywhere else. In fact, he'd even gone to college in Spokane, opting for Gonzaga University because it was both a great school and local. Well, that and GU had an awesome basketball team.

Lorna wasn't cutting him any slack. "Bull. You do know. You both know I'm right. It's settled. You two can haul ass back to Spokane tomorrow. Load up your stuff and bring it back pronto. No sense waiting around and spending more money on rent and utilities when you can live here. We'll be one big happy family."

Big family maybe, she was right on that score. He wasn't so sure about the happy part. It wasn't like they'd lived in the same household lately. It had been a pretty long time since they'd lived under the same roof, and when they were kids, well, they'd been known to disagree. Then again, they were all adults now and this was a really big house, not like the moderate-sized rancher they'd grown up in. Maybe Lorna was right. This could be the solution to their immediate needs. Wasn't like it had to be forever, and for a little while it could be a fun adventure.

If only he didn't still have that sick feeling in the pit of his stomach.

❖

Lorna couldn't sleep. Not until she knew how Jolene was doing. The fact that she was still unconscious when they'd loaded her into the ambulance was more than a little concerning. The only sound she'd made was the tiny moan when Clancy licked her face. That had been encouraging, but only a little.

When Renee called at a little after one to tell her Jolene had regained consciousness, her relief was enough that it almost made her cry. The initial diagnosis was a small skull fracture and understandably, a concussion. At this point, they weren't giving Renee an estimate on how much time Jolene would need to stay in the hospital. From the sounds of things, it was going to be a day-by-day process. The encouraging part was they expected a full recovery.

After regaining consciousness, Jolene related an odd thing to Renee. She told her she'd been standing at the edge of the bluff looking out at the ocean when it felt like someone put two hands on her back and shoved. As far as she'd known, she was alone, so to feel someone's hands on her back shocked her. Jolene hadn't had time to react: she was tumbling down the hill. The next thing she knew, she woke up in a hospital bed with a worried daughter holding her hand.

Renee tried to coax a little more detail from her mother. That didn't happen. The head injury had made her drowsy, and there was little more to be discovered tonight. She told Lorna everything she knew and promised she'd call in the morning.

Lorna wished Renee wasn't so far away. The hospital in Seattle was the best place Jolene could be right now. They would give her the kind of care she deserved and would need to recover from her injuries. Still, she wanted to be with both Renee and Jolene. They felt like family, and family stayed together.

After a few hours, Clancy had given up his vigil at the window, sort of. He was no longer sitting like a statue in front of the glass. Instead, he was now curled up on the rug resting while still close enough to the window that he wouldn't miss a thing that might happen outside. She understood how he felt. She wanted to do the same thing. Just curl up, wait, and watch.

Jeremy and Merry would be on their way back to Spokane first thing in the morning, leaving her alone in the house except for Clancy. They were getting some much needed rest before beginning the long drive across the mountains. After they left tomorrow, it was going to be terribly quiet with shadows looming in every corner.

Even now, the looming vacancy made the house feel lonely. She should go to bed. Get some sleep instead of rattling around in the quiet feeling alone. The best thing she could do right now was grab some rest before she took a drive into the city tomorrow to check on her girls.

She laughed thinking how natural it felt to call Renee and Jolene her girls. Aunt Bea must have had some kind of psychic ability herself. She'd gifted this home to Lorna seemingly knowing that she needed something in her life to ground her. As it turned out, this place was exactly what she'd needed.

The only tiny little problem with Aunt Bea's plan: the ghosts. Lorna's laugh this time was even heartier, and it made Clancy raise his head from his paws to stare at her.

"Not to worry, buddy, I'm not going wacko. Exactly." Clancy continued to stare for a moment longer and then put his black head back down on his paws. Apparently, he decided she wasn't as crazy as she sounded.

As much as she loved this house, and that love grew more and more each day, some lingering malevolence refused to give up its hold. Or would it be more accurate to say, give up *his* hold? The talk with Alden Swan clicked with her at a spiritual level. On the surface, any rational person would say bullshit. Rational zipped right past her a couple of visions ago.

Alden seemed like a pretty together guy. He was educated and successful, and yet at the same time held on to his spiritual beliefs in a way that all made sense. His official opinion was that unfinished business rested within this house, and at this point, she had no problem whatsoever buying in.

Now all she had to do was figure out how to complete the unfinished business put on her plate. To complete whatever had been started way back in John McCafferty's day. For the life of her, Lorna couldn't understand what made her so unique that she'd have the kind of ability needed to pull that off. Why would anyone, alive or dead, be waiting for her? She was far from special, as Anna pointed out to her rather brutally the last night they were together. In fact, according to Anna, she was a nobody.

In reality, maybe that wasn't very fair. In the heat of the moment, they both said things they regretted. For her part, if she could, she'd take back pretty much everything she'd spewed like hot lava that horrible night. It didn't matter whether Anna felt the same way or would say those terrible things all over again. Even before now, Lorna realized she didn't want to be that kind of woman. Just because Anna had hurt her, didn't give her a pass to be cruel. Her parents would not be proud, and even though they were gone, she wanted to be the kind of person who honored them.

That was not to say she wanted to hang out with Anna ever again. On the contrary, if she never saw her again it would be too soon. Her heart was forever broken, and that wasn't going to change. Renee's presence was beginning to make her believe that perhaps she could experience passion again, but love? Not gonna happen. That died the day Anna crushed her soul.

In her room, she changed into comfy sweats and a pair of old slippers. She didn't even look at the bed. No way was she going to be able to sleep. Instead, she looked over at the whalebone necklace and then with a big breath, picked it up, fully expecting to drop into a vision. It didn't happen.

"Huh." As she rolled the beads between her fingers, she stared at the lovely piece of jewelry. "Got nothing for me tonight? You get to pick and choose when we meet?"

She was stilling carrying the necklace as she went into the living room. Since it didn't seem to want to play tonight, she set it aside on the end table. She stoked the fire she'd built earlier. As it always did, the fire filled the room with a lovely aroma of tamarack. The fire crackled and sparked, rolling out warmth to every corner. She put the fireplace poker down on the hearth and lowered herself to the floor. With her back against the sofa, she stretched her legs out and let the warm air wash over her.

"Clancy," she said loudly. "Come sit with me."

He was still resting in front of his window, his head on his paws. He hadn't moved far from that window all night. She didn't think he was going to either, and then she heard the click, click, click of his nails on the hardwood floor. Much to her surprise, he came in, settled beside her on the rug, and put his head back down on his paws. His black eyes stared at the fire for a moment before closing. Soon, his chest rose and fell with easy rhythm. She gently rubbed the top of his head and realized how glad she was to have him here.

Her gaze traveled up to the table where she'd laid the necklace and curiosity took hold again. She reached over to snag the necklace. For whatever reason, it seemed to draw her attention like a moth to a flame. It was pretty and it was interesting, but it was more than either of those things. In the back of her mind it was like a siren's song played, and she was compelled to pick it up. Unlike earlier when she'd touched it, now electricity shot up her arms the moment her fingertips touched the whalebone. Her gasp made Clancy jump and whine.

"We must hurry," Tiana said as she dragged Catherine along by her hand. "He must not catch us."

Catherine giggled as she ran beside Tiana. "He will not catch us, for we run like the wind."

Tiana smiled in spite of her fear. How was it that whenever Catherine was at her side, the weight of the world disappeared and she felt as light as a feather? Even so, she carried in her heart a mighty worry that he was watching. Dear God, he was always watching, his face a dark mask of disapproval and, she feared, hatred. Most thought him a kind and generous family man who did much for his community. He threw lavish parties where he paraded her out like a precious doll. She always smiled and did exactly as he told her. Little did they know the terror he instilled in his only child.

He wanted, no demanded, unquestioned obedience from her. She was more like his property than his child. He'd never held her in his lap and read her a story. He'd never kissed her cheek and wished her a wonderful day. He'd never looked upon her with the kind of pride that she saw in the faces of other fathers. For her, it was always unreadable dark eyes and a twisted expectation that sent ice into her veins. Though he'd never said it, she was certain the only feeling he had for her was loathing.

How she longed to be free and to no longer exist within the walls of her stunning prison. The house her father had built was the talk of the Pacific Northwest, and scores of important people thought it an honor to stay in one of its glorious rooms. Her own room was no less magnificent. He might hate her, but he would never make his true feelings obvious to those he admired. He didn't have the room built for her. No, he built it so others would think he did it for her.

Tonight was the last night she intended to sleep in the soft bed with the fresh-smelling sheets and feather pillows. The silk spread brought from China would never again be pulled back by the maids. Neither would she light the Tiffany lamp on the bedside table. She didn't care if she ever spent a night in such luxury again as long as she was free.

The full moon illuminated the long expanse of grass carefully landscaped by an army of men who came each day and in whose eyes she saw pity. Unlike the guests who came to stay in the lovely rooms, he did not bother to temper his treatment toward her when in front of mere workers. In his world, they did not matter, just as she did not matter.

Tonight, she continued to hold Catherine's hand as they briskly crossed the lawn before anyone might catch a glimpse of them racing through the night. The air smelled of ocean and the life that lived within the cold waters. The mist upon her lips brought the light taste of salt and sea.

This she would miss. Despite her lifelong imprisonment within the beautiful home, here where the stars filled the sky and the ocean waves broke against the rocks and sandy shores, her heart felt full.

For it was on the shores of the ever-flowing ocean that she first glimpsed her love. Though she didn't realize it until she gazed upon Catherine's face, her soul had been waiting for the one who could make her complete.

It wasn't any within the parade of men, both young and old, that her father brought to their table in his quest to secure for her the perfect husband that made her feel alive and open to love. Unable to even feign attraction, she turned away from every one of them, not fully realizing why she felt nothing at their touch. Each time she spurned their attentions, his fury grew until now it was a beacon that filled her with dread. The day she gazed upon Catherine's face for the first time, she understood and her world became whole for the first time in her life.

In the end, he had come to discover the truth as well, and with it the anger that had before only simmered now flared into a fire so hot it could burn the noonday sun. If there was a way to please her father, surely she would have taken it in both hands and done whatever it took to earn even a tiny bit of affection. She did not want to be the disappointment to him that she had turned out to be. Perhaps she never really had a chance. She was, after all, a mere woman. He'd wanted a son, and Mother had given him one for ten full days. Then her precious little brother had been taken by death, a mere infant who never had a chance to make his place in the world.

It broke her heart the day her brother died. Had he lived, her life would have been so much different. Her mother might not have withdrawn from the world, and the attention her father focused so intently on her would have gone to another. She might have been free to love this beautiful woman outside the circle of his disapproval.

Or perhaps not. He did not understand that Catherine was the one, the only one, who made her feel alive and complete. But it was not the way of the world they lived in. Their love had to be secret, and only in the dark corners and shadows could she hold her in her arms and kiss her sweet lips. It wasn't just her father. Few understood the depth and need of their love. Expectations were laid out for her on the day she was born and nothing could or would change them. A prominent marriage was expected. Children were demanded.

Success in society an absolute mandate. She'd disappointed him on every front.

She didn't care. As she held tightly to Catherine's hand and scurried across the damp grass, all she could think of was that from tonight on they would be together. Forever.

And then she saw him.

CHAPTER EIGHTEEN

How's Clancy doing?" With the phone pressed to her ear with one hand, Renee was in the hospital waiting room, staring out the window and running her other hand through her unruly hair. She missed her dog and was anxious to get back to see him. Well, him and Lorna, if she were being honest.

She could hear the smile in Lorna's words. "He's great. You probably know this already. He's awesome company. Since you've been in Seattle, he's gone for a couple of runs with me, and after the first night watching out the front window for hours, has even slept on the bed with me."

"Oh, Lorna, you're spoiling him." Inside, she was delighted that she was bonding with her dog even if it didn't really make sense. What did it matter if she liked Clancy? It wasn't like they'd be staying there forever. Ultimately, they'd go back to Seattle and get back to the business of rebuilding. That's where her life was, after all.

"Naw, we're pals. The problem you really have to worry about is whether I'm gonna let you take him back. I may just have to hide him when you decide you have to leave."

This time, Renee laughed and it felt good after the last week of uncertainty and fear. "We can always hammer out a custody and visitation agreement."

Her heart warmed thinking about Lorna's words. Maybe they were given offhand, but they meant a lot to her. She'd realized over the last few days that she really liked Lorna…as in *REALLY* liked her. Deep in her heart, she hoped the feeling was mutual, and given their interaction before Mom's accident, she had reason to be hopeful.

Still, it had been a full week since they'd discovered her mother at the base of the bluff, and most of that time she'd spent here quietly waiting. It was all she could do. All the hospital and doctors could do. The concussion and skull fracture had to heal themselves. It was simply a case of hurry up and wait. Nothing like spending a week feeling helpless.

Today, there was good news. Mom was going to be discharged and allowed to return home. She'd be down for a while, and that was fine with Renee because she intended to stick to her Mom like glue until she was certain she was healed up. She hoped it was going to be fine with Lorna too.

"I'm bringing Mom home, and I plan to stay with her until she's given a clear bill," she told Lorna, holding her breath as she waited for a response. *Please, please, please let her say okay.*

"What time? It'll take me a few to get there, but with a little speeding, I can be there before you know it."

Renee silently breathed a sigh of relief. Her reaction was more than she expected and what her heart longed to hear. "You don't need to come all the way into the city. My car is still here, remember?"

Lorna laughed, the sound wonderful to Renee's ears. The week had been sorely lacking in lightness. "Oh yeah, forgot that little detail, although I don't know how. That was a fun night."

Fun and precious, but she didn't say that. "They're going to discharge her first thing in the morning, and we'll leave right from here. I'll take my time so Mom's as comfortable as possible on the drive home."

"Sounds like a plan. We'll be waiting."

Tears welled in her eyes, and she was glad no one was around to see them. "Thank you, Lorna."

"For what? Renee, there isn't a single thing you need to thank me for. This is your mother's home, always will be, and you're as welcome as she is. Even if I didn't already feel that way, you know

Aunt Bea would come back from the grave and kick my ass if I said otherwise."

"I appreciate that."

"Blah, blah, blah, just load up your mama and get your ass back here. I've been busy since you've been hanging around the hospital drinking coffee and flirting with nurses. Sister, I have some cool stuff to show you."

"I will get my ass back there as soon as I can. And, Lorna..."

"Yeah."

"I didn't flirt with a single nurse."

Lorna was laughing when Renee ended the call. She smiled too as she slipped the phone back into her pocket. She could hardly wait to get on the road. Not only was she anxious to get home because she was really tired of the hospital, but Lorna's news intrigued her. She missed the challenge of trying to uncover the mysteries of the house. They'd had such a great time at the Seattle Library as well as with Alden Swan, and she'd felt like they were on the verge of unraveling something quite curious. She wasn't exactly sure what, but it was definitely something. Life, in spite of the devastating fire, had become very interesting.

❖

Jeremy stood on the steps of the apartment building and tossed the keys up and down in the air. As he looked around, he grimaced. He hated to admit it, but Merry and Lorna had been right. Looking at it from their perspective, they had a valid point. This *was* a sucky neighborhood, and why he had decided to stay here for as long as he had was certainly a topic for conversation with a good shrink.

No more. It was past time to move on, and that's what he was about to do in a big way, sans the shrink. After dropping the keys into the manager's drop box, he crawled behind the wheel of his SUV and pulled away from the curb. The trailer he pulled was only about a third full. He had to go around the block so he could catch Maple Street, a one-way, and head south to Merry's place.

The last week had been a long one spent sorting, packing, and discarding. He did way more discarding than Merry, but then again, he needed to do way more discarding than Merry. Some of the crap he'd held on to was, well…crap. Time to clean house had sailed past him quite a while ago.

Her stuff, on the other hand, was pretty nice. Might have something to do with why he always felt so comfortable when he was at her place. With her roommate already gone, they'd been able to work through her house without interruption. Like his stuff, all of her belongings were now ready to be loaded into the enclosed trailer.

Once he had her furniture and boxes stacked and secured, they could be on their way. Spokane would be a distant memory in the rearview mirror and the Washington coast their new home. If he gave himself time to think about it, the move was scary even though Lorna was there with the net to catch him and Merry.

He'd never started over before. Not like this anyway. For that matter, his entire life had been spent inside the Spokane city limits. Relocating never occurred to him before now, let alone finding himself on the verge of getting married and becoming a father. In less than a year, his life would be about a hundred eighty degrees from what it looked like now. Talk about life changes. This was almost too much to take in.

Scared as he was about all the changes, he was also thrilled. It had taken a good many years and a good many women before he found the one. In the back of his mind, he'd known Merry was the one since the get-go. That's why the thought that she was pulling away scared the daylights out of him. He'd have been broken forever if she'd left him. He wasn't being dramatic either. That's just the way it would have gone done if he'd dumped him.

Now, it was a bright new world awaiting them both. It was all an unknown world to be sure. At the same time, it was really exciting. Together, they would find their way, and it would be good. How could it not be great? Together, they just worked, and he wasn't about to second-guess the magic.

He was still feeling good hours later when they pulled into Lorna's driveway. Merry slept through most of the drive, but he didn't mind. The early stages of her pregnancy were kicking her butt and sleep was exactly what she needed. Besides, the quiet time was relaxing to him. The drive across state was a long haul, and he'd driven it pretty much straight through except for stops for gas and restrooms. They grabbed food on the go and just kept ticking away the miles. Big fat pain in the ass as he was driving it. Worth it now that they were here.

The most surprising thing to him was he thought he'd feel sad as they left Eastern Washington, but he didn't. As the clouds rolled in at the top of Snoqualmie Pass, rather than washing him in a sense of gloom, it had made him smile. Adventure was awaiting them on the downside of the pass, and he was anxious to reach the ocean shores. The reality was maybe he more ready for a change in his life than he realized.

At the house, he parked the SUV and trailer close to the back door. He'd start unloading later when they figured out exactly where he and Merry would make their new home. The room he'd stayed in earlier was great, but there was a whole wing of the house he needed to explore. With a place this size there was no reason any of them had to be on top of each other.

In the kitchen, they both stopped and stared. He started to laugh and Merry shook her head.

"Jolene is going to kill her if she sees this," Merry said somberly.

No shit was his first thought. Lorna's mud-splattered tri bike was leaning against the kitchen counter, her helmet hanging from the handlebars. Running shoes with the laces splayed were tossed just inside the door. A glossy black wetsuit was wadded up in the sink, one sleeve hanging over and dripping water onto the floor where it puddled on the granite tile.

Then there was the kitchen table. Lorna's laptop was open, surrounded by piles of printed paper and books. A legal pad with sheets torn off lay next to the computer, and tossed aside were sheets covered with Lorna's distinctive writing. He counted five coffee mugs nestled in the midst of the paper chaos.

"Oh yeah," he said as he held up one piece of paper displaying coffee soaked rings. "Jolene is most definitely going to kill Lorna."

"Who's gonna kill me?" Lorna walked into the kitchen, dressed in jeans and a sweatshirt, her hair wet. Clancy trotted in behind her, his tail wagging. She walked past them to the back door, opened it, and Clancy trotted through without giving any of them another look.

"Kinda obvious, sis. She might be injured, but once she gets an eyeful of this place, Jolene is going to be smoking mad. You have completely trashed her kitchen. This is impressive, even for you."

"Even for me?"

"Even for you."

"Humph." Lorna looked around and shrugged. "What can I say? I've been busy. No time to tidy up."

"No time to clean up because you've been too busy making a hurricane."

"Not exactly, Mr. Clean." She opened a cupboard door and pulled out another coffee mug. He wondered if there was an endless supply inside there. "Good research takes time. Just wait until you guys see what I've found."

"When is Jolene coming back?" While he wanted to hear what Lorna had dug up, he was more concerned about getting this cleaned up. Jolene already had a head injury, he didn't want to give her a heart attack too when she saw her normally spotless kitchen looking like a tornado had blown through. He'd get it straightened away before he touched anything else.

Lorna took a sip of her freshly poured coffee. "In the morning. Plenty of time to get things back in tip-top shape."

"Depends," Merry said, her brow drawn together and her expression stern. "Does the rest of the house look like this? We may have to pull an all-nighter."

Rolling her eyes, Lorna said, "What do you guys think I am?"

He raised one eyebrow and stared at her. "Right now, a slob, and I'm trying to be nice here." It reminded him of her bedroom when they were teenagers. She was a walking disaster in those days, and he thought she might be having flashbacks now.

"Come on, Jeremy. So I dropped a few things. What's the big whoop?"

"A few things." He did a full circle, looking at the bike, the muddy shoe prints, the dripping wetsuit, and the piles of coffee mugs. "Lorna, your bike is in the kitchen!"

This time, she flinched. "Yeah, you might have a point there, bro. Don't think Jolene would be too amused by that. Probably not my wetsuit in the sink either."

This time he rolled his eyes. "You think?"

"Come on." Merry was holding up the wetsuit between her thumb and forefinger as it dripped water into the sink. "You two quit snapping at each other like little kids and let's get cleaning. We're burning daylight here, folks."

❖

The sun dropped below the horizon shoving out the light and ushering in deep, inky darkness. From his usual spot, the Watcher stepped around the tree and studied the three as they unloaded boxes from the long white trailer and carried them into the house.

The sight pleased him. Though the woman had been making progress in the days she'd been here alone, having the others back would give her both added power and help. She could draw strength from them, and perhaps at last this would all come to an end. They could finally be brought home and *his* reign of terror would be stopped.

Still, a nagging worry plagued him. Evil vibrated throughout the grounds despite his best efforts to keep it at bay. *He* was growing stronger with each passing day feeding off of something unseen. Now that the man was back, he would draw from him as he'd done before, and that frightened him. The danger grew every moment they failed to see and act, and his ability to guide them was limited.

It seemed hours before they finally locked the trailer and made their final trip into the house where they gathered around the table. From where he stood, he had a clear view into the lighted kitchen. There they sat talking and reading, handing papers back and forth.

She seemed to be the one holding court, and the other two listened, their faces full of interest. The seriousness with which they studied and listened gave him hope.

The man stepped to the window and gazed out as he drank from a long-stemmed glass filled halfway up with amber liquid. His high spirits sank as he watched him, the hazy glow around his body growing in intensity. Its origin was undeniable. In the short time since he'd returned to the house, *he* had once again invaded his body and soul. *He* always found a way, a vessel that would carry his energy into the present. In this life, it was the young man with the kind face and pale eyes. Preying on gentle souls was what he liked to do best. Taking what was good and corrupting it gave him power even in death. It was time to take that power away from him.

He closed his eyes and began to pray. Though he'd been cast from his rightful place in heaven, if God would hear him now, just maybe this time it would all end differently.

CHAPTER NINETEEN

So here's what I found." Lorna turned the wineglass in her hand, watching as the beautiful Shiraz swirled inside. "We have Tiana McCafferty, twenty years old, a 'spinster' still at home with her parents. Everything I could find seemed to show that despite living so far from the city, she and her family were very active in the Seattle social scene. From all accounts, her father was working hard to set her up in a successful marriage. Like really hard if you catch my drift."

"Pretty woman," Merry said as she studied a copy of an old photograph Lorna had uncovered. "I wouldn't think it would have been too tough a challenge to find a rich guy to take her for a walk down the aisle."

"I don't think finding a willing man was the problem. I found snippets of gossip about men vying for her attentions. It seems, however, that she didn't give any of them the time of day. All those eligible bachelors and not a single mention in any newspaper that she dated even one. I don't think our girl was interested in the bachelors."

"Must have burned her daddy's ass," Renee said with a smile. "A beautiful girl and no rich hubby to add to Daddy's coffers."

"She was beautiful and so was her lover, Catherine Swan. She kicked all the men to the curb because she was in love with another woman. Man, oh man, that must have driven Mom and Dad crazy.

Think about it. I mean even today, people can be far from accepting. Those two women did nothing wrong except fall in love. In that day and age it had to have turned most everyone against them."

Jeremy, who'd been standing in front of the windows looking out, turned around to study her and then shook his head. "People can be so narrow-minded, even these days. Think about how horrible it had to have been for the two of them. So what happened? I mean beyond Tiana killing herself?"

All Lorna had were her own deductions drawn from reading everything she could find. With a lot of work, she'd finally uncovered a number of stories about the wealthy heiress and her sad death. How she'd thrown herself from the roof of this very house, breaking her neck in the fall. Stories of how her mother had grieved deeply while her father acted as though she had never existed in the first place. It was love and hatred all written up in politically correct stories that said nothing and everything all at the same time.

A good psychiatrist would have lots to say about the esteemed Mr. McCafferty. Lorna was no medical professional, but in her opinion, he was a world-class horse's ass. Here was a self-made man who created an empire of wealth and influence. Everything pointed to the fact that he gave his family everything money could buy. On the surface, it was the American success story. Reading between the lines, she found something very different. To his daughter, his only living child, he'd denied her the one thing that mattered the most: unconditional love.

Perhaps that's what Tiana was searching for and ultimately found in the lovely Makah woman, Catherine. Though it might be a hundred years late, acceptance could heal, and she had no doubt that Tiana and Catherine needed that even in the beyond. It occurred to her as she'd pieced together the story that's why the women came to her now. Giving them what they needed might come late, but that's the least she could do for the two tragic souls.

Except she didn't think that was all. The mystery of Catherine's disappearance screamed for resolution, at least to her. As the days crept past while she was waiting for everyone to return, Lorna had the growing sense that understanding where Catherine had gone and what had happened to her was equally as important.

It was entirely possible she was creating a devious scenario in her own head, and it may have been a case of the pressure becoming too great for Catherine to bear even given her intense love affair with Tiana. Sometimes going against the grain was a burden impossible to handle. Lorna had witnessed it firsthand with two of her own friends. Catherine might have been one of those people, especially considering they were fighting not just on one front but two—she was a lesbian and an Indian. Tiana's father would have despised Catherine on every level.

Lorna got up and retrieved the open bottle of wine from the counter. She refilled her glass and topped off Jeremy's. For Merry, she pulled a bottle of apple juice from the fridge and poured her a big tumbler.

She handed Merry the tumbler of juice and said, "The day before Tiana jumped from the roof, Catherine disappeared. I don't think that was a coincidence."

Merry held the glass without taking a drink. "The police came looking for her?"

"They had to investigate, didn't they?" Jeremy spoke from where he still stood with his back to the windows.

Lorna shook her head, feeling anger at the prejudice and dismissal of those long ago times. "No, not even close. Remember, bro, this was a hundred years ago. They didn't care about one pretty girl from the Makah Nation."

He was shaking his head a look of disgust on his face and she knew he felt it too. Still, he asked, "How do you know she went missing then?"

"Alden Swan, one of her distant relatives, and the guy Jolene sent us to talk with. The story of her disappearance has been passed down since the day she vanished. One day, she was there and the next, she wasn't. He believes I'm the one who's going to find her."

Jeremy raised an eyebrow. "So are you?"

"Damn straight I am."

❖

By the time Renee pulled into the driveway it was nearly midnight. For a couple of minutes, she sat in the car with her head tipped back. Exhaustion washed over her so heavy it was like it seeped into her bones. What she wouldn't give for about twelve hours of uninterrupted sleep.

Her original plan called for at least a seven-hour stretch because she'd wanted to make the trip in the morning after they'd had a good night's rest. Her plan went out the window the second the doctor told her mother she could leave. Mom was up and dressed as soon as the doctor left the room, and they were out of there despite her best arguments to the contrary.

The right thing to do, in her mind, was to stay one more night, but no, Mom was having none of that. Not that she really blamed her. If she'd just spent a week in a hospital bed, she'd be running out of there as fast as she could too.

Of course, Mom got in the car and promptly went to sleep, and stayed asleep all the way from Seattle to here. Renee didn't have that luxury. She had to be wide-eyed and alert as they left the city behind, traveling the scenic highway to the coast. Traffic was light, not too surprising at this time of night, and she played music softly, humming along. All in all, the drive had turned out to be fairly pleasant. Under the circumstances, it was the best she could ask for.

Now that they were here, she sighed and rubbed her eyes. She should get up and out of the car. After all, sitting here wasn't going to get either one of them into bed, and while Mom might be feeling rested, she sure didn't. Bed sounded fantastic. Soft pillows, warm blankets, and the sound of the ocean out the window were exactly what she needed.

Renee pushed out of the driver's seat and went around the car to the back door of the house. Once the door was unlocked and open, she returned to the car. Though groggy, her mother roused enough to let Renee help her out of the car and into the house. Thirty minutes later, she had her tucked into her own bed. Though she hated to admit it, Mom had been right. Being home and in her room was a much better place for her to be even if it was the middle of the night. The look on her mother's face was far more peaceful here than what she'd seen at the hospital.

One more trip to the car and she had the bags inside, dropping them just inside the back door. She locked up the back door and thought about taking their bags to their rooms. That thought lasted a second or two before she decided against it. Tired to the point of exhaustion, all she wanted to do was go to bed herself. There was nothing in those bags that couldn't wait until morning.

She left the bags where she'd dropped them and walked into the kitchen, stopping abruptly. Lorna was leaning against the doorway to the hall. The last thing she expected this time of night was anyone to be up.

"Hey," Lorna said, her eyes a little sleepy, her hair messed in a way that looked cute. She wore a T-shirt and baggy flannel pants.

"Hey back at ya." It was lame, but it was all she could think to say. Her heart was hammering, and while she'd known she would be happy to see Lorna again, she didn't realize how happy she'd feel.

"Missed you." Lorna's eyes stayed on hers. "Kind of growing accustomed to both you and your mom being around. It was pretty quiet here all by myself."

"Really?" She wanted to believe it and was afraid. It had been a long time since she'd wanted someone to like her this much. It was kind of stupid at her age. Except that argument didn't seem to matter. She still wanted Lorna to like her.

Slowly, Lorna crossed the room until they were inches apart. She smelled like sweet soap. Her skin was creamy and clear, her eyes steady as she met Renee's. "Really." The single word was soft but confident.

Tears welled up unexpectedly in her eyes. This was something out of her dreams. "I missed you too."

When Lorna's head dropped toward hers, she didn't hesitate. She moved into the kiss that was sweet, gentle, and breathtaking. It made her heart swell, and she realized it wasn't enough. Not even close. She wanted so much more, and she was going to take it. Her tongue touched Lorna's lips, pushing its way between them.

In the quiet moments of the last week, she'd fantasized about an interlude like this, and now that it was happening, it was far more thrilling than anything she'd imagined. Her hands came up and tangled in Lorna's soft hair. Lorna's arms came around her, and they pressed together, the heat between them intense.

As wonderful as this was, it still wasn't enough. She wanted it all and didn't care that maybe it was rushing things. This woman, this wonderful woman who opened her home to Renee, made her crazy with desire. All her life, she'd been waiting to feel like this, and for so long believed it would never happen for her. Now that it had, to hell with restraint.

As she pulled out of Lorna's embrace, she saw dismay cross her features. Lorna mumbled, "I'm sorry—"

Renee smiled and put a finger to Lorna's lips, stopping any further apology. "Oh, I'm so not sorry."

Confusion replaced the dismay. "I thought—"

She laid her hand on Lorna's cheek and said, "Quit thinking."

Renee took Lorna's hand and started toward the door. "I don't want to think or talk. I want to…well, let me show you what I want to do." In the hallway, she paused and looked around. Then she smiled and asked, "My place or yours?"

Lorna hesitated for only a second and then pulled briskly her down the hall. "My place. Not so close to everyone else."

She made an excellent point. The master suite that Lorna called her own was not only on the main floor but also on the opposite side of the house from the other bedrooms. It was perfect for privacy. She hurried with Lorna to the door at the end of the hall. Once inside, Lorna turned the lock and then stared at Renee.

"You're sure?"

"Absolutely." Renee began to slowly unbutton her shirt, her eyes on Lorna the whole time. When it was fully open, she let it slide to the floor. Her shoes were next, flying across the room when she kicked them off. Her jeans followed. Finally, her bra and panties dropped to the pile of clothes on the floor.

When she was naked, Renee put her hands on her hips. "Well? What's the hold up?"

❖

His back hurt and sweat soaked through his shirt. He wiped at his forehead with the back of his hand, his eyes stinging with the salty sweat that dripped into them. A light drizzle was making his already damp shirt even wetter, and it stuck to his black like it was glued there. If he didn't hurry, the drizzle was bound to turn into outright rain. It was the way of things here on the ocean's fringe.

Shovel after shovel of dirt piled beside him until the hole grew too deep for him to continue to stand beside it and keep working. He clambered down into the damp earth so he could continue to increase the depth. Shoulders screaming, he refused to bend to the pain and slow down. Mind over physical discomfort always won. It had to be deep enough to erase do to the job perfectly.

The time had come to end the stupidity. He'd tried reason. He'd tried discipline. Nothing worked. His demands were met with stubborn defiance. No one dared to cross him in this way. No one, that is, except her.

Well, no more. He was not challenged in his command of business, and it had made him a very rich man. He was going to be equally successful at home. His wife was of the highest breeding, her family one of honor and wealth. She never crossed him or questioned any decision. His child was going to be a reflection of her parents. He demanded she be proper, ladylike, and most of all, obedient. She would marry the man he chose for her, and never again would she do one single thing that would bring shame or embarrassment to him.

If only the boy had survived, it would all be different. He would not have caused him the problems that she did. He would have carried their name into the future with pride and dignity, and more importantly, with no hint of shame. The complete opposite of her.

Why did she find it impossible to do the right thing? It was difficult for him to believe she was actually from his seed. He often wondered if she was fathered by another and that in fact his only true progeny had died. It made more sense than the travesty he had to endure day in and day out.

He stopped shoveling dirt out of the hole and looked at his work. Satisfied, he climbed out of the hole and laid the shovel on the damp grass. The drizzle had turned to rain, just as he'd known it would. The rain worked well and he welcomed it for it would ultimately wash away any sign of tonight's work. No one need know, not that many would care. Some lives simply were not worth as much as others. That was the case now.

Again, he wiped rain from his face, not caring that it probably left streaks of mud across his skin. Soon enough, he would be clean, dry, and vindicated. He took a deep breath, squared his shoulders, and strode across the grass, his footsteps sure and steady.

Jeremy bolted upright in the bed with his heart thudding. "Fuck me…not again," he muttered.

The odd feelings he'd had before they'd left for Spokane were gone by the time they hit the Spokane County limits. It had been great to be back to feeling like himself and it had lasted until they returned. Now, two hours into slumber in Lorna's house, the weirdness was back like a bad rash.

The open drapes let in moonlight, and it spilled golden across the blankets. Merry slept peacefully on her side, her face beautiful and serene in slumber. He gently touched her hair, the feel of it silky and comforting against his fingertips. She always brought him back to peace and happiness no matter what was going on.

Except now. Even Merry's presence wasn't enough to banish the ugliness that the dream brought on. Waking from it left him feeling alien and, even worse, bitter. He'd awakened with the urge to scream his lungs out, only he didn't know why. Dreams were usually easy for him to shake off. This one wasn't.

It was this place, this beautiful place. Everything about it was confusing and in some ways unsettling. He loved it and he hated it. On one hand, it made him feel as though he really was home where he could rest and restore. On the other, it was like an angry spirit wanted to ravage his body and infuse it with a rage that was the polar opposite of his normal demeanor. That was pretty damn creepy.

He wasn't going to let the dream rattle him regardless of how creepy it was. This was a great place to be, and he was going to hold on to that belief. He also planned to hold on to his beautiful bride-to-be as tight as he could. Nothing was going to hurt her or even disturb her sleep. Jeremy lay back down against the pillows and turned his face to the window. It was time to go back to sleep. No more creepy dreams; he would will it to be so.

He was just dozing off when a shadow moved across the shaft of moonlight coming through the window.

❖

It was a gamble, and she was up for it. Renee wanted more, and for the first time ever, was going for it. She'd never been very good at being the one who took the lead. It occurred to her that maybe all this time she'd been opting for the coward's way out. Waiting around for something to happen here was nuts. For way too long, she'd depended upon others for her happiness and was then discouraged when it didn't work out. It was high time for her to make her own happiness. To take it with both hands and then run as fast as she could

For a second, she feared Lorna was going to turn around and leave despite the passion of her kisses only minutes before. Her stomach tightened as she stood naked and exposed. Nothing happened, and she fought the urge to grab her clothes and run. She'd taken a risk and it appeared she'd taken it at the wrong time and in the wrong place.

Before she could grab her clothes and flee, Lorna became a flurry of frantic movement. Her shirt went flying right before sneakers and pants zoomed across the room. She wore only underwear and no bra on her high, firm breasts. Renee's breath caught in her throat and all thoughts of running away disappeared. God, Lorna was beautiful.

Not in the curvy way of a woman, but in the muscled and toned way of an athlete. Spectacular was the single thought rolling through her mind.

Sudden shyness washed over her. Lorna was so beautiful, while she was nothing special. While not heavy, neither was she thin. She was all rounded curves and softness. What would a woman like Lorna find desirable in her? The answer was crystal clear: nothing.

Lorna must have read her mind, for she whispered, "You're beautiful. Absolutely beautiful." She took a step forward and pulled Renee into her arms. The moment their flesh touched, desire washed away any lingering doubts.

She pulled Lorna to the bed, and once more, her urge to take control surged. Where it came from, she didn't know and didn't care. It was awesome. She wanted this woman so much it almost hurt, and savoring every moment was an absolute must. If this was a one-night stand, she was going to make the most of it. She kissed Lorna deeply, loving her feel and her taste. Once again, she thought, this is what I've been waiting for all my life.

Her lips moved down her neck, across her shoulders, and down to her breasts. They were so firm, the nipples round and dark. She took one into her mouth and suckled as she ran her tongue over the nub as it grew harder. Lorna moaned, her hands in Renee's hair and tugging gently.

As she continued to do service to Lorna's extraordinary breasts, she ran her palm over her flat stomach. Lorna's muscles tensed as she stroked her hot skin, dropping farther down. Lorna's hips moved in response. Her fingers skimmed through the fine hair before parting her swollen lips. She slid her fingers into her heat.

For a moment, she thought she might come right here and now, the feel of Lorna was so incredible. She forced a breath and began to stroke as Lorna's moans grew deeper. Bringing her lips back to Lorna's, she kissed her deeply at the same time her fingers slid inside and out meeting heat and wetness.

Hips rose to meet the thrusts of her fingers while she trailed her tongue once more down Lorna's skin until she captured a nipple again. Lorna jerked, her hips pushing against the thrust of her fingers. She could feel the pressure growing and inhaled the scent of passion. She moved her hand faster.

Lorna cried out, and Renee felt her come against her hand. She smiled against the nipple still held in her mouth. This was everything she hoped for.

And so much more.

Outside, day was trying to push aside the night. Clouds hung dark and low, rain falling light but steady. A woman, dressed in a long white gown, her waist-length hair streaming down her back, hurried across the wet grass toward the bluff.

Lorna squinted trying to get a better look. She didn't recognize her, and more than that, couldn't figure out what she was doing here. They weren't exactly on the beaten path. The house was set far away from the main road, and there were no such thing as a close neighbor. People didn't accidently stumble upon the estate.

A couple hundred yards before the drop off, the woman slumped to the ground. It didn't look like she stumbled, though she crumpled as though something heavy bore down on her. It was hard to tell in the dim light what she was doing.

Okay, her curiosity was piqued. Lorna had to know what was up. She grabbed a pair of sweats, a shirt, and her sneakers. Once dressed Lorna slid out the door and left Renee still sleeping in the bedroom. At the back door, she grabbed a hooded jacket, pulling the hood up over her head. Cold air slapped her when she stepped outside, and what had looked like light rain from her bedroom window turned out to be a heavy and steady downpour.

If the woman heard her approach, she gave no indication. She didn't even so much as turn her head in Lorna's direction. Rain had soaked her hair and her dress, which, as she drew closer, Lorna could see was some kind of cotton nightgown. That didn't make sense. How in the world would someone make it all the way out here in the dark, in the rain, in a nightgown? Things around here were getting stranger by the hour.

The second thing she noticed as she came close was that the woman was sobbing. Her face pressed to the grass, her hands pounding at the earth, she sobbed in silence. Silence? How was it possible that not a sound was coming from the sad figure who had to be flirting with hypothermia in the chilly morning rain?

"Hello," Lorna said as she continued to walk toward her. The woman didn't move, didn't act as though she heard. "Do you need some help? Is there someone I can call for you?"

CHAPTER TWENTY

The first weak rays of daylight poked through the windows by the time Lorna's eyes fluttered open. At first, she thought last night was a dream, and then she realized it was incredibly, wonderfully real. Renee was beside her, warm and naked, her chest rising and falling in easy sleep.

She couldn't help smiling as she thought about what had happened between them. All her worries about being able to feel for another woman were for nothing. Renee not just made her feel but cracked the ice that had formed around her heart when Anna left. It was amazing in so many ways.

She thought of all the things they could do together and then stopped herself. This was putting the cart before the horse. One night with Renee and she was plotting forever. She didn't know how Renee was feeling. This could be a casual fling for her, and if it was she had to respect that. No expectations. That was the best course take. Expectations had set her up for trouble before; she didn't w to play that game again.

She was still gazing out the window when she saw the sh of a person pass by the window.

"What the hell," she whispered, slipping out the bed so as not to disturb Renee. She grabbed her robe and slip before she moved to the window. Chill air drifted off the she pulled the robe tighter.

All of a sudden, the woman shot up and stared back at the house. Her gaze swept over Lorna as though she hadn't seen her at all. Or perhaps it was more accurate to say her gaze went right through Lorna. With a look of terror, the woman picked up her damp skirt and ran straight toward the house. Lorna stared after her, stunned by the way she totally ignored her. As she watched, her heart nearly stopped when the woman simply disappeared.

She was still thinking about the vanishing woman when Jeremy walked into the kitchen an hour later. The sun was completely up by then though it was an obscenely early hour for folks who did not have to get up and drive into an office.

"What made you roll out bright and early?" She asked as she got up to pour him a cup of coffee. "After your long drive, I'd have thought you'd be dead to the world."

He sighed as he took the offered cup and sipped. "Thanks, I needed that. I guess I'm so used to getting up in the morning I haven't gotten out of the habit yet."

She was watching his face as he talked and wasn't convinced. Sure, his unemployed status was still new enough that he hadn't had time to grow accustomed to sleeping in. His face, however, said it was something else. "What's up, Jer?"

He shook his head and sighed. "I don't know. I was actually sleeping pretty well, and then boom...had another crazy ass dream. You know, when I was in Spokane, this didn't happen. As soon as I get back here, it starts again. Gotta be this house, Lorna. I don't have dreams like this. They're creeping me out."

She patted his hand. "You're preaching to the choir, brother. I am convinced this place is seriously haunted. Reach out and touch from beyond, if you know what I mean. I'm pretty creeped out myself."

"I wonder why Aunt Bea never said anything about it. Or for that matter, why hasn't Jolene said something to us about the guests who came and never left?"

She'd wondered the same thing, rolling it over and over in her head. Her final conclusion was they didn't know. "I don't think any of this happened until I got here, and then by extension, you."

He furrowed his brow and studied her with a skeptical expression on his face. "That doesn't make sense. We're nothing special. Just a couple of regular folks from Spokane. Ghosts magnets we're not."

"Yeah, that's what I always thought too, but I'm beginning to wonder if that's really true. We might have to consider the possibility that we could be ghost magnets."

For a moment, he said nothing, just studied her face. "What happened while I was gone?"

She shrugged and debated whether to tell him. To her it seemed as though he had enough on his plate without her weirdness added to the mix. Then she made a decision. In for a penny, in for a pound. "Another vision while you were gone. Another vision this morning. Except the one this morning…"

"Spit it out." He set his mug on the table with a thud. "You know you can always trust me, both to have your back and to tell you the truth. So spill."

She blew out a long breath before saying it out loud. "Okay, you're right and I know it. It's just that it gives me the chills thinking about how it all went down. I was wide awake, Jeremy, as in WIDE awake." There was a reason she didn't want to verbalize it. It sounded way too much like she had finally stepped aboard the crazy train.

He seemed to grasp the enormity of why she was afraid to share. "All right, weird enough that's for sure, but really, Lorna, I think it sounds more like a hallucination than a vision." He gave her a crooked smile. "What have you been smoking while we were gone?"

She smacked him on the arm. "I wish the explanation was that simple. Come on, Jeremy, you and I both know I'm not losing my mind, and I'm not smoking a damn thing. I know what I saw."

"So let's assume for the moment you really are quite sane. Now, tell me what happened and what you saw. We can figure this out together just like we've always done."

She took a deep breath, her heart still pounding as she rolled through her mind what she'd seen out there. The answer came back the same no matter how she rationalized it, and the truth of it rang crystal clear in her heart. "Tiana McCafferty, though it was different this time. In my dreams it's like I'm her. Not this time."

At first, she hadn't realized who it was she'd seen kneeling in the grass. Not until the apparition turned to run back toward the house anyway. Even then, she'd wavered. The possibility seemed remote. At least until the woman disappeared, and then any doubts she'd had vaporized into thin air right along with the woman. The blunt reality of it, if it could be called reality, was that Tiana was back. If she'd ever left, that is. She was trying to show Lorna something important. All she had to do now was figure out what that was.

"Woo," he said with a whistle. "Okay, you now have my undivided attention. This I gotta hear right now."

Her reluctance to tell what she'd seen fled. Sharing with him felt right, and so she did, filling Jeremy in on everything that happened once she looked out the window and saw the woman crossing the grass. When she told him how the woman had disappeared into thin air, he raised a single eyebrow.

"Freaky."

"Don't doubt the messenger," she told him. "I'm not unbalanced or blind. I saw a woman in a soaking wet white nightgown running toward the house, and then poof, in a flash of a second, she was gone. That simple and that quick. Instead of dreaming I'm here, this time it's like we're together in the flesh. You think your dreams are fucked up, I think I've taken the game to a new level."

Jeremy was rubbing his forehead now and looking down at the table. His earlier jovial attitude had evaporated to be replaced by a more somber reflection. "Yeah, sister, I believe you and I believe what you saw. To tell you the truth, I'd rather not believe, because it's too out there for somebody like me. It would be a hell of a lot easier if you were just crazy and all this was happening only inside your pretty little head. The problem is, if you're heading toward the psychiatric ward, then unfortunately, so am I."

❖

Renee stretched, loving the way her body felt. What a fantastic night. Given all that happened with her mom and the fire, she never expected to feel so gloriously alive. Lorna was incredible, and she'd never understand how that woman in Spokane could leave her.

Renee would never leave someone like Lorna. Or maybe it would be more accurate to say she would never leave Lorna. Yes, this was all new, and she was basking in the afterglow of incredible sex. The problem as she saw it was that she understood the difference between casual hookups and meaningful sex. Theirs had been the latter. Lorna didn't need to verbalize a thing; it was in her touch, her sighs, and her comforting arms as they both drifted off to sleep. A casual hookup it was not.

Yes, whether they liked it or not, there was far more between them than a simple roll in the hay. The thought made her heart sing. With not a clue how it would all shake out, she nonetheless felt happy. For the moment, it was more than enough. She would settle for happy and the rest would take care of itself.

She rolled out of the bed, grabbed her clothes, and snuck down to her own room. A nice warm shower and some clean clothes would be the crowning glory to her perfect night. Twenty minutes later, she was heading toward the smell of coffee. One thing about staying here, the coffee was always on in the morning, hot, black, and wonderful. She could get used to this.

Lorna and Jeremy were sitting at the table talking in low voices when she walked through the door. Both of them snapped around to look at her as she came in. "Hey," she said in greeting, hoping at the same time she wasn't interrupting something, because that's sure what it felt like.

Lorna's face took on softness that warmed Renee's heart and banished any worry that maybe she should have backed out of the room. She had a hunch the same sort of look crossed her own face. Jeremy glanced first at her and then at Lorna, and it occurred to her that it might have been better to try to rein her emotions in. Lorna might not want her brother to guess what happened between them.

Jeremy raised his eyebrows and smirked. "Anything you ladies want to tell me?"

So much for her attempt to throw off suspicion by looking innocent, because it appeared Jeremy could see right through both of them. It was too late, and she really hoped it wasn't a problem for Lorna.

Didn't seem to be when Lorna turned back to Jeremy and cocked her head. "What?" she asked with a sly smile.

"I asked," he drew out the words slowly. "If there's anything you or your pretty friend here would like to share with me?"

She wasn't about to say a word and so she didn't. This was one minefield she intended to stay out of. Instead, she walked to the kitchen counter, grabbed a mug, and filled it with coffee while keeping her back to the other two. Or was it more like keeping her head in the sand? Either way, it worked for her. Maybe she should go check on her mother.

"Don't know what you mean."

Jeremy's laughter was hearty and good-natured, the sound easing the tension bunching up her shoulders. "Really, Lorna? You don't think I know you well enough to figure out when you've been bed hopping? Oh, my dear sister, you are so terribly transparent."

Lorna blurted, "Jeremy!" at the same time Renee started to laugh, which made her spit out the coffee she just sipped. That made her laugh even harder.

"Oh, come on, you guys. I wasn't born yesterday. And besides, why tiptoe around and pretend? Personally, I think it's great. No offense, sis, but the nun thing just doesn't suit you. Ever since you and Anna broke up, you've been a real downer. I like this Lorna a whole lot better. It's my sister coming back to the land of the living and the loving."

A flush raced up Lorna's face, and it was all Renee could do not to laugh again. If Jeremy kept this up, they'd be doing CPR on Lorna any minute. Perhaps she should have kept that CPR card current. She took her coffee mug and headed back toward the door. This seemed like a private sibling discussion to her.

"I'm going to check on Mom."

She wasn't sure, but she thought she heard Jeremy say "chicken" as she walked out the door.

CHAPTER TWENTY-ONE

"All right, you big brat! If you must know, yes, Renee and I hit it off."

"As opposed to hitting it?"

Lorna threw a spoon at him. It bounced on the table in front of him. "You are such an—"

"Don't say it. Mom wouldn't like it." He was smiling broadly. "Seriously, Lorna, I think it's great. You've needed someone in your life, and not someone like Anna. She wasn't right for you. Face the facts, my dear sister, she was a bitch. Not true of Renee. There's something about her that brings out the good in you. Give it a chance. You never know where it might take you. She could be the one." He winked.

Her heart warmed. God, how she loved her little brother and she hoped he was right. "Thanks, I appreciate that. I like her a lot too. Now that you've chased her out of here and embarrassed the crap out of me, maybe you can finish telling me why you don't think either one of us is crazy."

Jeremy smiled his I-have-no-idea-what-you-mean smile. "Oh come on, Lorna, a guy has to take his fun where he can. Besides, you opened the door for me. You want to try to convince me you didn't jump Renee's bones last night? You can try. It won't do you any good. I know you, and your face is an open book. I like that about you because it gives me the opportunity to tease you and watch you squirm. Big fun."

"I didn't jump her bones." Her protest was weak even to her own ears. Except she didn't think of it like that. What they'd shared last night was a whole lot more than mere sex. Almost scary more, but she wasn't going to delve too deep into that right at the moment. A smart woman would only put one toe at a time back into the pool, and she liked to think she was a smart woman.

"Yeah, you did, but really that's your business. The only other thing I'll say about it and then I'll shut up is, I like her. She's a real bright light. I think you've traded up."

His simple words warmed her heart. Whether she wanted it to or not, his opinion did mean so very much to her. They were family, and she didn't want a woman to come between them. She'd already lost her parents; she wasn't about to lose her brother over a woman.

"Thanks, Jer, I appreciate that."

"I calls it like I sees it." He was smiling big.

"So get on with it already." She wanted to know what he was thinking in terms of the visions plaguing her. The fact that he didn't believe she was going around the bend eased some of her worries. Oh hell, who was she kidding? It eased a lot of her worries.

"It's this house," he said simply as he waved his hands as if to encompass the entire structure. "My educated opinion is that it's haunted or maybe even cursed. In fact, the more I think about it, cursed seems the more likely scenario."

She was this close to buying into the idea that the house was haunted. Tiana McCafferty seemed to be reaching out from the grave as if she wanted to tell Lorna something important. The thing was it didn't feel dangerous or evil, just important. Cursed didn't seem to fit for her.

She shook her head. "I don't think it's cursed."

He was holding the spoon she tossed at him and tapping it on the tabletop. "Well, maybe not in your case, but it sure as hell seems that way to me every time I close my eyes."

"Your dreams?" A good look in his eyes and she could see how deadly serious he was. "Tell me about them." A sick feeling settled in her stomach.

"Nightmares, my dear sister, nightmares."

He'd always been a dreamer, and through the years recounted some doozies. He was one of those people who dreamed every night and actually remembered most of them. To say he was having dreams really didn't mean much. Usually, they were quirky and funny. He hadn't had scary dreams since he'd been a little boy. So when he said nightmare, he had her undivided attention.

He held up a hand before she could say as much. "These are not my normal midnight movies. These are specific and mean-spirited. Not just that, Lorna. They really are only happening when I'm here. When Merry and I were back in Spokane—nothing. The first night I come back to this place, and all of a sudden I'm evil incarnate."

Lorna closed her eyes and ran her hands through her hair. Her head was beginning to throb. "We're missing something," she said at last.

"Like?"

She opened her eyes and looked at him. "I don't know. We know that Tiana McCafferty killed herself. We know that she did it right after Catherine Swan disappeared. We know that her father was an asshole. We know her mother pretty much ignored her. But there's a thread of something else in there that we're missing."

"Like why you and me?"

"Exactly." It occurred to her as Jeremy was telling her about the nightmares that for some reason, the McCafferty family was touching hers. Or maybe it would be more accurate to say bitch-slapping hers. But why? Renee essentially grew up in this house, and none of the voodoo was happening to her. Jolene had been here for decades and nada. So why was it targeting her and Jeremy?

Merry walked in as she and Jeremy sat in silence staring at each other and pondering. "Good morning," she said cheerfully.

"Morning," Lorna mumbled, her mind still a thousand miles away.

Merry stopped next to Jeremy and kissed him on the lips. Then she stood straight and stared from one face to the other. "Earth to Jeremy and Lorna. Hellooooo."

"Uh." Lorna turned her head toward Merry. "What?"

She laughed and hugged Jeremy, kissing the top of his head this time. "I don't know what you two have been doing down here, but you are both in la-la land. What have you been doing that has you so distracted?"

That was a loaded question. After Lorna filled her in, Merry sipped on a glass of orange juice and said, "I have an idea. Let's go on a scavenger hunt. I say we dig through the attic and all the paperwork your aunt left and see what we come up with. Maybe we can find the answers there, or at the very least, a clue. We've dug up what we can from outside sources; why not begin again only this time start from home?"

Lorna smiled. "See, now this is exactly why I said you two need to be here. Apparently, solving mysteries takes a minimum of three heads."

❖

Sitting cross-legged on the floor of the attic with a dusty hat, circa 1920s, on her head, Renee read with deep interest. She was going through a steamer trunk full of ledgers, diaries, and one old Bible, the kind where a family member dutifully kept track of births, marriages, and deaths. It was fascinating on so many levels.

After she'd checked on her mother and made sure she was comfortable, she'd gone in search of Lorna. All she'd found in the kitchen where she'd left them half an hour earlier were abandoned coffee mugs and an empty room. With her best detective skills, she followed the low murmur of voices until she located Lorna, Jeremy, and Merry in the attic.

The attic was incredible, something found in movies but not in real life. Spanning the entire length of the house, it was a massive open area broken up by supports of unfinished pine. The floor was, like the supports, unfinished hardwood deeply colored by age and the ever-present dust. Scattered throughout the space like forgotten pieces of history were furniture, trunks, boxes, and discarded clothing spanning multiple decades. She was all in before Lorna even told her what the game plan was for the day.

"I found something. I think." She picked up her glass and took a big swig of white wine. Jeremy was right. He'd brought the bottle up around four saying it was from a local Spokane winery, Nodland Cellars, and it was one of their best. He was so correct. She loved it.

Now, the Bible in her lap, she stared down at the faded handwriting crisscrossing the pages like a spider web. She'd been staring at it for at least ten minutes making sure she was seeing what she thought she was. It didn't change, and a very interesting story just revealed itself to her. If she was a betting woman, she'd lay odds that Lorna and Jeremy had no idea about this little twist.

"What do you have?" Lorna said, standing up and stretching her arms over her head. Her shirt slid up as she stretched, and her smooth stomach was revealed, as was the small tattoo of a skull Renee had discovered last night. The sight sent shivers through her body. All she could think was how that stomach felt against the palm of her hands and the tip of her tongue. Or how many times she placed kisses against that tiny skull. She shivered just remembering.

She brought her thoughts away from the feel of Lorna's body and back to the Bible. Tapping the page, she told them, "You need to come and see."

Like Renee, Lorna wore a hat. Hers was a straw version complete with white tulle gone gray with time and ribbons that she thought might have been blue once upon a time. Undoubtedly, it had been someone's Easter bonnet. Renee smiled as she looked at her, the hat so out of place with her jeans and fleece pullover.

Merry came over and sat next to her on the floor. She'd wrapped herself in crimson brocade coat she'd found hanging on a tall carved coat rack. It was a style at least a century old, and it hung to the ground when she was standing and pooled around her like a lake when she sat on the floor. Made to go over the full dresses of an era long gone, it dwarfed the diminutive Merry.

Not to be left out, Jeremy snagged a bowler hat as he crossed the room from where he'd been digging through a box of old ledgers. She hated numbers, and it would have taken a death threat to get her to even open one of those things. Jeremy was, in her opinion, a weirdo on that front. When he grabbed that box, he'd been like a little kid with a brand new toy box declaring spreadsheets, ledgers, and flow charts to be fun. She had one word for that: ick. She much preferred the Bible and it's tale of intrigue.

Renee glanced down and then back up, doing a double take as Jeremy walked toward her. For a second, when he twirled the hat and then popped it onto his head, it was as though the face she saw was not his own. When the shimmering visage faded, his aura became clear and the black streak was back in force. Thick and dark, it almost pulsed. She shook her head. Obviously, she'd spent too many hours sitting up here staring into boxes and reading old books. Top it off with wine on an empty stomach, and it was possible she was making something out of nothing. Usually, she'd just get sick when she drank on an empty stomach; today it was minor hallucinations. Or not, and that's the part that was scaring her.

"Okay, what do you have for us?" Lorna asked when they were all clustered close to her.

Renee looked up at Lorna and winked. "Wait until you see this." She opened the Bible to the pages she'd marked with scraps of paper. "Ta da…the McCafferty family history." She ran her finger along the edge of the paper with the intricate family tree.

Starting with the first page of the family tree that went back to Drogheda, Ireland, the history of the McCafferty family began to unfold for them. Like she'd done earlier, she showed them the names as they tracked down through the generations. It recorded all the births, the marriages, and the births of the subsequent generations. The deaths were as one would expect: some of old age, some tragically young. On the faces clustered near to her own she could see the same curiosity she'd experienced when she'd first come across the Bible. She had found it interesting but didn't expect anything beyond that until she came to the last page, and that's where everything changed. There was John McCafferty, and recorded next to him, his marriage to Susanne. There was the birth of Tiana, followed by the birth and death of her younger brother. Then came Tiana's far-too-early death. Susanne was the next to pass, some five years after her daughter. John, however, did not follow his wife and daughter for fifteen years.

None of that was a big surprise or even particularly interesting. They pretty much knew all of it from their visits to the libraries. What did surprise them was what came next. By all rights, the family tree should have ended with the death of patriarch John McCafferty. That's what Renee expected. That's what they all expected. For at least a full minute, no one said a word.

Jeremy broke the silence, rocking back on his heels and exclaiming, "Son of a bitch."

❖

The crash of thunder brought his eyes heavenward. Rain began to pummel his head, yet he did not move. Tonight was it. The lights had been on in the attic for hours, and whatever they had touched inside that room had opened the door to the other world. Like a snake waiting for a chance to strike, *he* was stepping through. Lightning sliced across the sky, and the storm raged its fury preternaturally strong, as well it should be. This was not a storm born of nature.

He was out of time. They were out of time. It all came down to this night. If she did not see and act, once more, he would fail in his promise. The gates of heaven would remain closed to him, and the souls of the two lost women would remain lost.

The evil one had returned. His strength had grown as it had in life, until now, the Watcher feared he could not stop him. Each time he returned, he grew stronger and more malevolent. If she failed to stop him now, how long would it be before another would come? He did not want to think about it. She had to defeat him this time. She had to.

Thunder crashed again, and this time he looked up at the windows of the attic. The lights still glowed, and he prayed they would find what he'd left for them. If they read and if they understood then perhaps they would have a chance. If not? Tears streaked down his massive cheeks.

His eyes strayed to the wet expanse of grass that ran along the bluff. In his mind's eye, he could see them standing there hand in hand, the light of the moon shining off their hair. Love had radiated around them like rays of sunlight. Truth had a way of doing that. So did true love.

Evil turned their precious light to darkness. He'd tried to save them, but he'd been too late. All he could do was give them his promise that he would one day make it right. He was in danger of failing once again. He'd done all that he could from his world of exile. It all rested in her hands now. With his eyes turned once more heavenward, he quietly prayed:

"Our Father who art in heaven, hallowed be Thy name. Thy kingdom come, Thy will be done, on earth as it is in heaven. Give us this day our daily bread, and forgive us our trespasses as we forgive those who trespass against us. And lead us not into temptation, but deliver us from evil..."

CHAPTER TWENTY-TWO

L orna, like all of them, was reeling after seeing Renee's mind-boggling discovery. It didn't diminish their need for food, and they all declared they were starving when they trooped down the stairs sounding like a herd of cattle. Renee left them to go check on her mother who was, as the doctor said would happen, sleeping away the day. Good thing he forewarned her or Lorna had no doubt, she'd be even more worried than she already was. Sleep, the doctor had explained, was the magic that would ultimately heal her wounds.

In the kitchen, Lorna began directing Jeremy and Merry in the production of dinner. The entire time they chatted and cooked, her mind was racing. In a best-case scenario, she wanted to believe the connections were nothing more than coincidence. Realistically, this wasn't best case, and it wasn't a coincidence. Jeremy had been correct earlier when he said it was this house. No denying he was a sharp guy, and as usual was dead-on.

Renee's friend had been so adamant that Lorna possessed psychic abilities, and that's why she was experiencing these visions. If that were true, and she still wasn't totally convinced it was, then it appeared to be a family trait. Something was happening to Jeremy too, although whatever it was with him appeared only to occur during sleep.

Still, for both of them, it all came back to this beautiful house on the shores of the Pacific Ocean. Except when she really thought about it, it wasn't really the house that was tragic. No, it was the people who had lived in the house, and it was their spirits that lay heavy on the wood and plaster that made up the walls they stood inside.

All through dinner, she turned over in her mind everything they'd discovered so far and wondered what it was Tiana wanted from her. Maybe it wasn't so important to discover why Tiana was with her now as it was to discover what she needed from Lorna. The funny thing was she was invested in the history of the house and its occupants as well as in finding out where Catherine Swan disappeared to. Though she had no rational reason for feeling this way, she had to find the truth behind whatever it was that separated the two women who so obviously loved each other.

She would discover the truth, whatever it turned out to be, and then perhaps she'd know why Tiana came to her.

They were sitting by the fire watching the storm and drinking a bit more of the fabulous wine when the lights sputtered and went out. Lorna got up and found the matches so she could light some candles. Merry yawned and Jeremy stood, pulling her to her feet.

"I think I better take sleeping beauty to bed." He grabbed one of the candles. Saying their good nights, they left to go to their room.

Renee took one of the candles and hurried to her mother's room. Five minutes later, she returned.

"How's she doing?" The fire not only kept the room warm and cozy, it also bathed it in a lovely gold glow. With the sound of the rain outside, it was romantic. She found that not having electricity wasn't too bad.

Renee lowered herself to the floor and sat beside Lorna. With their backs against the sofa and feet stretched out so that the fire warmed their soles, it was incredibly comfortable.

Once more, Lorna marveled at how quickly things could change. She wasn't the same woman she'd been when she'd come here hoping for solitude. She'd wanted to run away to hide, and right now that was the last thing she wanted to do. She hated to think how lonely it would be here without Renee.

"I think she's actually doing a bit better," Renee said as she leaned her head back against the sofa cushions. "She's still incredibly tired, but the doctor said she was going to be for a few weeks, so I was expecting that. Healing a skull fracture takes a whole hell of a lot of rest."

"She's going to be all right." Lorna could feel the truth of her words. Despite the seriousness of her injuries, she felt the strength in Jolene. She was a fighter, and more importantly, a survivor. No tumble down a hill was going to defeat her.

Renee tilted her head until it rested on Lorna's shoulder. "Yes, she is. Thank you, Lorna."

"Stop with all the thank yous already. I've explained to you that you don't have to do that."

"I know, and that's what makes it all the more important to thank you. You are one in a million."

Lorna kissed the top of her head. "You know I didn't think I'd ever be able to love someone again."

Renee's voice was soft and filled with regret. "I didn't either."

"Anna broke my heart. For so long, I've felt like I was unlovable and unable to love. That's why I came here. Hiding from everyone seemed the easiest way to survive."

Renee looked into the fire, and for a moment, Lorna thought she'd said too much. Maybe shared a little more than she should have at this point. Sometimes she just didn't know where the line was and plunged right over it.

Renee's voice was soft, but the bitterness was hard to miss. "Better than being the one who did the breaking."

With one finger, Lorna turned Renee's face to hers. "You? I don't believe it."

She nodded slowly, her eyes closed. When she opened them again, there were tears. "Lorna, I lied to him. I promised him that I would love him forever, and the truth is I don't think I ever really loved him at all."

"Him who?"

"My husband. Or more precisely, my ex-husband. I promised him forever, and then I turned my back on him and walked away. I made him feel unlovable. What kind of person does that?"

"A confused person. One who is good in their heart and who when she realizes the undeniable truth makes a hard choice that will ultimately save them both."

Renee closed her eyes against the tears that threatened to fall and willed herself to stay strong. "I hurt him terribly, and that was wrong."

She kissed her cheek and then kissed her gently on the lips. "But in the end you saved him. Is he happy now?"

Renee opened her eyes, and her gaze met Lorna's. She nodded and the ghost of a smile crossed her lips. "Yes, I think he is."

Lorna smiled. "Okay, that's a good thing. Are you happy now?"

Her gaze slid away from Lorna's to where Clancy lay sleeping peacefully at the edge of the hearth. Then her eyes came back to meet hers again. "Yes."

Lorna couldn't help smiling. "Yeah, me too."

She kissed her deeply and felt the flutter of her heart. She pushed her tongue between her lips to touch Renee's. Every nerve in her body came alive, and somewhere in the back of her mind she wondered why in all the years with Anna she'd never felt like this. Vaguely, she had the sense that until now, she'd never been truly alive.

Renee pulled back and took Lorna's face between her hands. "What do you see in me? You have it all, Lorna. You're attractive with a body to die for, you're successful, have a fabulous brother, and this beautiful home. All I have left is my mother and my dog. Pretty slim pickings all the way around if you ask me."

Lorna couldn't help it; she laughed. "Are you kidding me? You think that's all you have going for you? God, Renee, you're bright and shining and full of life. You've made hard choices, the right choices, and then moved forward. You've taken a huge hit, losing everything you had, and still you laugh and you smile and you make everyone around you feel good. I would give anything to have even a touch of your magic."

Tears glistened in her eyes again, but this time they sparkled. "You're just trying to get my pants off me."

Lorna laughed even harder. "Well, that's totally true, but cross my heart, Renee, everything else I've said is true too. All of it, and best of all, you made me believe in love again, and in my wildest dreams, I didn't think that was possible."

The tears spilled down Renee's face, but a smile let her know they were not tears of sorrow. Renee leaned in and kissed her, first softly and then with passion that took her breath away. No way would she ever grow tired of this.

With the crackle of the fire and the sound of rain against the windows, she made love to Renee and knew that her heart had been captured as surely as if they'd promised each other a thousand tomorrows. She didn't have to hear the words. The softness of Renee's touch, the sweetness of her lips, the fire in her passion, was all she needed on this night. Her heart was full.

❖

No more! He was at the end of his rope. He would tolerate no more of this ungodly behavior. It went against everything he had taught her about right and wrong, and everything they believed in. God was watching over her, as was their community. Her disregard for the honor of their family was something he could not turn a blind eye to for one more second. Judgment day had arrived.

He'd awakened to the sound of thunder, the storm alerting him to what was happening beneath the roof of this honorable home. Not for the first time, she was disgracing herself and her family.

His bare feet touched the cool hardwood of the floor. The air was chilled and carried the scent of rain and ocean. He didn't notice. All he could think of was what she was doing in his home. Of the disrespect she continued to throw in his face. The room was dark; the only light an occasional flash of lightning. He knew the way without need of any illumination.

As he descended the stairs, his feet silent on the steps, the sounds of their moans and sighs grew louder. His blood roared, and his breath came quicker. How dare she? It took every ounce of his considerable self-control not to scream. But he could not, for he dared not wake any of the good and decent people who slept blissfully unaware of the sick and unholy thing happening on the floor below.

In the doorway, he stood silent, motionless. Flesh intertwined with flesh. One creamy white, one touched with color that reminded him of coffee softened by cream. Their clothing littered his magnificent imported rug, an insult to the beautiful craftsmanship of the room's centerpiece. The sight sent his rage soaring.

His hands shook as he watched, unable to tear his eyes away from the sight of their writhing bodies, unable to close out the sound of their cries of passion, the womanly scent. Finally, his good Christian soul could stand no more. He strode through the door and right up to where the two women made love before the flickering firelight. He grabbed the darker skinned woman by her long black hair and hauled her roughly to her feet.

"No more!" With an arm around her neck, he dragged her to the front door.

"Jeremy!"

He heard her screams as though they came from a great distance away. The name meant nothing to him. His pace did not slow. His arm did not loosen.

"Jeremy, for the love of God, STOP. You're hurting her."

He continued out the door, the fight in the woman fading as his hold around her neck forced the breath from her chest. His eyes on the far end of the grass, he moved through the night, rain soaking him to the skin.

❖

Lorna was frantic. Something was terribly wrong with Jeremy. Except it wasn't Jeremy. The face that stared out at her wasn't her brother's. The angles were sharper, the eyes dead. Gone were the light and the laughter that made Jeremy so special to her and everyone else who had the joy of knowing him.

She grabbed at her clothes where they'd fallen on the floor at the same time she scrambled to her feet. "Tiana," she cried as she slipped her shirt over her head. "Help me." She hopped on one foot and then the other while pulling on her jeans. Feet bare, she raced out the door and into the storm.

Outside, the sound of Clancy's frantic barks soared over the pounding rain. He'd followed Jeremy out the door, barking and jumping, trying as she did to get Jeremy's attention.

As she'd been racing toward the door, the necklace on the end table caught her eye. It was lying right where she'd left it several days ago. Not knowing why, she grabbed it, holding it for dear life in one hand, and tore outside.

Cold struck her like a shot to the system as her feet touched the grass now soaked by hours of storm. Her fingers tightened around the necklace, the beautifully crafted beads cutting into the flesh of her palm. A shock ripped up her spine, and everything changed in an instant. Wind whipped through her skirt chilling her legs.

Wait? What? Her gaze dropped and she was stopped by what she saw. The jeans were gone replaced by a long white nightdress soaked through by rain and clinging to her naked body. Except it wasn't her body exactly.

Holy mother of God, she was no longer alone. Her heart raced and her hands shook. In a flash, it came to her she had two choices: freak out or let Tiana help her.

She went for option number two. "Tell me, Tiana. Show me."

It took only a moment for the shock to fade away. In a sense, Lorna figured she'd been waiting for this all along. All that had happened to her since she'd come here wasn't by accident. There was a reason and she finally understood what it was. Tiana's voice needed to be heard, for it had been silent far too long. It was her destiny to be Tiana's voice.

Not hampered by the wet skirts clinging to her legs, she continued to race across the grass until finally she caught sight of Jeremy. Watching the way he walked made her stop and stare. In her heart, she realized what had been eluding her since the moment he'd grabbed Renee and began to drag her away. Her brother was bigger, stronger, and younger. Like her, he was a seasoned athlete who moved with speed and grace.

John McCafferty wasn't any of those things.

With that sudden flash of understanding, she took off at a dead run. A couple of feet away, she pushed off, and tackled Jeremy.

Clancy, who'd been racing beside Jeremy and pulling on his T-shirt the whole time, went tumbling too. Taken off guard, his grip on Renee fell away, and she crumbled motionless to the grass. Jeremy thrashed beneath her, losing Clancy in the bargain but not Lorna. She held steady, vaguely aware that beneath her hands he felt different from the guy she'd grown up with. It was like holding on to a stranger. Clancy abandoned his assault on Jeremy and ran to Renee where he whined and licked her face. Her low moan reassured Lorna that she wasn't lost.

"Enough," she yelled into Jeremy's face, and wasn't sure if it she was talking to her brother or if Tiana was screaming at her father. It didn't matter either way because they were both trying to accomplish the same thing. To end this thing right here and right now before anyone else was hurt.

"You will not disgrace me again." His words were so full of venom it made her blood turn cold. He twisted hard and she lost her grip on him. Like a fox, he scrambled toward Renee, stopping only at the low growl from Clancy.

Question asked. Question answered. John McCafferty. "It's over," she said and understood the words were not hers. Tiana was speaking to her father.

His face was almost purple with rage, raining slashing across it until it looked as though it was sliding away from his skull. It distorted his face so much there wasn't so much as a trace of Jeremy left. "NO."

"It's over, Father. It's over."

"No, it will never be over." John McCafferty appeared to have no intention of releasing his hold on either this place or his daughter. Not in life and certainly not in death. In a lightning fast movement, he lunged past Clancy and grabbed Renee once more. Her body hung limp in his arms. He didn't seem to notice. The cliff was at his back as he began to back slowly toward it while dragging Renee with him.

Lorna's heart lurched at the sight and she began to run toward them. No way was he going to reach that cliff with her woman in his arms. This time she joined her voice with Tiana's, their shared strength loud and clear on the night air. "Let her go!"

"No." His voice was flat and ice cold.

"Father, it is time."

"I will kill her again and again. However many times it takes to keep your soul from damnation and my family name from disgrace. I will bury her here once more and you will do as I tell you."

"Let her go." Their voices joined. Lorna felt the despair and sadness that filled Tiana's heart. She loved Catherine, but she loved her father despite everything.

His arm once more went to Renee's neck, and Lorna could see the way it tightened. He was going to kill her. She didn't remember doing it, but somehow the shovel that had been lying on grass was in her hands. Almost as if she watched from a distance, her arms came up and the shovel began to move through the air. The vibrations went up her arms and through her body as it connected with Jeremy's head. She screamed and he crumbled to the ground at the same time his hold on Renee fell away.

"Holy mother of God." She dropped to his side, tears mixing with the rain that refused to relent. "Please don't die," she pleaded.

She almost started laughing as he moaned and murmured. "Ow."

Only then did she look up and just as quickly looked back down. Her jeans were back. She was alone. Slowly she turned head and gasped. There beside her was the ghostly visage of Tiana kneeling beside the crumpled body of a man.

"I'm sorry, Father," she whispered as she leaned down and placed a kiss on his cheek. "It was time for this to be over."

Thunder shook the night followed by a flash of lightning that pulled Lorna's gaze to the sky. When she looked down again, Tiana and her father were gone.

Jeremy moaned again and his eyelids popped open. He stared up at her with confusion. "What the hell are we doing out here?"

She didn't answer, just kissed him on the cheek and then scooted over until she knelt beside Renee. "Are you all right? Did he hurt you?" Her hands were trembling as she ran them over Renee's body. Her skin was cold and wet, her eyes slightly unfocused.

Renee's voice was raspy and shaking. She blinked and seemed to focus. "I'm all right, I think."

"If he hurt you…"

Renee pushed up to a sitting position and looked over at Jeremy. She took a big breath and let it out slowly. "It wasn't Jeremy. I could tell that the second he touched me."

She nodded. "Oh yeah, damn straight it wasn't him." She helped Renee to her feet and wrapped her arms around her. For just a second, she held her. Even soaking wet and cold, feeling the beat of her heart against her chest was glorious.

"I'm okay," Renee said into her ear before giving her a gentle kiss. "I promise."

"You better be," she said and didn't even bother to try to hide the emotion in her voice. Too damn close. It had been too damn close.

As fast as she could, Lorna hustled Renee back inside and next to the fire. She wrapped a blanket around her shivering body, put a pillow at her back, and turned to race into the kitchen. Hot tea was definitely in order. The fact that she was soaked to the skin didn't even occur to her.

Before she could move more than a couple feet, Jeremy came in. Like her, he was drenched, his shaggy hair plastered to his head, one hand rubbing the back of his head where the shovel had connected. His eyes were wide and scared. She didn't see her brother frightened often, and it pulled at her heart. "What *was* that?"

Renee surprised her with her simple statement. "It was the truth."

His words trembled as he looked at Renee, and uncharacteristic tears glittered in his eyes. "I was going to kill you and bury you right there."

Lorna nodded and tears welled in her eyes too. "It wasn't you, Jeremy. You weren't going to hurt Renee. He was."

"Everything's a great big blur. All I really remember is how angry I felt and how I wanted to choke the life out of Renee. I've never felt that pissed off before. Never want to again either."

"It wasn't Renee he wanted to kill. It was Catherine." She went back to the sofa and sat beside Renee, taking her hand.

His eyes cleared suddenly as if a heavy curtain had been lifted. "Yes, it wasn't Renee at all. In my head, it was another woman."

She nodded again, putting her arms around Renee. She'd finally stopped shaking. The tea could probably wait. This was more important. "Tiana showed me and now I understand it all. Go back to bed, Jeremy."

"But—"

"I'll explain it all in the morning. There's really nothing more we can do tonight."

He still didn't move. "What if he comes back?" The fear in his voice made her want to hug him.

"He won't. I can promise you that."

"How can you be so sure?"

"I just am. He lost this time and he knows it. It's almost over. By tomorrow, it will be. Trust me."

CHAPTER TWENTY-THREE

The first thing Renee noticed when she woke up was that the power had come back on. The alarm clock on the nightstand was flashing, and the bedside lamp was on.

The second thing she noticed was that she was alone. When she'd finally made it to bed last night, Lorna had been right beside her, and Clancy, ever vigilant, curled up at the foot of the bed. After everything that had happened, he was making darned sure he had eyes on Renee. He was such a good boy.

Now, though, she was alone in the big comfy bed. No Lorna. No Clancy. It felt empty and cold without them. Slowly, she pushed up and touched the tender skin on her neck. She flinched and pulled her hand away. For a few minutes last night, she thought it was all over. Judging by how tender the skin was, it had been a little too close for comfort.

Not that she blamed Jeremy. She'd known the second he touched her it wasn't him. The man who tried to force life from her body was an angry and bitter tyrant. John McCafferty might not have been there in body, but his spirit had been crushing the life out of both Jeremy and her. His anger survived the decades until it could no longer be contained. It was like a campfire that burst into a massive conflagration. Nearly all the color in Jeremy's aura had been obliterated by black. It was then she realized it was McCafftery's spirit that wrapped around Jeremy. Once it was over, Jeremy's own aura returned bright and full of the colors of his beautiful soul. Not even a shred of blackness remained.

McCafferty did not prevail, and that was all that mattered. Today was a new day, and she had the feeling it was going to be a good one. She got up, took a shower, and by the time she was dressed, she felt like a new woman, bruises and all. Sure, her throat was bound to be sore for a few days, but she could live with that. *Live* being the operative word.

After checking on Mom, she went in search of her woman and her dog. She found both out where she'd nearly lost her life last night. Lorna was dirty and sweaty, digging as if her life depended upon it. An odd time to be landscaping.

She tilted her head as she watched Lorna shoveling away. Like her brother, the aura around Lorna was now clear of any dark shadows. That alone made her spirit lighter although she was really curious about the task Lorna was so intent on. "What exactly are you doing?"

Lorna looked up from the hole she was standing in. It was probably five feet long and an easy three feet deep. She pointed down the deep dark earth as she leaned on the shovel. "Solving the mystery of course. You didn't think everything was solved last night, did you? I still have some work to do."

"Of course you do." Renee peered into the hole, and suddenly her breath caught in her throat as the full import hit her. "Is that...?"

"Oh yeah, it sure is. I think it's time we put in a call to Alden Swan and the Makah elders."

What she saw in the disturbed soil made her heart sad. At the same time it filled her with a sense of peace. Last night had been bizarre, unreal, and frightening. It had also been worth every second of the chaos.

She left Lorna working and went inside to call Alden. She suspected he'd been waiting for this call for a very long time. Six hours later, the police were gone, the medical examiner was gone, and they once more decided a bottle of wine was in order. Was it just her, or were they becoming very attached to the fabulous wine cellar Aunt Bea had left Lorna?

An hour later, Alden Swan pulled up in the driveway. Lorna took him out back first and then they came into the house. In the living room, Merry and Jeremy sat together on the sofa. Renee joined Lorna on the loveseat while Alden took one of the chairs. Her mother, feeling the need for company, joined them as well. Renee kept a close eye on her, still concerned by the pale cast to her skin and the constant fatigue. All things considered, though, she looked pretty good for all that had happened to her.

"Tiana showed me," Lorna was saying to them all. "It was as you predicted, Alden. She was reaching out to me. If I hadn't been so reluctant to open up to the her, I'd have seen what she'd been trying to show me all along. I was too dense and stubborn to see it. I'm a pretty sucky psychic if I do so say."

"Now you understand why she reached out to you?" Alden asked.

Lorna smiled though it was a sad smile. "Yes, I think we all do although it was my lovely lady, Renee, who figured out that piece of the puzzle. As it turns out, Jeremy and I are actually descendants of John McCafferty. After his wife died, he had another child with the woman who came in to help. She was our great-great-grandmother. That's how Aunt Bea ultimately came to own this place."

Despite understanding the blood connection Renee was still a little confused. "If you were all related to Tiana and John, why didn't any of this craziness happen to anyone else in your family before you two showed up?"

Lorna put an arm around her. "You know I've been thinking about that ever since I figured out what Tiana was trying to tell me. The only answer I've come up with that makes sense to me is it's because of you and me."

For a second, she didn't get it, and then it hit her. "Ohhhh, because we're…"

Lorna smiled. "Yeah, because we are and so was she. Tiana was waiting for someone who could really understand her love for Catherine. Family, and I don't mean the blood kind, if you get my drift. Enter you and me. The only two who could understand because we're living it, and the necklace?" She turned her gaze onto

Alden. "I think it has to do with the Watcher you told us about. All
along I've had a feeling someone or something else was out there.
I think he's the one who put the necklace where I could find it so I
could connect at an even deeper level with Tiana. Like I said, I'm
kinda dense and it took the equivalent of a sledgehammer to get my
attention."

"And me?" Jeremy asked. "What did I do to deserve the
asshole? You get a gracious, caring young woman and some kind of
dark angel to help you along, and I get a control-freak with violent
tendencies. That's messed up."

"My uneducated guess: luck of the draw. I think he's always
been here making sure no one tarnished his perfect castle. When
Renee and I—well, you know—shook up the status quo, his spirit
grabbed what he could to put a stop to it. Who better than a male
descendant? Blood is thicker than water and all that. Long story
short, in your case, wrong place, wrong time, bro. You agree,
Alden?"

Alden nodded. "I do."

That explanation actually made a lot of sense to Renee, and
at the same time sent shivers up her spine. It all fit together in a
very bizarre puzzle. Except for one final piece. "How did you know
where to find her?"

Lorna smiled. "Two things. John dragged you to the same spot
where he'd buried her body after he choked the life out of her. At
first, I thought he was going to dump you off the cliff except that
he didn't seem to want to get very far from that patch of grass. That
was clue number one. Tiana helped again too. The sorrow that filled
me when I stepped on that spot last night was so all-consuming it
was impossible to ignore. Only one thing could bring that depth of
emotion, and I just knew. That was clue number two."

Renee thought of the pale skull that had been in the dirt at
Lorna's feet. The sight had filled her with such a deep sadness. For
a hundred years, Catherine Swan lay beneath the lush green grass
of an estate honored for its natural beauty. There, in anonymity, she
was for over a century denied the love of her life and the respect of
a decent burial.

Until now. Lorna had found her, and now Catherine Swan's family would take her home at last. Somehow, it all seemed right.

❖

Darkness fell swiftly, obscuring the land where only hours before the grass was green and undisturbed. As dawn had broken, the sins of the father came into the light of day. The murder by John McCafferty was no longer a secret. His hold on the two beautiful souls denied their destiny was shattered. Never again would he hurt another.

Catherine Swan was on her way home, and his promise had at long last been fulfilled. His prayers had been answered. She had come, and she had made right what had been wrong for so many long years.

The house was silent now, the whispers of the past laid to rest. He was gone, and no more would he taint a love born of truth. They had been denied in life and in death. No more. She had made things right, as the universe had decreed.

The moon rose as he stood in the shadow of the trees. The golden light this hour free from the storm clouds that had passed away shone down in bright shafts across the lawn. As he watched, two women walked together hand-in-hand toward the bluff. One woman was tall and fair, the other one shorter with dark hair that fell down her back to below her waist. They were a striking couple not simply because they were both beautiful, but also because of the depth of the love they shared was so clearly evident.

At the edge of the bluff, they turned as one and looked in his direction. Tiana McCafferty was radiant in the moonlight, her joy undeniable. Beside her, Catherine Swan smiled, her quiet beauty unmarred by the years of sorrow and separation. Tiana's head tilted ever so slightly, and across the distance, he could read the movement of her lips. "Thank you."

The Watcher reached out his hand as if he could touch them. How he longed to go with the two as they began their journey, but as he watched them fade from this place, he understood his work in this world was far from complete.

For so long, he'd believed that to bring Tiana and Catherine together once more, his path to heaven would open. Now he knew it was not so but simply one more step on a path long and twisted.

His redemption lay not in just this one night, but in the woman he could see inside the house as she stood at the window gazing out. It was not Tiana he was brought here to save, but Lorna. For if he could save her, he would save himself.

About the Author

Sheri Lewis Wohl grew up in northeast Washington State and though she always thought she'd move away, never has. Despite traveling throughout the United States, Sheri always finds her way back home. And so she lives, plays, and writes amidst mountains, evergreens, and abundant wildlife. When not working the day job in federal finance, she writes stories that typically include a bit of the strange and unusual and always a touch of romance. She works to carve out time to run, swim, and bike so she can participate in local triathlons, her latest addiction.

Books Available from Bold Strokes Books

Courtship by Carsen Taite. Love and justice—a lethal mix or a perfect match? (978-1-62639-210-6)

Against Doctor's Orders by Radclyffe. Corporate financier Presley Worth wants to shut down Argyle Community Hospital, but Dr. Harper Rivers will fight her every step of the way, if she can also fight their growing attraction. (978-1-62639-211-3)

A Spark of Heavenly Fire by Kathleen Knowles. Kerry and Beth are building their life together, but unexpected circumstances could destroy their happiness. (978-1-62639-212-0)

Never Too Late by Julie Blair. When Dr. Jamie Hammond is forced to hire a new office manager, she's shocked to come face to face with Carla Grant and memories from her past. (978-1-62639-213-7)

Widow by Martha Miller. Judge Bertha Brannon must solve the murder of her lover, a policewoman she thought she'd grow old with. As more bodies pile up, the murderer starts coming for her. (978-1-62639-214-4)

Twisted Echoes by Sheri Lewis Wohl. What's a woman to do when she realizes the voices in her head are real? (978-1-62639-215-1)

Criminal Gold by Ann Aptaker. Through a dangerous night in New York in 1949, Cantor Gold, dapper dyke-about-town, smuggler of fine art, is forced by a crime lord to be his instrument of vengeance. (978-1-62639-216-8)

The Melody of Light by M.L. Rice. After surviving abuse and loss, will Riley Gordon be able to navigate her first year of college and accept true love and family? (978-1-62639-219-9)

Because of You by Julie Cannon. What would you do for the woman you were forced to leave behind? (978-1-62639-199-4)

The Job by Jove Belle. Sera always dreamed that she would one day reunite with Tor. She just didn't think it would involve terrorists, firearms, and hostages. (978-1-62639-200-7)

Making Time by C.J. Harte. Two women going in different directions meet after fifteen years and struggle to reconnect in spite of the past that separated them. (978-1-62639-201-4)

Once The Clouds Have Gone by KE Payne. Overwhelmed by the dark clouds of her past, Tag Grainger is lost until the intriguing and spirited Freddie Metcalfe unexpectedly forces her to reevaluate her life. (978-1-62639-202-1)

The Acquittal by Anne Laughlin. Chicago private investigator Josie Harper searches for the real killer of a woman whose lover has been acquitted of the crime. (978-1-62639-203-8)

An American Queer: The Amazon Trail by Lee Lynch. Lee Lynch's heartening and heart-rending history of gay life from the turbulence of the late 1900s to the triumphs of the early 2000s are recorded in this selection of her columns. (978-1-62639-204-5)

Stick McLaughlin: The Prohibition Years by CF Frizzell. Corruption in 1918 cost Stick her lover, her freedom, and her identity, but a very special flapper and the family bond of her own gang could help win them back—even if it means outwitting the Boston Mob. (978-1-62639-205-2)

Edge of Awareness by C.A. Popovich. When Maria, a woman in the middle of her third divorce, meets Dana, an out lesbian, awareness of her feelings brings up reservations about the teachings of her church. (978-1-62639-188-8)

Taken by Storm by Kim Baldwin. Lives depend on two women when a train derails high in the remote Alps, but an unforgiving mountain, avalanches, crevasses, and other perils stand between them and safety. (978-1-62639-189-5)

The Common Thread by Jaime Maddox. Dr. Nicole Coussart's life is falling apart, but fortunately, DEA Attorney Rae Rhodes is there to pick up the pieces and help Nic put them back together. (978-1-62639-190-1)

Jolt by Kris Bryant. Mystery writer Bethany Lange wasn't prepared for the twisting emotions that left her breathless the moment she laid eyes on folk singer sensation Ali Hart. (978-1-62639-191-8)

Searching For Forever by Emily Smith. Dr. Natalie Jenner's life has always been about saving others, until young paramedic Charlie Thompson comes along and shows her maybe she's the one who needs saving. (978-1-62639-186-4)

A Queer Sort of Justice: Prison Tales Across Time by Rebecca S. Buck. When liberty is only a memory, and all seems lost, what freedoms and hopes can be found within us? (978-1-62639-195-6E)

Blue Water Dreams by Dena Hankins. Lania Marchiol keeps her wary sailor's gaze trained on the horizon until Oly Rassmussen, a wickedly handsome trans man, sends her trusty compass spinning off course. (978-1-62639-192-5)

Rest Home Runaways by Clifford Henderson. Baby boomer Morgan Ronzio's troubled marriage is the least of her worries when she gets the call that her addled, eighty-six-year-old, half-blind dad has escaped the rest home. (978-1-62639-169-7)

Charm City by Mason Dixon. Raq Overstreet's loyalty to her drug kingpin boss is put to the test when she begins to fall for Bathsheba Morris, the undercover cop assigned to bring him down. (978-1-62639-198-7)

Let the Lover Be by Sheree Greer. Kiana Lewis, a functional alcoholic on the verge of destruction, finally faces the demons of her past while finding love and earning redemption in New Orleans. (978-1-62639-077-5)

Blindsided by Karis Walsh. Blindsided by love, guide dog trainer Lenae McIntyre and media personality Cara Bradley learn to trust what they see with their hearts. (978-1-62639-078-2)

About Face by VK Powell. Forensic artist Macy Sheridan and Detective Leigh Monroe work on a case that has troubled them both for years, but they're hampered by the past and their unlikely yet undeniable attraction. (978-1-62639-079-9)

Blackstone by Shea Godfrey. For Darry and Jessa, their chance at a life of freedom is stolen by the arrival of war and an ancient prophecy that just might destroy their love. (978-1-62639-080-5)

Out of This World by Maggie Morton. Iris decided to cross an ocean to get over her ex. But instead, she ends up traveling much farther, all the way to another world. Once there, only a mysterious, sexy, and magical woman can help her return home. (978-1-62639-083-6)

Kiss The Girl by Melissa Brayden. Sleeping with the enemy has never been so complicated. Brooklyn Campbell and Jessica Lennox face off in love and advertising in fast-paced New York City. (978-1-62639-071-3)

Taking Fire: A First Responders Novel by Radclyffe. Hunted by extremists and under siege by nature's most virulent weapons, Navy medic Max de Milles and Red Cross worker Rachel Winslow join forces to survive and discover something far more lasting. (978-1-62639-072-0)

First Tango in Paris by Shelley Thrasher. When French law student Eva Laroche meets American call girl Brigitte Green in 1970s Paris, they have no idea how their pasts and futures will intersect. (978-1-62639-073-7)

The War Within by Yolanda Wallace. Army nurse Meredith Moser went to Vietnam in 1967 looking to help those in need; she didn't expect to meet the love of her life along the way. (978-1-62639-074-4)

Escapades by MJ Williamz. Two women, afraid to love again, must overcome their fears to find the happiness that awaits them. (978-1-62639-182-6)

Desire at Dawn by Fiona Zedde. For Kylie, love had always come armed with sharp teeth and claws. But with the human, Olivia, she bares her vampire heart for the very first time, sharing passion, lust, and a tenderness she'd never dared dream of before. (978-1-62639-064-5)

Visions by Larkin Rose. Sometimes the mysteries of love reveal themselves when you least expect it. Other times they hide behind a black satin mask. Can Paige unveil her masked stranger this time? (978-1-62639-065-2)

All In by Nell Stark. Internet poker champion Annie Navarro loses everything when the Feds shut down online gambling, and she turns to experienced casino host Vesper Blake for advice—but can Nova convince Vesper to take a gamble on romance? (978-1-62639-066-9)

Vermilion Justice by Sheri Lewis Wohl. What's a vampire to do when Dracula is no longer just a character in a novel? (978-1-62639-067-6)

Switchblade by Carsen Taite. Lines were meant to be crossed. Third in the Luca Bennett Bounty Hunter Series. (978-1-62639-058-4)

Nightingale by Andrea Bramhall. Culture, faith, and duty conspire to tear two young lovers apart, yet fate seems to have different plans for them both. (978-1-62639-059-1)

No Boundaries by Donna K. Ford. A chance meeting and a nightmare from the past threaten more than Andi Massey's solitude as she and Gwen Palmer struggle to understand the complexity of love without boundaries. (978-1-62639-060-7)